CLOCK DANCE

Clock Dance

ANNE TYLER

Chatto & Windus
LONDON

3 5 7 9 10 8 6 4 2

Chatto & Windus, an imprint of Vintage,
20 Vauxhall Bridge Road,
London SW1V 2SA

Chatto & Windus is part of the Penguin Random House group of companies
whose addresses can be found at global.penguinrandomhouse.com.

First published in the United Kingdom by Chatto & Windus in 2018
First published in the United States by Alfred A. Knopf in 2018

penguin.co.uk/vintage

A CIP catalogue record for this book is available from the British Library

HB ISBN 9781784742430
TPB ISBN 9781784742447

Printed and bound by Clays Ltd, St Ives Plc

Penguin Random House is committed to a sustainable future
for our business, our readers and our planet. This book is made
from Forest Stewardship Council® certified paper.

PART I

1967

WILLA DRAKE and Sonya Bailey were selling candy bars door-to-door. This was for the Herbert Malone Elementary School Orchestra. If they sold enough, the orchestra would get to travel to the regional competitions in Harrisburg. Willa had never been to Harrisburg, but she liked the harsh, gritty sound of the name. Sonya had been but had no memory of it because she was a baby at the time. Both of them swore they would absolutely die if they didn't get to go now.

Willa played the clarinet. Sonya played the flute. They were eleven years old. They lived two blocks from each other in Lark City, Pennsylvania, which wasn't a city at all or even much of a town and in fact didn't even have sidewalks except on the one street where the stores were. In Willa's mind, sidewalks were *huge*. She planned never to live in a place without them after she was grown.

Because of the lack of sidewalks, they weren't allowed to walk on the roads after dark. So they set out in the afternoon, Willa lugging a carton of candy bars and Sonya holding a manila envelope for the money they hoped to make. They started from Sonya's house, where they'd first had to finish their homework. Sonya's mother made them promise to head back as soon as the sun—pale as milk anyhow in mid-February—fell behind the scratchy trees on top of Bert Kane

Ridge. Sonya's mother was kind of a worrier, much more so than Willa's mother.

The plan was that they would begin far off, on Harper Road, and end up back in their own neighborhood. Nobody in the orchestra lived on Harper Road, and they were thinking they could make a killing if they got there before the others. This was Monday, the very first day of the candy drive; most of the others would probably wait till the weekend.

The top three sellers would win a three-course dinner with Mr. Budd, their music teacher, in a downtown Harrisburg restaurant, all expenses paid.

The houses on Harper Road were newish. Ranch-style, they were called. They were all on one level and made of brick, and the people who lived there were newish, too—most of them employed by the furniture factory that had opened over in Garrettville a couple of years ago. Willa and Sonya didn't know a one of them, and this was a good thing because then they wouldn't feel so self-conscious pretending to be salesmen.

Before they tried the first house, they stopped behind a big evergreen bush in order to get themselves ready. They had washed their hands and faces back at Sonya's house, and Sonya had combed her hair, which was the straight, dark, ribbony kind that a comb could slide right through. Willa's billow of yellow curls needed a brush instead of a comb, but Sonya didn't own a brush and so Willa had just flattened her frizzes with her palms as best she could. She and Sonya wore almost-matching wool jackets with fake-fur-trimmed hoods, and blue jeans with the cuffs turned up to show their plaid flannel linings. Sonya had sneakers on but Willa was still in her school shoes, brown tie oxfords, because she hadn't wanted to stop by home and get waylaid by her little sister, who would beg to tag along.

"Hold the whole carton up when they open the door," Sonya told Willa. "Not just one candy bar. Ask, 'Would you like to buy some candy bars?' Plural."

"*I'm* going to ask?" Willa said. "I thought you were."

"I'd feel silly asking."

"What, you don't think *I'd* feel silly?"

"But you're much better with grownups."

"What will you be doing?"

"I'll be in charge of the money," Sonya said, and she waved her envelope.

Willa said, "Okay, but then you have to ask at the next house."

"Fine," Sonya said.

Of course it was fine, because the next house was bound to be easier. But Willa tightened her arms around the carton, and Sonya turned to lead the way up the flagstone walk.

This house had a metal sculpture out front that was nothing but a tall, swooping curve, very modern. The doorbell was lit with a light that glowed even in the daytime. Sonya poked it. A rich-sounding two-note chime rang somewhere inside, followed by a silence so deep that they could begin to hope no one was home. But then foot-steps approached, and the door opened, and a woman stood smil-ing at them. She was younger than their mothers and more stylish, with short brown hair and bright lipstick, and she wore a miniskirt. "Why, hello, girls," she said, while behind her a little boy came tod-dling up, dragging a pull toy and asking, "Who's that, Mama? Who's that, Mama?"

Willa looked at Sonya. Sonya looked at Willa. Something about

Sonya's expression—so trusting, so expectant, her lips moistened and slightly parted as if she planned to start speaking along with Willa—struck Willa as comical, and she felt a little burp of laughter rising in her chest and then bubbling in her throat. The sudden, surprising squeak that popped out seemed comical too—hilarious, in fact—and the bubble of laughter turned to gales of laughter, whole waterfalls of laughter, and next to her Sonya broke into sputters and doubled in on herself while the woman stood looking at them, still smiling a questioning smile. Willa asked, "Would you like—? Would you like—?" but she couldn't finish; she was overcome; she couldn't catch her breath.

"Are you two offering to sell me something?" the woman suggested kindly. Willa could tell that she'd probably gotten the giggles herself when she was their age, although surely—oh, lord—surely not such hysterical giggles, such helpless, overpowering, uncontrollable giggles. These giggles were like a liquid that flooded Willa's whole body, causing tears to stream from her eyes and forcing her to crumple over her carton and clamp her legs together so as not to pee. She was mortified, and she could see from Sonya's desperate, wild-eyed face that she was mortified too, but at the same time it was the most wonderful, loose, relaxing feeling. Her cheeks ached and her stomach muscles seemed to have softened into silk. She could have melted into a puddle right there on the stoop.

Sonya was the first to give up. She flapped an arm wearily in the woman's direction and turned to start back down the flagstone walk, and Willa turned too and followed without another word. After a moment, they heard the front door gently closing behind them.

They weren't laughing anymore. Willa felt tired to the bone, and emptied and a little sad. And Sonya might have felt the same way, because the sun still hung like a thin white dime above Bert Kane Ridge, but she said, "We ought to wait till the weekend. It's too hard when we've got all this homework." Willa didn't argue.

When her father opened the door to her, he had a sorrowful look on his face. His eyes behind his little rimless glasses seemed a paler blue, lacking their usual twinkle, and he was passing one palm across his smooth bald scalp in that slow, uncertain way that meant something had disappointed him. Willa's first thought was that he had found out about her giggling fit. She knew that was unlikely—and anyway, he wasn't the type to object to a case of giggles—but how else to explain his expression? "Hi, honey," he said in a discouraged-sounding voice.

"Hi, Pop."

He turned and wandered into the living room, leaving her to close the front door. He was still in the white shirt and gray pants he wore to work, but he'd exchanged his shoes for his corduroy slippers so he must have been home for a while. (He taught shop at the high school in Garrettville; he came home well before other fathers.)

Her sister was sitting on the rug with the newspaper opened to the comics. She was six years old and had gone overnight from cute to really ugly—all chewed-down nails and missing front teeth and disturbingly skinny brown braids. "How many'd you sell?" she asked Willa. "Did you sell all of them?," because Willa had left the carton of candy bars at Sonya's and she only had her book bag with her. Willa tossed her book bag onto the couch and shucked off her jacket. Her eyes were on her father, who had not stopped in the living room but was continuing toward the kitchen. She followed him. In the kitchen he reached for a skillet from the pegboard beside the stove. "Grilled cheese sandwiches tonight!" he said in a fake-cheerful voice.

"Where's Mom?"

"Your mother won't be joining us."

She waited for him to say something else, but he got very busy adjusting the burner under the skillet, dropping in a pat of butter, adjusting the burner again when the butter began to sizzle. He started whistling under his breath, some tune that didn't go anywhere.

Willa returned to the living room. Elaine had finished reading the comics now and was folding up the paper—another bad sign: taking such care, for once; trying to be good. "Is Mom upstairs?" Willa asked in a whisper.

Elaine gave the smallest shake of her head.

"Did she go out?"

"Mm-hmm."

"What happened?"

Elaine shrugged.

"Was she mad?"

"Mm-hmm."

"What about?"

Another shrug.

Well, what was it ever about, really? Their mother was the prettiest mother in their school, and the liveliest and the smartest, but then all of a sudden something would happen and she would have this big flare-up. It started with their father, often. It could start with Willa or Elaine, but most often it was him. You'd think he would learn, Willa thought. Learn what, though? To Willa, he seemed perfect just the way he was, and she loved him more than any other person in the world. He was funny and kind and soft-spoken, and he never got grumpy like Sonya's father or belched at the table like Madeline's. But "Oh," their mother would say to him, "I know you! I see right through you! All 'Yes, dear; no, dear,' but butter wouldn't melt in your mouth."

Butter wouldn't melt in his mouth. Willa wasn't sure exactly what that meant. Still, he must have done *something* wrong. She sank onto the couch and watched Elaine place the folded newspaper neatly-neatly on top of a stack of magazines. "She said she'd had it," Elaine told her after a minute. She spoke in a tiny thin voice and barely moved her lips, as if to hide the fact that she was talking. "She said he could just try running this house himself, if he thought he could do any better. She said he was 'holier than thou.' She called him 'Saint Melvin.'"

"Saint Melvin?" Willa asked. She screwed up her forehead. That sounded to her like a *good* thing. "What did he say back?" she asked.

"He didn't say anything, at first. Then he said he was sorry she felt that way."

Elaine settled on the couch beside Willa, just on the very front edge.

The living room had had a do-over recently; it was more up-to-date than it used to be. Their mother had borrowed decorating books from the library in Garrettville, and one of her Little Theatre friends had brought over swatches of fabric that they laid here and there on the couch and the backs of the two matching armchairs. Matching furniture was passé, their mother said. Now one chair was covered in a bluish tweed and the other was blue-and-green-striped. The wall-to-wall carpet had been ripped up and replaced with a fringed off-white rug, so that the dark wood floor could be seen all around the edges. Willa missed the wall-to-wall carpet. Their house was an old white clapboard house that rattled when the wind blew, and the carpet had made it feel solider and warmer. Also she missed the painting above the fireplace that showed a ship in full sail on a faded sea. (Now there was a, kind of like, picture of a fuzzy circle.) But she was proud of the rest of it. Sonya said she wished Willa's mother would come and redecorate *their* poky old living room.

Their father appeared in the doorway with a spatula in his hand. "Peas or green beans?" he asked them.

Elaine said, "Can't we go to Bing's Drive-In, Pop? Please?"

"What!" he said, pretending to be insulted. "You would turn down my famous Grilled Cheese Sandwiches à la Maison for *drive-in* food?"

Grilled cheese sandwiches were all he knew how to make. He fried them over high heat and they gave off a sharp, salty smell that Willa had learned to associate with their mother's absences—her sick headaches and her play rehearsals and the times she slammed out of the house.

Elaine said, "Tammy Denton goes to Bing's with her family every single Friday night."

Their father rolled his eyes. "Has Tammy Denton backed a winning horse at the races lately?" he asked.

"What?"

"Did a rich aunt die and leave her a fortune? Did she find a treasure chest buried in her backyard?"

He started advancing on Elaine with the fingers of his free hand wriggling comically, threatening to tickle her, and Elaine shrieked and shrank away, laughing, and hid behind Willa. Willa held herself apart. She sat rigid and drew in her elbows. "When is Mom coming back?" she asked.

Her father straightened and said, "Oh, pretty soon."

"Did she say where she was going?"

"No, she didn't, but you know what? I'm thinking we three should have Cokes with our supper."

"Goody!" Elaine said, popping up from behind Willa.

Willa said, "Did she take the car?"

He passed a palm across his scalp. "Well, yes," he said.

This was bad. It meant she didn't just walk down the road to her friend Mimi Prentice's house; she had gone off who-knows-where.

"So, no Bing's Drive-In, then," Elaine said sadly.

"Shut *up* about Bing's Drive-In!" Willa shouted, turning on her.

Elaine's mouth flew open. Their father said, "Gracious."

But then smoke started coming from the kitchen, and he said, "Uh-oh," and rushed back to set up a clatter among the pots and pans.

Their car was old and it had one different-colored fender from the time when their mother had run it into a guardrail out on the East-West Parkway, and it was always full of their father's junk— paper cups and ruffle-edged magazines and candy wrappers and various coffee-ringed pieces of mail. For years their mother had been wanting a car of her own, but they were too poor. *She* said they were too poor. Their father said they were fine. "We've got enough to eat, haven't we?" he asked his daughters. Yes, and they had a fancy new living room too, Willa thought, and she felt scornful and bitter and unexpectedly grown up when these words flew into her mind.

The grilled cheese sandwiches had a scaly look where their father had scraped off the black parts, but they tasted okay. Especially with Cokes. Their vegetable was green beans—frozen, and cooked not quite long enough so that they had a wet feel and squeaked against Willa's teeth when she chewed them. Most of them she hid beneath the crusts of her sandwich.

When their father was in charge of dinner he didn't bother with the frills, like completely clearing the table of its clutter before he set it; or folding the paper napkins into triangles under the forks; or lowering the shades against the cold dark that was pressing against the windowpanes. This gave Willa a hollow feeling. Also, he seemed to have run out of steam as far as conversation went. He didn't say much during supper and he barely touched his food.

After they were done eating he went into the living room and turned the news on the way he always did. Usually Elaine went with him, but tonight she stayed in the kitchen with Willa, whose job it was to clear the table. Willa stacked the dirty dishes on the counter beside the sink, and then she took the saucepan from the stovetop and went out to the living room to ask their father, "What'll I do with the beans?"

"Hmm?" he said. He was watching Vietnam.

"Should I save them?"

"What? No. I don't know."

She waited. Behind her she felt the presence of Elaine, who had trailed her like a puppy. Finally she said, "Would Mom maybe come home later tonight and want to eat them?"

"Just throw them out," he said after a moment.

When she turned to go back to the kitchen she bumped smack into Elaine; that was how closely Elaine had been following her.

In the kitchen, she dumped the beans into the garbage bin and set the saucepan on the counter. She wiped the table with a damp cloth and draped the cloth over the faucet, and then she turned the kitchen light off and she and Elaine went back to the living room and watched the rest of the news, even though it was boring. They sat close on either side of their father, and he put an arm around each of them and gave them a squeeze from time to time, but still he was very quiet.

Once the news was finished, though, he seemed to gather himself together. "Anyone for Parcheesi?" he asked, rubbing his hands briskly. Willa was sort of over Parcheesi, but she said, "I am!," matching his enthusiastic tone, and Elaine went to fetch the board.

They played at the coffee table, the two girls on the floor and their father on the couch because he was too old and stiff, he always said, to sit on the floor. The theory was that Parcheesi would be good for Elaine's arithmetic; she still counted on her fingers when she did addition. Tonight, though, she didn't seem to be trying. When she threw a four and a two she announced, "One-two-three-four; one-two," plopping her token down on each space hard enough to rattle the other tokens. "Six," their father corrected her. "Add them together, honey." Elaine just settled back on her heels, and when it was her turn again she counted to five and then three. This time their father said nothing.

Elaine's bedtime was eight o'clock and Willa's was nine, but tonight when their father sent Elaine upstairs to get into her pajamas Willa went with her and got into her own pajamas. They shared a room; they had matching single beds along opposite walls. Elaine climbed into her bed and asked, "Who will read to me?," because most nights it was their mother who did that. Willa said, "I will," and she slid under the covers next to Elaine and took *Little House in the Big Woods* from the nightstand.

Willa always thought of Pa in this book as looking like their father. This made no sense, because a picture right on the cover showed Pa with a lot of hair and a beard. But he had that quiet, explaining manner that their father had, and whenever he said anything in the story Willa tried to read his words in their father's furry voice, dropping her final g's just the way he did.

At the end of the chapter, Elaine said, "Another," but Willa snapped the book shut and said, "Nope, you have to wait till tomorrow."

"Will Mom be home by tomorrow?"

"Sure," Willa said. "What did you think? She'll be home tonight, I bet, probably."

Then she got out of Elaine's bed and went to the door, planning to call down the stairs and ask their father to come tuck them in, but he was on the phone; she could tell by his extra-loud voice and the silences between sentences. "Great!" he said energetically, and then, after a silence, "Seven fifteen will be fine. I have to be in pretty early myself." He must be talking to Mr. Law, who taught algebra at the high school, or maybe Mrs. Bellows, who was the assistant principal. Both of them lived here in Lark City and occasionally gave him a ride if Willa's mother needed the car.

So she would *not* be home by tomorrow, was what it sounded like. She had never stayed away a whole night before.

Willa turned off the light and padded over to her own bed and slipped under the covers. She lay on her back, eyes wide open. She wasn't the least bit sleepy.

What if their mother never came back?

She wasn't *always* angry. She had lots of good days. On good days she invented the most exciting projects for the three of them—things to paint, things to decorate the house with, skits to put on for the holidays. And she had a wonderful singing voice, clear and sort of liquid-sounding. Sometimes, when Willa and Elaine begged her, she would sit in their room after bedtime and sing to them, and then as they drifted into sleep she would rise and back out of the room still singing, but more softly, and she would sing all the way down the stairs until she faded into silence. Willa loved it when she sang "Down in the Valley"—especially the part where she asked someone to write her a letter and send it by mail, send it in care of Birmingham Jail. It was such a lonesome song that it made Willa ache just to hear it now in her mind. But it was the sweetly heavy, enjoyable kind of ache.

The next morning, her father whistled his special wake-up whistle in the doorway. *Tweet*-tweet! he whistled—like the first two notes of "Dixie," Willa always thought. She had been awake for ages, but she made a big show of opening her eyes and stretching and yawning. She already knew that their mother wasn't back yet. The house had an echoey sound, and it seemed too exposed in the flat white light from the windows.

"Hey there, sweetheart," her father said. "I let you sleep as long as I could, but I'm going to have to leave before your bus comes. Will you be able to get the two of you ready for school?"

Willa said, "Okay." She sat up and looked across at Elaine, who lay on her side facing her. Elaine opened her eyes just then and blinked. Willa had the feeling that she hadn't been asleep either.

"I've put the key on the kitchen table," her father said. "Hang it around your neck, all right? Just in case you have to let yourselves in when you get home this afternoon."

"Okay," Willa said again.

He waited to make sure she was actually out of bed, and then he gave them both a little wave and went back downstairs. A moment later a car horn honked outside and she heard the front door opening and closing.

They dressed in what they'd worn the day before, because Willa didn't feel like making a bunch of choices. Then she yanked a brush through her hair. Elaine's hair was still in its two skinny braids and she claimed they didn't need redoing, but Willa said, "Are you kidding? They're falling apart." She unbraided Elaine's hair and brushed it, with Elaine squirming and wincing away from her, and braided it again. As she snapped the second rubber band in place she felt capable and efficient, but then Elaine said, "They're not right."

"What do you mean, not right?"

"They feel too loose."

"They're the same as Mom always makes them," Willa said.

This was absolutely true, but Elaine went over to look in the mirror on the closet door and when she turned back her eyes were filled with tears. "They're *not* the same!" she said. "They're all floppy!"

"Well, I did the best I could! Gee!"

The tears spilled over and rolled down Elaine's cheeks, but she didn't say anything more.

For breakfast they had Cheerios and orange juice from a carton and their chewable vitamin pills. Then Willa cleared the table and wiped it. The counter was crowded now with dirty dishes, the ones from last night and the ones from breakfast, and they were very depressing to look at.

Their father had made himself coffee, she saw, but he hadn't left a bowl or a plate so he must not have eaten anything.

She worried they might miss the school bus—she wasn't used to timing this on her own—so she hustled them both into their jackets and mittens and they hurried out of the house and up the road to the bus stop and got there way too early. The bus stop was a lean-to with an old snuff ad peeling off it and a bench inside, and they sat close together on the bench and hugged their book bags for warmth and breathed out miserable rags of white air. It was better when the others arrived—Eula Pratt and her brother and the three Turnstile boys. They all crowded into the lean-to and jiggled up and down and made shuddery noises, and Willa started feeling halfway warm.

On the bus Elaine usually sat with Natalie Dean, but this morning she followed Willa to the rear where Sonya was saving Willa a seat and she settled in the empty seat across the aisle from the two of them. It was true that her braids looked kind of draggly. And the tails at their ends were too long. Their mother only left about an inch of tail.

Sonya said she'd been thinking it over, and she believed that if they sold their candy bars just to family they wouldn't have to go around ringing strangers' doorbells. "I've got four uncles on my mom's side," she said, "and an uncle and two aunts on my dad's side, except my aunts live far away. But that's okay; they can *mail* me the money, and I can keep their candy bars for the next time they come to visit."

"You have a way bigger family than I do," Willa said.

"And then my grandma Bailey: well, that goes without saying. But my other grandparents are dead."

Willa's grandparents were still alive, both sets, but she didn't see them much. Well, her father's parents she didn't see at all, because Willa's mother said she had not one thing in common with them. Besides, they were country people and they couldn't leave their animals. Her mother's parents did sometimes come down from Philly for holidays, although not that often and not for very long, but her mother didn't really like her brother and sister and they hardly ever visited. She said her brother had always been the favorite because he was a boy, and her sister was a favorite too because she was the youngest and cutest; her sister was spoiled rotten, she said. Willa was almost sure that if she suggested selling candy bars to either of them, her mother would make a snorting sound. Anyhow, they would probably say no if they were as awful as all that.

"Maybe I'll just go around to the people in my own block," she told Sonya. "That's easier than strangers, at least."

"Okay, but Billy Turnstile's on your block, remember. You better hurry or he'll get to everyone first."

Willa sent Billy a slit-eyed look. He was tussling with his brother, trying to wrest some kind of cellophane-wrapped snack from his hands. "Billy Turnstile's a back-of-the-room boy," she said. "What do you want to bet he doesn't even bother."

"Oh, and I have a godmother, too," Sonya said.

"You are so, so lucky," Willa told her.

When she grew up she was going to marry a man who came from a big, close, jolly family. He would get along with all of them—he'd be the same kind of man her father was, friendly and easygoing—

and all of them would love Willa and treat her like one of their own. She would have either six children or eight children, half of them girls and half boys, and they would grow up playing with their multitude of cousins.

"Your sister's crying," Sonya pointed out.

Willa glanced over and saw Elaine wiping her nose with the back of one mittened hand. "What's the matter?" she called across the aisle.

"Nothing," Elaine said in a small voice. The back of her mitten had a shiny streak now like a string of glue.

"She's okay," Willa told Sonya.

But halfway through the school day, just after Willa's lunch period, the nurse came to the classroom and asked the teacher to excuse Willa Drake. "Your little sister's got a tummy ache," she told Willa as they walked to her office. "I don't think it's anything serious, but I can't seem to get ahold of your mother, and your sister asked if you could come sit with her."

This made Willa feel important, at first. "It's probably all in her mind," she said in a knowledgeable voice, and when they reached the office Elaine sat up on her cot looking glad to see her and the nurse brought over a chair for her. But then Elaine lay back down and covered her eyes with one arm, and Willa had nothing to do. She watched the nurse filling out some papers at her desk across the room. She studied a brightly colored poster about the importance of washing your hands. Somebody knocked on the door—Mrs. Porter from sixth grade—and the nurse went out to speak with her, leaving the door partly open behind her so that Willa could see the seventh-graders crowding past on their way to lunch. One of the seventh-grade boys elbowed another and caused him to stumble, and Mrs. Porter said, "I saw that, Dickie Bond!" Her voice rang out in the hall as if she were speaking from inside a seashell, and so did a seventh-grade girl's voice saying ". . . weird pinky-orangeish shade that made my teeth look yellow . . ."

Did all these kids come from perfectly happy families? Weren't any of them hiding something that was going on at home? They didn't seem to be. They didn't seem to have a thing on their minds but lunch and friends and lipstick.

The nurse came back in and shut the door, and the sounds from the hall fell away. Still, Willa could hear when orchestra practice started. Darn. She loved orchestra. They were learning "The Gliding Dance of the Maidens" by Borodin. The first few notes were so soft and uncertain—*weak* notes, she always thought—that it took her a moment to sort them out, but they grew stronger on the main melody. It was the "Stranger in Paradise" melody, and the back-of-the-room boys always crooned, "Take my hand, I'm a strange-looking parasite . . ." till Mr. Budd tapped his baton against his music stand. Mr. Budd was very handsome, with longish golden curls and bulging muscles. You could mistake him for a rock star. If Willa sold the most candy bars and got to go to dinner with him, she would be completely tongue-tied. She almost didn't *want* to go to dinner with him.

The orchestra broke off and started over. Same weak beginning, same "Take my hand . . ." but growing louder now and more sure of itself.

"Is Mom going to be there when we get home today?" Elaine asked.

Willa glanced at her. She had lowered her arm and was crinkling her eyebrows worriedly.

"Of course she is," Willa said.

Of course she was going to be there, but even so, Willa told Sonya on the bus that she couldn't go home with her after school. "I have to babysit my sister," she said. She said it just in a murmur, so that her sister wouldn't hear. Her sister was sitting all by herself across the aisle from them again.

It was hard to tell from the front of their house whether anyone was inside. True, the windows were dark, but it was daytime, after all. The grass had a flattened, beaten-down look and the leaves of the rhododendron bush by the porch were rolled up tight as cigars; that was how cold it was. Willa fished for the key on its string inside her jacket. She could have tried ringing the doorbell first, but she didn't want to make her sister stand waiting and then have nothing happen.

In the foyer, there was a ticking silence. In the living room the only motion was the stirring of a curtain hem above a radiator. "She's not here," Elaine said in that small voice of hers.

Willa threw her book bag onto the couch. "Give her time," she said.

"But we already gave her time! We gave her all last night!"

"Thinking time," their father called it. Their mother would shout at him and stamp her foot, or slap Willa in the face (such a stinging, shameful experience, being slapped in the face—so scary to the person's eyes), or shake Elaine like a Raggedy Ann, and then she would grab her own hair in both hands so that even after she let go of it, it stayed bushed out on either side of her head. Then next thing you knew she'd be gone, with the house standing shocked and trembling behind her, and their father would say, "Never mind, she just needs a little thinking time." He wouldn't seem perturbed in the least. "She's overtired, is all," he'd say.

"Other people get overtired," Willa had told him once, "but they don't act the way she does."

"Well, but you know she's very high-strung."

Willa wondered how he could be so understanding when he himself *never* lost his temper—had never even raised his voice, as far as she could remember.

She wished he were here now. Generally he was home by four, but they couldn't count on that today because he'd be riding with someone else.

"You want a snack?" she asked Elaine. "How about milk and cookies?"

"Well, cookies, maybe."

"No milk, no cookies!"

That was what their mother always said; Willa used their mother's merry, singsong voice. It was an effort, though.

In the kitchen she poured a glass of milk and set it on the table along with two Oreos. She didn't take anything for herself because she had this weird feeling that something was stuck in her throat. Instead she fetched her book bag from the couch and carried it into the dining room, where she always did her homework. Before she'd even started on it, though, Elaine arrived, bringing her cookies but not her milk, and settled opposite her. First-graders didn't have homework, so Willa asked her, "Want to color in your coloring book?"

Elaine just shook her head.

Willa made up her mind to ignore her. She drew out her math assignment and set to work, but she was conscious all the while of her sister's eyes on her. Every now and then she heard a mousy crunching sound as Elaine took a nibble from an Oreo.

By the time Willa started on her history questions, Elaine had finished both cookies and was just sitting there, every now and then heaving loud sighs that Willa pretended not to notice. Then the telephone rang. "I'll get it!" Elaine said, but Willa beat her into the kitchen and grabbed the receiver first. "Hello?" she said.

"Hi, sweetheart," her father said.

"Hi, Pop."

"Everything okay there?"

She knew what he was really asking, but all she said was "Yup. I'm doing my homework and Elaine's just had her snack."

There was a pause. Then he said, "Well, I ought to be there before long. I'm just waiting for Doug Law to finish meeting with a student."

He was riding with Mr. Law, then. That was better than Mrs. Bellows, who sometimes stayed in her office as late as six or seven. Willa said, "Okay, Pop."

"Get ready for the world's best grilled cheese sandwiches!"

"Okay."

She hung up and turned to Elaine, who was watching her closely. "He says he'll be home before long," Willa told her.

Elaine heaved another sigh.

Willa looked around the kitchen at the counter crowded with dirty dishes, more dishes in the sink, Elaine's untouched glass of milk sitting on the table along with the clutter from yesterday. "We should clean up," she said. "Want to help me do the dishes? Me washing and you drying?"

"Yes!" Elaine said. She sounded excited about it; ordinarily it was their mother who washed and Willa who dried. "Do I get to wear an apron?" she asked.

"Well, sure."

Willa tied one of their mother's aprons just under Elaine's armpits, to keep it from dragging on the floor. Then she filled both sides of the sink with hot water, and Elaine hauled the step stool over so she could reach the counter. After Willa had washed the first plate and dipped it into the rinse water, she set it in the dish rack and Elaine picked it up carefully and dried every little crevice with a towel. She took ages at it, but that was all for the better, Willa figured. She started moving more slowly herself, drawing out the process, and when she'd finished washing the dishes she wiped down every surface, including the stovetop, and she cleared the clutter from the table and returned Elaine's milk to the fridge.

"I did good, don't you think?" Elaine asked when she'd dried the last dish.

"Yes, you did, Lainey," Willa said.

It wasn't so bad, really, being in charge. She began to imagine it as a permanent situation—just the three of them forever, coping on their own. Why, she and her father between them could keep things going just fine! They both liked systems, and methods. If her mother ever came back, she'd say, "Oh." She'd look around her and say, "Oh. I see you're doing better than I ever did."

"Know what?" Willa asked Elaine. "I vote we make a dessert."

"Dessert!" Elaine said. She started smiling hugely, showing the gap in her teeth. She smoothed her apron down her front. "What kind of dessert?"

"A cake, maybe, or a pudding. Chocolate pudding."

"Yes! Do you know how to do that?"

"I'm sure we can find a recipe," Willa said. She was warming to the idea now. As a rule they didn't have dessert. She had always envied Sonya, whose mother served dessert every night of the week. And chocolate pudding was their father's favorite—that and chocolate silk pie, but Willa thought a piecrust might be complicated.

"We'll keep it a secret from Pop till after supper," she told Elaine, "and then we'll bring it out. He's going to be amazed." She was moving the step stool as she spoke, climbing up on it to look through the books on their mother's cookbook shelf. *The Bride's Kitchen*," she read. "That would have the easiest recipe, I bet." She brought it down with her and opened it on the counter. Elaine came to stand at her elbow, her eyes on Willa's finger as it traveled down a column. "Chocolate cake, chocolate milk . . ." Willa read out. "Chocolate pudding. Two sixty-one." She flipped to page 261. "Sugar, cocoa powder, salt. Half-and-half, vanilla . . . uh-oh. Cornstarch." She didn't even know what cornstarch looked like, but she went over to check the cupboard where their mother kept the flour and such, and there it was. She set the box on the counter and Elaine said, "Can I stir, Willa? Can I?"

"Sure," Willa told her.

Elaine wasn't allowed to do anything on the stove yet, so Willa put a saucepan on the kitchen table and had her mix everything there. Of course Elaine made a mess of it, splashing enthusiastically over the rim of the pan, and the cornstarch and cocoa powder sat there in lumps instead of blending in, but Willa said, "Good job, Lainey," and then she moved the pan to the stove and stirred it herself, more gently, while it was heating.

But she had no better luck than Elaine had. The lumps remained, even after the mixture began bubbling around the edges. It looked like plain milk with brown-and-white gravel in it. "What's happening? Is it turning to pudding?" Elaine asked, because she wasn't tall enough to see for herself. Willa didn't answer. She raised the heat even higher, and the pan would have boiled over if she hadn't snatched it up and moved it to a cool burner, but still the gravel remained. "I don't understand," she told Elaine. She snapped off the right-hand burner, which was glowing a deep, dark red, and then she stared down into the saucepan.

"What? What?" Elaine asked.

"I don't—"

Out in the living room, their father called, "Hello?"

Willa and Elaine looked at each other.

"Anyone home?"

"Hide it!" Elaine whispered. "Put it in the fridge."

"I can't! It's not pudding yet!"

"What is it?"

"Whatcha up to, ladies?" their father asked from the kitchen doorway.

Willa turned to face him, trying to block his view of the saucepan, but he came closer and looked over her shoulder. He was still in his wool jacket and he smelled of winter air. "Cocoa?" he asked her.

"It's chocolate pudding," Willa told her shoes.

"It's what?"

"It's chocolate pudding, Papa!" Elaine shouted happily. "We made it for your dessert! It was going to be a surprise!"

"Well, gosh. I *am* surprised," he said. "I didn't know you two could cook. Why, this is really something!"

"We ruined it," Willa said.

"Say what?"

"It's all lumpy!" she burst out. "It won't mix in, and we've been stirring and stirring."

"Oh, now. Let's have a look," he said.

She moved aside, unwillingly, and he stepped up next to the stove and took hold of the spoon that slanted inside the saucepan. In a testing sort of way, he gave the mixture a stir. "Hmm," he said. "I see."

"It's a mess!" she told him.

"Well, not a mess, exactly; it's just a little ... Where's your recipe?"

She poked her chin toward the cookbook lying open on the counter, and he went over to check it. "So," he said, "you mixed the sugar and the cocoa and the salt. Then you stirred in all but a quarter-cup of the half-and-half over very low heat."

"Well ..."

"Then in a separate bowl you made a paste of the cornstarch and the remaining quarter-cup of half-and-half—"

"What? No. We just stirred everything together all at once."

"Ah," he said.

"Is that why it's doing this way?"

"Why, yes, I believe so, honey."

"But I didn't know!"

"When you're trying out a recipe, you'll find it pays to read all the instructions before you set to work."

She went back to staring at her shoes, because she didn't want him to see the tears in her eyes.

"First you check the list of ingredients, to make sure you have everything—"

"I *did* that."

"Well, good, honey. Then you assemble them on the counter—"

"I did! I was being so careful!"

"Then you read through the whole process, you see. It's kind of like what I tell my students when they're working on a carpentry project. You figure out what to do right away and what to do later, which step ought to come first and which step—"

She couldn't stand the way he *drilled* at her, pushing on so persistently no matter what she said back. She said, "I get it! Good grief. I'm not some dummy."

"Well, of course you're not, sweetheart. This is a learning experience, that's all. Next time, you'll know better."

"But I knew *this* time! I lined up all my ingredients . . . And now look. I wanted to surprise you!"

"Honey. It doesn't matter. Believe me."

"Doesn't matter?"

She raised her eyes and stared at him. She didn't care now if he saw that she was crying. She hoped he *did* see. "How can you say it doesn't matter," she asked him, "when I went to all this trouble?"

"No, I just meant—"

"Oh, forget it," she said, and she spun on her heel and left the kitchen. She went back out to the dining room and sat down in her chair and picked up her pencil.

Her father followed, with Elaine a shadow behind him. "Willa, honey," he said.

"I'm studying."

"Willa, don't be this way."

"Will you let me do my homework, please?" she asked him.

He waited a while, but she kept her head lowered, frowning steadily at her notebook, and finally he went back to the kitchen. Elaine stayed there a moment longer, watching her, but then she turned and left too.

Willa drew a fierce black line through her last history answer.

For supper they had grilled cheese sandwiches with peas. Willa ate silently, keeping her eyes on her plate, but Elaine and their father talked all through the meal in way-too-bright voices. Elaine told their father about the rabbit that Dommie Marconi had brought in for show-and-tell, and their father said, "Speaking of which, eat your peas, little rabbit," and Elaine popped a single pea in her mouth and tried to wriggle her nose up and down as she chewed, which made their father laugh. It was disgusting.

Willa said, "May I please be excused?"

"You didn't like your sandwich, honey?" her father asked, because she'd left half of it on her plate.

She said, "I'm not hungry," and stood up and pushed her chair back.

Her father and Elaine were the ones who cleared the table. Willa heard the chinking and scraping from where she sat in the dining room, and then she heard water running. So they must be washing the dishes, too.

Her father had not said one word of thanks for how she'd washed the dishes from earlier.

By now she had finished her homework, but she went on sitting over her books because they were her excuse for not helping out in the kitchen. Then her father came to the doorway and said, "Care for a game of Parcheesi?"

"It's my bath night," she said stiffly.

"What, so early?"

She didn't answer. Keeping her face turned away from him, she stood up and left the dining room and climbed the stairs to her room.

In the mirror on the closet door she looked streaky-faced and rumpled. Her frizzes were sticking out crazily all over her head, and her eyelashes were spiky from tears.

She yanked the closet door open and her reflection vanished. She took her pajamas from their hook and went to the bathroom to run a bath.

Sitting up to her armpits in hot water, watching her fingers turn smocked-looking, she started wondering if something terrible had happened to her mother. Maybe she had left intending to come right back but then had wrecked the car. Would anyone know to call them? She might be lying in the hospital unconscious.

Or dead.

Why hadn't that thought occurred to her father? Oh, there was just something *wrong* with this family! Willa was the only one who was normal.

When she'd finished her bath she went straight to bed, although it wasn't even eight o'clock and she didn't feel the least bit sleepy. She lay in the dark with her arms straight by her sides and stared up at the ceiling. Downstairs she heard her father talking and her sister giggling. A bit later she heard her sister climbing the stairs and she closed her eyes. Elaine hesitated in the doorway and then crossed to her bed and undressed by the light from the hall. Willa could make out the shape of her through her squinched eyelids; she saw Elaine hopping about as she put one foot and then the other into her pajama bottoms. When she was done she picked up her *Little House* book from the nightstand and went back downstairs, and then Willa heard their father's voice rumbling indistinctly as he read aloud.

He came upstairs with Elaine when they'd finished their chapter. Willa had just enough time to turn on her side with her face to the wall before he walked in, and she listened to him tuck Elaine into bed and wish her a good night. Then he came over to Willa's side of the room and whispered, "Willie? Wills? You awake?" But she didn't answer, and finally he went away.

His footsteps thudding down the stairs sounded so humble and disappointed that Willa had the feeling something was tearing apart in her chest.

When she woke, the morning sun was slanting across her quilt, and the house smelled of bacon and toast, and she heard quick, light foot-steps tripping up the stairs. "Rise and shine, duckies!" their mother said as she arrived in the doorway.

"Duckies" was what she called them when she was in a good mood, and to Willa it always seemed that she said it in a ducklike voice—fat-sounding and happy, like the voice women used on the radio when they wanted to show they were smiling. Willa couldn't help feeling cheered any time she heard it, but this morning she stayed flat on her back even so.

Elaine, though, sat up and cried, "Mommy!"

This was really annoying, because ordinarily she said "Mom." But "I've missed you so *much*, Mommy!" she cried, and she jumped out of bed, and when Willa sat up herself Elaine was wrapping her arms around their mother's waist and beaming up at her, and their mother was smiling and hugging her. She was wearing her rosebud house-coat, so she must have come home at some point during the night. "Where *were* you, Mommy? Where'd you go?" Elaine asked, but their mother just said, "Oh, hither and yon," in an airy tone, and then she flashed a smile at Willa and said, "Good morning, sleepy-head."

"Morning," Willa said in a low voice.

"I can fry your eggs, or scramble them, or poach them. What's Your Highness's preference?"

Which was how she often did after flare-ups—pretending nothing had happened. Never mind that she'd walked out on them without a thought; it didn't *mean* anything, she seemed to be saying. Heavens, just get over it! She could come back to find them dead in their beds, Willa thought, and all she'd say would be "Goodness! What's all *this* about?"

Although a few times, the really awful times (the time she slammed a serving spoon across Willa's cheekbone and gave her a black eye, the time she threw Elaine's lovey doll in the fire), she apologized like a heroine in a movie, sweeping them into her arms and crying, "Dear hearts, can you ever forgive me?" and burying her face in their necks and weeping hot tears. In the old days that had made Willa weep too, and cling to her and blurt out how scared she'd been and how of *course* she forgave her; but now it embarrassed her to remember that. Now she stayed stiff in her mother's arms on such occasions and turned her face to one side, and eventually her mother would draw back and say, "Oh, you're a cold one, Willa Drake."

Still, this morning her mother was looking so fresh and attractive, with the rosebuds bringing out the pink-and-white of her skin, and the house was smelling so cozy, and the world was back to how it should be. So Willa said, finally, "Scrambled, I guess."

"Scrambled it is! Lainey? For you?"

"Scrambled too, Mommy," Elaine said in her stupid baby voice, and when their mother caroled "Coming right up!" and turned to leave, Elaine went with her, even though she was still in pajamas.

Then Willa climbed out of bed and spent a long while washing and dressing, and clamping her hair down with two barrettes, and staring at her own serious face in the bathroom mirror.

By the time she got downstairs, the others were halfway through breakfast—the three of them in the dining room, as if it were Sunday. The table was set with the good china and they were even using the toast rack, with the toast standing up in a row like the teeth of a comb. "Morning, honey," her father said.

"Morning," Willa said, not looking at him. She slid into her seat.

"*Somebody* took her time," her mother said. Which made Willa send her a sideways glance, checking the set of her mouth. Was it held a little bit crooked, the top lip not quite aligned with the bottom lip because she was gritting her teeth? But no, her lips were soft and curved, and when she rose to pour Willa's father more coffee she touched him lightly on the shoulder before she sat down again.

The scrambled eggs were lukewarm by now but they still tasted good, with a little cheese stirred in just the way Willa liked, and the bacon was nice and crisp with no fatty white spots. She helped herself to three strips.

"I guess I should let Doug Law know I won't be needing a ride," her father was saying, and her mother said, "Oh, I meant to tell you. I think the car seems to be having this teensy little problem."

"What kind of teensy little problem?" he asked.

"Well, any time you turn it on a red dot shows up on the dash-board."

He raised his eyebrows. He said, "You've been driving all around with the idiot light lit?"

"The idiot . . . ?" she said, and Willa tensed, worrying that she had taken it the wrong way. But then she said, "Oh. Well, yes, I suppose I have been."

"And you didn't think to get it looked at?"

"I know! I'm awful," she said gaily. "I'm so hopeless with mechanical things." And she made a silly-me face at Willa and Elaine.

"Can you believe her?" their father asked them. But he seemed amused, more than anything. From his expression, he might have been asking, "Don't you think she's *wonderful*?"

Elaine was too busy spreading jam on her toast to notice. Willa just looked at him and said nothing.

Their mother peered into the cream pitcher and shook it a little, and then she got up and carried it out to the kitchen. Elaine, meanwhile, started talking again about Dommie Marconi's rabbit, except now she was calling it a bunny. "Bunnies are real quiet and Dommie says they don't need walking," she said. "Can *we* get a bunny, Pop? Please?"

But he was studying Willa. He said, "Willa, honey? Are you still mad at me?"

She shrugged.

"I didn't quite understand about last night," he said. "What *was* that? Can we talk about it?"

His voice was meek but pushy, Willa thought, and she didn't feel like answering him, but she knew he would keep on pressing her until she did. So she shrugged again and said, "I was just overtired, I guess."

"Oh," he said

That seemed to satisfy him. At least, he didn't ask anything more.

In the silence that followed, Willa's eyes met her sister's, and the two of them exchanged a long, stunned, stricken gaze.

1977

WILLA'S COLLEGE had a jitney that made several runs to the airport before any major holiday. She herself had never taken it—plane travel was expensive, and she went home by Greyhound bus if she went at all—but in the spring of her junior year her boyfriend suggested that he come meet her family over Easter weekend, and it was his idea they should fly. What else, he asked: ride sitting up on a bus all night only to do the same thing going back again two days later? Well, yes, that was what *she* would have done. But she didn't argue.

Derek paid for her ticket out of his monthly allowance, but Willa told her parents he had happened upon it for nothing in a buy-one-get-one-free deal. Heaven only knew if there *were* such deals, but her parents weren't used to flying themselves and they took her word for it.

In the jitney he and she were surrounded by friends, mostly his, and they couldn't carry on much of a conversation. Derek was president of the senior class and captain of the tennis team; he had a warm, friendly way about him that everybody liked. So there was a lot of backslapping and wisecracking and calling from seat to seat, while Willa held her purse in both hands and looked on, smiling. She had dressed up for the plane, which she would not have done for the bus. She wore a powder-blue wool suit and her hair was smoothed into a bun. (Derek said she was the prettiest girl in the school when she did her hair that way.) He, on the other hand, was in jeans and his usual tan corduroy blazer, because he came from California and flying was not such a big deal to him. But he was so square-jawed and clean-cut, a full head taller than anyone else—and *two* heads taller than Willa—and with his short blond hair he could not have looked sloppy if he'd tried, Willa believed.

Kinney College was in northern Illinois, surrounded by farmlands as flat as pool tables, and on this April afternoon the few trees they passed were still stark and bare. At home it would be spring already. The Lenten roses had come and gone, her mother had written; they always finished up before Easter. Derek was going to like seeing some green for once. He couldn't get over the long midwestern winters.

At the airport their friends split off to go to their different airlines, and Willa and Derek were finally on their own. She was glad he was there to take care of things. She wouldn't have known what to do at the metal detector or how to check her luggage. When everything had been seen to, he shepherded her to the waiting area and settled her in a plastic chair, and then he went off to buy soft drinks. She had the feeling while he was gone that she was all alone on the planet. The passengers sitting around her seemed not quite real, and she was conscious of herself from outside, from a distance—her back very straight, her patent-leather pumps set primly together, her eyes wide and wary. The sight of Derek heading toward her finally, with a paper cup in each hand, filled her with relief.

"What do you think I should call your folks?" he asked as he plopped down next to her and passed her a cup. "Mr. and Mrs. Drake? Or use their first names?"

"Oh, Mr. and Mrs., at the start," she said. She didn't even have to consider. Her parents would be horrified if a young person acted so free and easy with them. Or her mother would, at least. "After they get to know you, though," she said, "they might suggest you use their first names."

"What *are* their first names?"

For some reason, she hesitated. Maybe she worried he would ignore her advice and start right off using them. But then she said, "Melvin and Alice."

"Hi there, Melvin and Alice!" he said. He put on a resonant, deliberately smarmy-sounding voice that made her laugh. "May I please have your daughter's hand in marriage?"

Willa stopped laughing. She couldn't tell if he was serious.

"Too soon?" he asked her. He set an arm around her shoulders and looked into her face. "Too sudden? Did I surprise you?"

"Well . . ."

"It must have crossed your mind, Willa. I'm in love with you. I've wanted to marry you from the day I first laid eyes on you."

His face was so close to hers that she could see the sprinkling of freckles across the bridge of his nose, as fine as grains of sand. His freckles rescued him from handsomeness, she always felt. They made her trust him. Without a second thought she had turned her back on those overconfident football players pressing sweet mixed drinks on her; she had covered sheets of notebook paper with "Willa MacIntyre" and "Mrs. Derek MacIntyre," and dreamed of being surprised one night with a diamond engagement ring. They could be engaged throughout her senior year, she figured, and marry the summer after she graduated.

But "I can't imagine just going off and leaving you behind when I start my job," he was saying. "I need to have you with me."

Willa said, "What . . . ?" Then she said, "You're starting your job this June, though."

"Right."

"You want to get married in two months?"

"Or it could be three, if you need more time to plan the wedding," he said.

"You mean before I finish school?"

"You can finish in California."

"But at Kinney I have a full scholarship!"

"So? You could get a scholarship in California, too. With those grades of yours? Any place would be dying to have you."

She didn't bother telling him that scholarships were not that easy to arrange. Instead she said, "And Dr. Brogan."

"What about him?"

"He's got a whole plan for me, Derek. Next fall I'm taking his honors course in linguistic anthropology."

"You think they don't teach foreign languages in San Diego?" he asked.

"No, I just—"

"Willa," he said, "do you not *want* to marry me?"

"Oh, I do, but—"

He took his arm away and slumped back in his chair. "I messed up, didn't I," he said. "I should have made you a formal proposal."

"It isn't that! I really do want to marry you, Derek; honest. But couldn't we just, maybe, get engaged for now?"

"Sure," he said.

This wasn't very satisfying. She studied his face, which gave nothing away. "Are you mad at me?" she asked him.

"No."

"I don't want you to be mad at me."

"I'm not mad in the least," he said, "because I'm counting on changing your mind by and by."

"Derek—"

"So! I call your parents Mr. and Mrs. I do not use their first names until they tell me to. And how about your sister? Is she 'Miss Drake'?"

"No, silly," Willa said, forcing a laugh. "She's Elaine."

"Or maybe Miss Elaine," he said consideringly. "Miss Elaine and Miss Willa, the two spinster sisters of Lark City, Pennsylvania."

Willa gave him a playful slap on the knee. But she couldn't help feeling that something unsettled still hung in the air between them.

In the magazine ads for airlines, stewardesses wore trim skirts with matching tailored jackets and military-looking hats. But the young woman who greeted Willa and Derek when they stepped onto the plane wore a boxy pantsuit—pantsuit!—and no hat at all. And the seats were arranged not in twos but in threes, which made them seem less luxurious. Willa and Derek had a window seat and a middle seat. Derek stood back to let her in next to the window, but she said, "Oh, I'll take the middle," because she needed less room. She settled in after he did and fastened her seat belt and then tentatively pressed the button to tilt herself farther back, till Derek told her she shouldn't do that until they were in the air.

Even if it wasn't as glamorous as she had imagined, she was still excited. The interior of the plane had an unfamiliar plastic smell, and the sounds seemed different, too. Some sort of sealed-off, plugged-up silence lay just beneath the voices of the other passengers.

The man who dropped into the seat on her right was gaunt and whiskery, and he wore a black-and-red lumber jacket over thread-bare jeans. She decided against saying hello. She merely smiled at him with her mouth closed, but he was figuring out his seat belt and might not have noticed.

When they took off she was reading the safety instructions, and she folded them immediately and returned them to her seat-back pocket. It was lucky she did, because their trip down the runway seemed very long and bumpy. (Willa tended to get carsick if she read in a moving vehicle.) After a while she started wondering: Were they not ever going to leave the ground? Was the pilot trying to lift off but failing? She shifted her eyes from the airport buildings outside the window to Derek, who was reading the *Sports Illustrated* he had brought along. He seemed relaxed, so she decided not to worry. And just then she felt a shift of some kind and the plane tipped upward. She saw the scenery dropping away below them, but they couldn't be actually flying, could they? It didn't *feel* like flying. She still felt earthbound; she was still weighing down her seat cushion. Some-how she had expected more of a floating sensation. And once they had leveled off it was even more disappointing, because any sense of motion gradually ceased. They could be just sitting on the ground with the engines roaring, except that the scenery had vanished.

The stewardess came to stand near them in the aisle and dem-onstrate the safety equipment, including an inflatable life vest. Life vest! For what? Nobody watched except Willa and the whiskery man beside her. Willa made sure to keep a rapt expression on her face so the stewardess wouldn't feel ignored.

Then a different stewardess wheeled a cart down the aisle and offered people free drinks. Derek ordered a Coke but Willa said, "Nothing, thanks," because she would feel shy about asking her seatmate to let her out if she needed to use the bathroom. He didn't take anything, either, just shook his head and went on staring glumly straight in front of him.

She told Derek, "I wish we were on a flight where they gave us a meal."

"No, you don't," he said. "Believe me."

"I wanted one of those teeny saltshakers like my roommate got on her trip to New York."

He gave her an indulgent smile and went back to his magazine.

Willa had brought a paperback, but she didn't think she could concentrate so she let it stay in her purse. She resumed looking out the window. Thin shreds of clouds passed like wisps of cigarette smoke. She tried to convince herself that these were the pillowy puffs she used to imagine bouncing on when she was a little girl, but they didn't seem related. Judy Collins came into her head, singing "Both Sides Now." All at once the lyrics seemed more meaningful.

Willa glanced at Derek again. He was still absorbed in his reading. His face in repose was so serene that it seemed childlike, with his lashes casting a shadow on his velvety cheek. So this was the person she was going to end up marrying! After all her years of wondering. She had to keep trying the notion out, the way she would try out her image in the mirror after she got a new hairdo. Each time she returned to it, she felt a thrill all over again. And yet... Nobody had told her that you could want to marry a person but still have conflicting thoughts about him. (She was sometimes a little put off by his single-minded interest in sports, for instance. Also he had a bit of a temper and twice to her knowledge had got into a shoving match with guys at football games.) Well, but of course you could have such thoughts. This wasn't a Hollywood movie.

Something nudged hard into her right side, and she drew away, but the nudging object followed her. She looked over at the stranger. "Keep your eyes straight ahead," he muttered. He was staring straight ahead himself, and his lips were barely moving. Whatever was pressing into her side went on pressing, no matter how she shrank from it.

She blinked and focused on the seat back in front of her.

"This is a gun," he said quietly, "and it's loaded. Move and I shoot. You're not allowed out of your seat, and neither is he."

In a thin, whimpery voice that didn't sound like her own, Willa asked, "How am I going to explain to him that he can't get out of his seat?"

Derek said "Huh?" and looked over at her.

The gun jabbed her harder. She said, "I didn't say anything," and Derek returned to his magazine.

A few minutes later the stewardess came down the aisle again. This time she was carrying a plastic bag. "Trash? Any trash?" she asked at each row, and she gave the bag a shake. Willa looked up into the stewardess's face when she reached them and sent her a silent message: *Please. Please.* "Trash?" the woman said, shaking her bag. Without taking his eyes from his magazine, Derek held his empty cup out, and Willa raised a hand to pass it along but the gun jabbed her again. She gasped aloud, but Derek just extended his cup slightly farther and the stewardess took it from him and continued on down the aisle.

Willa could see that the stranger's right arm was folded across his stomach, but his gun was concealed by Willa's armrest. Her mind was racing. She had heard that phrase often, "mind was racing," without realizing what it would actually feel like—the skittery, frantic speed of her thoughts. Should she scream? Poke him with her elbow? Jump out of her seat? But then he might shoot Derek.

Derek said, without looking up from his magazine, "My ears are popping; are yours?"

"What?"

"You know to swallow, right?"

"What?"

The jab of the gun was vicious this time, painful and insistent, and she said, "Oh!"

Derek glanced over at her. Then he closed his magazine, leaving a finger inside as a marker, and undid his seat belt and stood up. "Trade places with me," he said.

Willa gazed up at him imploringly.

"Come on. Move."

She fumbled for her seat belt. She undid the buckle, holding her breath, and then she clutched her purse and sat forward, wincing as she braced for the slam of the bullet. Nothing happened. Derek took her arm to help her to a standing position and guide her past him to the window, after which he settled in the middle seat and opened his magazine again.

At first she was so tense that her spine didn't touch her seat back. She was wondering when Derek would feel the gun nosing his ribs.

All he did, though, was turn a page, and when she dared to slide her eyes past him she saw that the stranger's hands were resting loosely on his knees now, and there was nothing in them.

She sat back. She was shaking. She turned her face toward the window, but she was conscious only of Derek's thigh near her own thigh, and his corduroy sleeve rasping her own sleeve each time he turned another page. She felt deeply grateful for his certainty—his matter-of-fact conviction that he could handle any of the many, many dangers in the universe.

She had been anxious about their landing, back in what seemed that long-ago time before she'd *really* had something to be anxious about, but in fact she noticed only the mildest bump, followed by a long, hard pulling-back sensation. Then a voice came over the loud-speaker welcoming them and thanking them and hoping to see them again. Outside her window, Willa could see pale lavender mountains far in the distance.

The whiskery man was the first to stand up and the first to step into the aisle, and while Willa and Derek were waiting their turn to step into the aisle themselves he was already pushing past the people ahead of him and making his way to the front of the plane. As soon as he was safely out of hearing, Willa touched Derek's elbow and asked, "Did you know what he was up to?"

"What who was up to?" Derek asked, turning slightly to look at her.

"That man sitting next to us," she said, and she tipped her head in the man's direction. He was sidling past a fat woman now. All they could see of him was his scrawny black-and-red back, and then not even that. "He was pointing a gun at me."

Derek said, "Say what?," but at the same time he was entering the stream of passengers moving forward.

"He poked a gun in my side," Willa said, following close behind. "He said don't move or he'd shoot."

"What kind of gun?" Derek asked over his shoulder.

"What *kind* of gun?" she echoed. "How would I know what kind? It was poking into my ribcage! I couldn't see it."

Derek sent a sharp glance back at her, but he didn't comment.

They arrived at the exit door and Derek thanked the stewardess. Willa hadn't known they should do that; she hurriedly thanked her too. Then they stepped out onto the staircase. It was warm here, and sunny, with a soft breeze brushing their faces. Below them she saw their seatmate—a slouched stick figure loping toward the terminal building, pulling open the glass door before anybody else, vanishing inside without a backward glance.

Derek made no attempt to talk as they descended the stairs, but once they reached the tarmac he said, "I don't understand. He aimed a gun at you but you couldn't see it?"

"He had it hidden under the armrest," she said. They were walking side by side now; she had to take an extra little skip from time to time to keep up with him. "He poked it into my ribs and he said, 'Move and I shoot.' And I couldn't think of any way to tell you! How did you guess that something was wrong, finally?"

"How did I . . . ?"

"What made you say we ought to change places?"

"Well, I was reading and you weren't," Derek said. "You were just spacing out, there. I thought it would make more sense for you to take the window seat."

"You didn't notice anything odd?"

"Let me get this straight," Derek said. He stopped walking and turned to look at her. "The guy who was sitting next to us pointed a gun at you."

"Right."

"A real, actual gun."

"I think so."

"Well ... Willa? What was he planning to do? Make you take the controls and fly us to Cuba?"

"I don't know, Derek!"

"I mean, it doesn't add up, sweetie. I don't see how this would have worked. Don't you think it was maybe a joke?"

"A joke!"

"Okay, so not a very funny one, but—"

"He scared me to *death*, Derek! I was shaking. I felt it was just him and me alone in this, and I didn't know how to tell you about it, so I was really glad when you caught on of your own accord. Or I *thought* you caught on."

"Oh, well, all's well that ends well," Derek said. He was looking around now. The air smelled like flowers, and the afternoon sun was almost hot, and people were trickling out of the terminal to greet the arriving passengers. "*Cute* little place," he said. "Do you see your folks anywhere?"

"They'll be out front," she said shortly. They would be idling the car at the curb so they wouldn't have to pay for parking, but she didn't want to tell Derek that.

She felt a lot less grateful to Derek now than she had when they were on the plane.

They entered the terminal, which did seem very small, and waited beneath the Baggage sign till a worker wheeled in a trolley loaded with suitcases. Other passengers were waiting too, but not their seatmate. Maybe he was hiding until they left the building. Or he'd been traveling with no luggage; that seemed even more likely.

Derek reclaimed his duffel bag and Willa's blue vinyl suitcase, and then they headed for the exit. Willa spotted her parents' car almost as soon as they stepped outside—a Chevy her father had bought a few years ago from one of his students. You couldn't mistake its distinctive finish, which was a hand-painted, nonshiny purple. She said, "There they are," and deliberately did not look over to see Derek's reaction.

Both her parents got out of the car when she and Derek approached. "Willa girl!" her father said. He was in his work clothes, but her mother had dressed up a bit. She wore a flowered shirtwaist that Willa hadn't seen before and her hair was tied back with a floppy bow. Willa said, "Mom and Pop, I'd like you to meet Derek," and Derek said, "How do you do, Mrs. Drake. Mr. Drake," and set down Willa's suitcase to shake hands. They didn't suggest he use their first names, but they were both smiling and putting in some effort, Willa could tell. This made her feel a little sad for them, in a way that had been happening more and more often since she had started college. While her father loaded their luggage into the trunk her mother hugged her and said, "Welcome home, darling." Then her father hugged her too, in his usual shy, held-back way, and asked, "Flight go okay?"

"It went fine," she said.

She and Derek were settled in the rear seat and the car was pulling away from the curb before she added, "But a passenger pointed
a gun at me."

"What!" her mother said, twisting around to stare at her. "A
gun?"

"He was sitting right next to me, and I felt something poke into
me and he said, 'Don't move or I shoot.'"

"Are you serious?"

"*Yes,* I'm serious."

"Well, my lord," her father said, while her mother twisted even
farther around so that she could see Derek. She said, "What did *you*
do, Derek?"

"Oh, I didn't even know about it," Derek said cheerfully.

"Did you call for help?" her mother asked Willa.

"I couldn't! I didn't dare open my mouth. Finally Derek said to
change seats with him, and that seemed to be the end of it."

"Merciful heavens," her mother said. "I hope you reported it
afterward."

"Who to, though?" Willa asked. "I mean, it was the weirdest
thing. The whole situation just seemed to get . . . swept under the
rug, finally."

Derek cleared his throat. "Also," he said, "it might not have been
exactly what it looked like."

Willa's mother swiveled toward him again.

"I'm guessing the guy was just some kind of joker," he said. And
then, to Willa, "After all, sweetie, you had only his word for it that
there even *was* a gun. Guy was probably just sitting there bored out
of his skull, and he thinks to himself, 'I know what: I'll have myself
some fun with this snippy little college girl.'"

Willa's mother looked expectantly at Willa.

"Well, maybe," Willa said after a moment. She wasn't sure why she felt offended. Finally, changing the subject, she asked her parents, "Where's Elaine? I was thinking she might come with you."

"Oh, *Elaine*," her mother said, facing forward again. "Elaine wouldn't be caught dead with us. Wait till you see her, Willa. She gets all her clothes at Goodwill these days and she listens to what I wouldn't even call music and her friends are downright strange."

"Now, now," Willa's father said. "It's not as bad as all that."

"Yesterday," Willa's mother told Willa, "I asked her to clean her room because your side of it was completely submerged. I mean, I couldn't even see your bed for all the clothes piled on it. But later I went up to check and she hadn't done a thing. She'd gone off by then with her, I don't know, boyfriend? Friend? Partner in crime? This boy who's a whole foot shorter than she is, Marcus, his name is, all dressed in black and wearing one earring; has never so much as given me the time of day. So anyhow, when I saw the state of the room do you know what I did? I opened the window and I heaved all her clothes down into the backyard."

Derek gave a little hiss of amusement, and Willa's mother sent him an appreciative glance. "Jeans, tops, sweaters," she told him, "these dead old men's pajamas she favors . . . all of it. Out the window. Clean across the yard. Long black skinny tights straggling over the barbecue grill."

Now Derek laughed aloud.

"My wife is very tempestuous," Willa's father told him.

Willa hated when he said that. He always made it sound like a virtue. He gave a prideful lilt to the word, and when he sought out Derek's face in the rearview mirror his eyes were rayed with smile lines.

"Well, I don't get it," Willa told her mother flatly. "All you did was spread her mess around further. I don't know what good *that* did."

"Oh, honey, just you wait till you have a teenage daughter yourself and you'll understand," her mother said. "My life is a living hell."

Willa sank into silence. Derek set a hand on top of hers, and she let it stay there, but she kept her face turned toward her window.

The countryside here was much more interesting than Illinois, she felt. She hoped Derek was noticing that. (He always talked as if California were so special.) There were tumbling green hills resembling bunches of fresh parsley, and mysterious hollows already darkening in the late-afternoon shadows, and nearer to the highway little cabins sat surrounded by rickrack fences and ramshackle sheds, washing machines on their front porches, hound dogs splayed in the dirt yards, tractors rusting out back. The trip from the airport took over an hour, and Willa watched the scenery that whole time without speaking while her mother, up front, was all charm and gaiety and hostessy curiosity. Did Derek have brothers and sisters? Yes, two brothers, both younger. And did she understand correctly that he was about to graduate? Right, and not a moment too soon; he was ready to start his real life. What did he plan to do next; did he know? He already had a job back home in San Diego; a friend of his dad's owned a sporting-goods chain and he had offered Derek an executive position. Willa's mother said, "Oh, how lovely! Because of your tennis skills, I guess," which was embarrassing because it revealed that Willa must have discussed him with her family. "Yes, ma'am," Derek said. Willa had never heard him say "ma'am" before. It seemed he had switched to a foreign language to accommodate the natives. She scowled at a passing pickup with three overalled boys lounging in the rear, their backs slouched against the truck's cab. How they would have hooted at all this genteel small talk!

The house had been spruced up for their visit, Willa could tell. There was a pot of pansies on the porch that must have been bought within the last couple of days, because her mother could kill off a plant in no time, as she cheerfully admitted herself. In the foyer Willa smelled a combination of lemon Pledge and Mr. Clean, and when she took Derek upstairs to the guest room she could see the fresh vacuum-cleaner tracks on the carpet. "This is where you'll be sleeping," she told him, entering first. The window was open and a breeze was stirring the curtains. A vase of daffodils stood on the dresser. Clearly, her mother had gone to a lot of trouble.

Ordinarily the sight of the guest-room bed, with its multiple rows of giant pillows and fussy, overstuffed cushions slanted against the headboard, made Willa's toes curl in protest as she imagined how her feet would jam against the footboard. But Derek said, "Nice," and he set his duffel bag on the new foldout luggage stand, and Willa saw that it *was* nice, actually.

"Where's *your* room?" he asked. He took hold of her wrist as he spoke and drew her toward him.

"Oh, down the hall," she said vaguely.

Now he had her nestled against him, and he murmured, "Do I get to visit in the night?," with his breath ruffling the top of her head.

"No, silly, I share with my sister," she said, but she didn't pull away.

"So you will have to visit *me*, then."

"Not a chance!" she said, laughing. Then she looked up to see her sister glancing in as she passed the doorway. She was wearing what looked like a man's long overcoat, brown tweed and much too warm for the season, and her hair hung in two straight curtains that barely parted to make room for her face. "Oh, Lainey," Willa said, hastily separating from Derek. Elaine came to a reluctant halt. "I'd like you to meet Derek. Derek, this is my sister, Elaine."

Elaine raised her left eyebrow—or the part of her left eyebrow that could be seen, at least. Her eyes were so heavily outlined in black that she resembled a pileated woodpecker. "Don't let me interrupt anything," she said, and she continued down the hall.

Derek and Willa exchanged a wry look.

"So!" Willa finally said in a bright voice. "Bathroom's directly across from you, towels are on the shelf above the tub . . ."

Derek reached out to encircle her wrist again, and she allowed it, but she said, "Let's go downstairs and see what's for supper, shall we?"

Downstairs, Willa's mother was setting a tray of juice tumblers on the coffee table. An uncorked bottle already stood there—cream sherry, Willa saw as her mother began pouring. She was surprised. She was shocked, in fact. Her parents didn't drink. Her father had never found any liquor he could stand the taste of, he always said, and her mother just didn't have the habit of it, although she'd been known to accept a flute of champagne at a wedding reception. But now her mother said, "Sherry, Derek?" delicately lifting a brimful glass with just her fingertips, and he said, "Oh, well, thanks," and accepted it.

"Sherry for you, Willa?"

"Thank you, Mom," Willa said.

She couldn't bear for Derek to show any sign he found this laughable: the sweet, thick sherry served just before supper and the squat, slightly sticky juice glasses. But no, he acted perfectly solemn and respectful, holding his glass in front of him without taking a sip until Willa's father arrived from the kitchen with his own drink (iced tea). Then Derek said, "Cheers, everybody," and everyone murmured, "Cheers," and took a sip.

"Shouldn't we call Lainey?" Willa's father asked her mother, but her mother gave a grimace and said, "Lots of luck with *that*." She told Derek, "Willa's sister wouldn't be caught dead hanging out with her family these days," and Derek chuckled.

Willa didn't know why her mother was putting on such a show. It must be because Willa had finally, finally found herself a boyfriend. (Had her parents been worried about that?) It was true she had not been popular in high school. The only boys who ever asked her out had been geeky, bespectacled misfits whom she had turned down without a thought, preferring instead the back-of-the-room boys—juvenile-delinquent types in leather jackets, lounging almost horizontal at their desks and yawning at the ceiling during class, roaring out of the parking lot in their souped-up trucks as soon as the last bell rang. But none of those boys had ever given her a glance.

Maybe her parents had been asking each other, year after year, "Is she all *right*? Is something wrong with her? Do you suppose she'll end up an old maid?"

Derek was telling her mother that he had once been like Elaine himself; used to avoid his parents like the plague ("I find that hard to believe," her mother murmured), but *now* look: he couldn't think of any two people he'd rather spend an evening with.

Willa took another sip of sherry. It coated her throat like cough syrup.

．　．　．

The experience with the man on the plane lurked behind every-thing, casting a shadow, causing the back of her neck to tingle, sur-facing now and then during the most unrelated conversations, but neither Derek nor her parents referred to it again. It seemed her par-ents had decided to go along with Derek's interpretation of it.

When she was showering that night she examined her right side for a bruise, but there wasn't one. When she went to bed she made a conscious effort to focus on other subjects so that she wouldn't have bad dreams—think of how to entertain Derek tomorrow; think of whether he'd made a good impression on her parents—and it worked, more or less, but then in the middle of a deep sleep she felt a steady, blunt nudge in her ribs, and she woke with her heart pound-ing so violently that she fancied she could see her top sheet trem-bling over her breasts in the dark. She searched with her fingers for the spot where she'd felt the nudge and it seemed to her that it was, in fact, slightly sore, but maybe that was just from her own prodding earlier. After that she lay awake a long time, staring up at the ceiling and listening to her sister's snuffly breaths across the room.

Okay, then: think of Derek's proposal.

He had no idea how much he'd asked of her, suggesting she give up her work with Dr. Brogan. The discovery of language had been her great epiphany in college. Not just Spanish and French and such, which she already knew from high school, but the origins of lan-guage in general, and what the various languages revealed about the various cultures that spoke them, and—most interesting of all—how many things the different languages had in common. Wasn't it amazing that most people the world over agreed upon the need to distinguish between "he did" and "he was doing"? And idioms: funny how often the same illogical and unlikely idiom had been arrived at independently by widely separate nationalities. She could listen to Dr. Brogan discuss such issues all day.

Still, it was tempting, just for a moment, to consider the adventurousness of throwing everything over to marry Derek. Ditching all that was familiar, tying herself almost arbitrarily to this whole new person entirely unrelated to her. The suddenness, the extremeness.

Finally she slid back into sleep, and as far as she knew she had no dreams at all, good or bad, either one.

After breakfast the next morning she took Derek on a walk through town, keeping up a stream of chatter. "There's where the Pearsons live," she said. The Pearsons were the people she worked for during the summers, tending their two children while the parents took city folk whitewater-rafting. "And here's Miss Carroll's house who taught me clarinet, except one day I rang the doorbell and got no answer and it turned out she'd run off with Mr. Surrey from the auto-parts store who was married and had five children."

Derek said, "I didn't know you played the clarinet."

She drew in a breath to speak but then just stared at him, because *what*? Oh, boys were such foreigners. (Not for the first time, she wished she'd had a brother or two.) A girl would have begged for every detail about Miss Carroll's running off. "Well, not anymore," she said finally. "I wasn't very musical."

For their lunch she packed sandwiches and a thermos of lemonade and they went for a hike up Bert Kane Ridge. They ate on the wrinkled mound of granite at the top—Elephant Rock, it was called—which was covered with names and hearts and initials dating all the way back to the 1920s. From time to time other hikers passed, so it wasn't as private as she had hoped, but she and Derek sat close together and exchanged a few discreet kisses. Willa pointed out the distant road where her parents lived, and the steeple of their church just below them. "Looks like a nice place for a wedding," Derek said, even though he could not have known that from where he sat.

Willa was worried he might start talking again about marrying this summer, so she said, "Oh, look, jack-in-the-pulpits! I haven't seen jack-in-the-pulpits for ages," and the subject of the church was dropped.

For supper that night her parents took them to the area's best restaurant, the Nu-Deal Inn out on the East-West Parkway. Willa had been hoping that Elaine would come along to dilute the conversation (was how she thought of it), but Elaine wasn't even around to turn them down, so they went without her. The Nu-Deal was family-style, with long, linen-draped tables where the diners all sat together and helped themselves from giant platters of fried chicken and barbecued ribs and sliced ham and turnip greens cooked with fatback. Willa's mother got involved in a conversation with a woman who was a huge fan, she said; she'd seen Willa's mother play Amanda in a production of *The Glass Menagerie* at the Garrettville Little Theatre. Willa's mother said, "Oh, aren't you nice to remember! Goodness, that was so long ago." So then of course Willa's father had to explain to Derek about his wife's acting hobby. "I think she really could have made something of herself if we'd lived in a big city," he said. "She's got this flair; I mean, when she is on the stage the audience looks only at her. Take that *Glass Menagerie*, for instance: why, *she* was not the star, this young crippled girl was, but Alice swoops in and she's so full of verve and just . . . uninhibited, you know, and enthusiastic—"

"Oh, Melvin, stop," Willa's mother said with a laugh, and she gave him an affectionate swat on the arm.

He beamed at her, his eyes twinkling behind his tiny, very clean lenses. "Well, anyhow," he told Derek, "maybe someday you'll get to see her in something and you'll understand what I'm talking about."

Did that mean he hoped Derek would be more than a one-time guest? Did it mean he approved of him?

Neither of Willa's parents had voiced an opinion about Derek so far. Several times during the day Willa had made a point of being conveniently at hand when Derek was out of hearing, but still they had said nothing. This was unlike them—or at least unlike her mother, who could have a very sharp eye when it came to Willa's friends. Her father was generally more noncommittal. Now, though, he told Derek, "Summers they always do a Shakespeare play, and she's bound to get a part in that. You should come back in the summer." Willa took that as an excellent sign. She looked over at Derek (please don't let him go into how he hoped they'd be married by summer), and he said, "Sure thing, I'd enjoy that." Willa relaxed.

The other unanswered question was how Derek felt about *them*. She'd had any number of opportunities to ask him, but she hadn't. Maybe she thought he would be more truthful if she didn't try to force it out of him.

Quietly buttering her biscuit, she felt important, suddenly. She was the sole reason these three people were sitting here. For once she was the absolute center of her world, and she took her own sweet time over the biscuit, keeping her eyes lowered and spreading the butter exactly to the biscuit's edges with slow, even strokes that felt languorous and self-indulgent.

The next day was Easter Sunday and they all went to church except Elaine, who said she wasn't a Christian. "What has *that* got to do with it?" her mother asked, but she didn't insist. When they got home, though (after a painful social interval where Willa and Derek had to chitchat with various inquisitive church ladies), Willa's mother went directly to the living room, where Elaine was lounging behind the Sunday paper, and said, "I just want you to know that you are joining us for lunch, missy; no ifs or ands or buts. Your sister's leaving this afternoon and you have not had one meal with us the entire time she's been here."

"Fine; whatever," Elaine said, not emerging from behind her paper.

Derek wasn't around for that conversation—he'd gone upstairs to pack—so when he walked into the dining room later and saw the table set for five he raised his eyebrows. "Whoa," he said, "Morticia's honoring us with her presence?"

"Who knows?" Willa said bleakly. She was beginning to feel a little hurt about Elaine. She had imagined that the two of them could have a few private talks together; commiserate about their mother's craziness as they used to and maybe discuss Derek. But it seemed that Elaine had begun to lump Willa in with their parents in her general resentment.

When lunch was announced, though, she did come to the table and drop into her seat. She was still wearing pajamas, striped flannel, with a huge moth-eaten cardigan sagging over them, but her sheets of hair were combed smooth and the heavy black slashes were freshly painted around her eyes. "Rabbit stew," she informed Derek, when her mother rose to lift the lid off the cast-iron pot in front of her.

Derek said, "Really?"

"You don't like rabbit?" Willa's mother asked him.

"No, I . . . sure, I like it fine," he said.

"It's a recipe from my aunt Rachel," she said, picking up a serving spoon. "*Civet de lievre.*" (She gave the *r* a fancy gargled sound that made Willa want to crawl under the table.) "Aunt Rachel was the gourmet cook in my family. The rest of them . . . oh, you wouldn't believe what dreadful meals my mother served."

Willa and Elaine had been told many, many stories about those meals. "A clump of mashed split peas glopped onto a plate . . . ," Willa began, and Elaine chimed in, ". . . topped with an iceberg-lettuce salad drenched in bottled orange-colored dressing . . ."

"On special occasions, tinned pineapple chunks were added to the salad," Willa said.

"On *non*-special occasions, dinner was canned baked beans on a slice of Wonder bread."

They were enjoying themselves; it was sort of like a comedy routine. Even their mother was smiling, although she said, "Now, girls, don't poke fun at your poor old grandma." She passed Derek his plate and reached for Willa's.

"I always liked her cooking," their father said wistfully.

"Oh, you just liked that she made a fuss over you," their mother told him.

"She made a fuss over him?" Willa asked. She hadn't known that. She'd always figured that her grandparents—longtime

Philadelphians—must look down on her father, with his backcountry origins.

But her mother said, "Well, I had been dating this boy they couldn't stand. He was infatuated with flying and once took me up in his father's Piper Cub and we had to crash-land on the New Jersey Turnpike."

She had finished filling everyone's plate now. She sat down and flashed a smile around the table before she unfolded her napkin. Derek blinked, but the others just started eating. (Her family always reacted to these tales with embarrassment. Not that they disbelieved them, exactly, but her elated tone made them uneasy—her feverish gaiety, her dramatic leaps in narrative. It seemed she might at any moment *cross the line,* as Willa put it to herself.)

"Speaking of flying," Willa's father said after a moment, "I was thinking, Wills, maybe you would want to pop in and speak to Security when we take you to the airport."

Willa said, "Security?"

"Just to report that guy on the plane's behavior. I mean, they must have a record of whoever occupied that seat, don't you think?"

Elaine said, "What guy on the plane?" at the same time that Willa said, "Would our airport even *have* a Security?"

"You don't want him going around doing that to other passengers," her father said.

"What guy are you talking about?" Elaine asked Willa. While Willa was figuring out how to word it (how not to sound like their mother telling one of her tales), their father said, "The man sitting next to Willa poked something in her ribs that he said was a gun and told her not to move."

"He *what?*"

"He was probably just some disturbed person," Derek told her.

"What did you do?" Elaine asked Willa.

"Well . . . nothing," Willa said.

"You didn't do anything?"

"Derek said we should trade places along about then and so we did and that was the end of it."

"You didn't tell anybody? You didn't press your call button?"

"Call button?" Willa asked.

Elaine let out a disgusted puff of a breath and set her fork down. "Geez, and then what?" she asked. "You just went back to reading your magazine?"

"Well, I didn't actually have a—"

"I cannot believe this," Elaine told them all. "How could she not make a fuss?"

"Oh, it isn't so hard to understand," her father said. "First of all, on a crowded plane it was probably best to downplay things. No point causing a ruckus. Also, none of us knows how we'd react ourselves in a situation like that."

"I know how I would react," Elaine said.

Willa said, "But that might have made things worse."

"When I was a student in Philly," their father told them, "I was taking out the garbage one night and this guy stepped up and pointed a knife at me. Set the tip of it just below my breastbone; I could feel it through my T-shirt. He said, 'Hand over your wallet,' and I said, 'I don't have a wallet.' I mean, I was only taking the garbage out, right? He said, 'Don't you lie to me.' 'Honest,' I said, 'all I have in my pockets is a pack of chewing gum,' and he says, 'What the—?' Then, 'You're just this wimpy weak *white* guy,' he says, and I say, 'You think I don't know that?' and he says, 'Huh?' I said, 'You think I don't feel like I'm too white, too thin, too Waspy?' Guy folds his knife and says, 'Shoot, man'—only he didn't use the word 'shoot'—'you're just a *loser*,' he says, and walks off shaking his head."

Willa laughed, but Elaine said, "Oh, for Pete's sake," and Derek said, "Wait. You can't let people get away with talking to you like that!"

Willa's father surveyed him mildly, but he didn't bother arguing. Then, just when Willa herself was about to speak (she could identify with her father's story; she had often had that too-white feeling), her mother said, "I agree, Derek. That story always makes me *furious*."

So it was everybody else against Willa and her father, it seemed. But her father didn't look perturbed. He tipped his chair back on its two rear legs (another thing that made her mother furious) and sent an amused smile around the table, but Willa was the only one who smiled back.

Willa was fitting her last few toiletries into her suitcase when Derek appeared, his duffel bag slung over his shoulder. "So this is your room," he said, looking around.

"Mm-hmm."

He set his bag down and came over to study the bulletin board. Once it had been plastered with Willa's things, but if any vestiges remained of her high-school days they were buried now beneath markers from Elaine's bewildering life—a bumper sticker reading "Nobody for President," ticket stubs bearing names of bands Willa hadn't heard of, somebody's penciled cartoon of Snow White smoking a joint.

"I guess before we leave we should tell them we're engaged," Derek said, seemingly addressing Snow White.

"What? Why?" Willa asked.

He turned and looked at her.

"You mean now?" she asked him.

He said, "Willa, have you changed your mind about this?"

"No, of course not," she said. "But we're going to be engaged for so long. We have lots of time to tell them."

"So?" he said. "I should think they'd be happy to hear about it. Won't they?"

"Well, sure, I guess," she said.

"You guess?"

"I mean . . . of course they would, but . . . you know. They might point out that I'm only a junior in college."

"You're twenty-one years old, for God's sake. And I am twenty-three."

"Yes, but—"

Just then Elaine arrived in the doorway, holding a can of root beer. She stopped short and looked at them. "Oops," she said. "*So* sorry." From the scornful smile on her face, you would have thought she had caught them stark naked.

Willa said, "What for?," and shut her suitcase. "Let's go," she told Derek. She angled her suitcase past Elaine, who grudgingly stepped aside, and Derek picked up his bag and followed. So did Elaine, after a moment. Willa heard the pop of her root beer tab as she descended the stairs behind them.

In the living room, Willa's mother was collecting scattered sections of the Sunday paper while Willa's father stood in front of the

TV gazing at a weather map. "You'll be flying straight into a belt of thunderstorms, looks like," he told Willa and Derek. "Ha! I knew you should've stayed through Easter Monday."

Derek dropped his bag and said, "Mr. Drake. Mrs. Drake."

It took no more than that to bring everything to a halt. Willa's mother stopped folding the sports section and grew completely still. Willa's father threw Derek a glance and then stepped forward to switch the TV off. Elaine, heading toward the dining room, stopped in her tracks and returned to stand in the living-room doorway, looking more interested than she had during any other point in their visit.

"Willa and I are engaged," Derek said.

Nobody reacted. Not even Willa could tell what her parents were thinking. She set her suitcase down inch by inch, without a sound.

"We love each other," Derek said, "and . . . we've decided, um, we want to spend the rest of our lives together." Something in his delivery, the words tumbling forth in short bursts, suggested that he was speaking almost at random, trying to fill what was beginning to be a noticeable silence. "I've asked her and she—she said yes and she wants to wait till she graduates although me, I'm thinking this summer would be good; I mean, she could finish school in California just as well as at Kinney, so I'm hoping to talk her around, but in any case—"

Willa's mother said, "Melvin?"

Willa's father stirred, as if he were slowly waking up. He cleared his throat. "Well, now, ah, Derek," he said, "that's very nice news, of course, but you realize Willa is only—"

"Nice news?" Willa's mother echoed. "You think it's nice news that he wants to 'talk her around'?"

Willa said, "No—"

And Derek said, "No, I just meant . . . I mean I was thinking we could discuss it *together*, like, but in any case—"

"Yes, forget about Willa's side in all this," her mother said. "Forget she's not even through college yet and has barely passed her twenty-first birthday, because *you*, Mr. Wharton Business School Type, you with your quote-unquote executive position—"

"Now, hon," Willa's father said, "calm down, now." Which he of all people should know was the wrong thing to tell her. "Now, we do have to accept the possibility that maybe Wills knows what she's doing."

Willa felt a bolt of panic shoot through her. She opened her mouth to speak, but then her mother told her father, "Oh, please." And to Willa she said, "Do you want to be like your friend Sonya, or the Barnes girl, or Maddie Lennox? All those girls who got hitched in their teens and have a houseful of babies now?"

Willa said, "I'm not in my—"

"This is someone who called you a snippy little college girl!"

"A what?" Derek asked, and then, apparently recollecting, he said, "Excuse me, Mrs. Drake. I was not the one who called her that." He spoke levelly, if a bit louder than usual. He didn't seem fazed in the least, whereas even Willa's father was sort of wincing and blinking in that way he did when he was just wishing this would all go away. "It was the man on the plane who called her that," Derek said. "Or who *maybe* called her that. Who maybe thought of her as that."

"Same thing, isn't it?" Willa's mother said. "You dismissed her story outright. She tells you a man aimed a gun at her and you just brush her off."

Willa looked at Derek, because her mother was right, in fact. But

Derek said, "Well, granted I didn't get all dramatic about it. Not like you, Mrs. Drake, with your actressy ways and your 'tempestuous' personality, stealing the stage from some poor young crippled girl who was supposed to be the star."

"That was the point, you fool," Willa's mother said. She actually seemed to be enjoying herself. She was smiling a terrible, bitter smile, and two patches like overbright rouge were showing on her sharp cheekbones. "Amanda's *supposed* to steal the stage; that was the point of the play."

Willa had never seen her mother expose her true self to outsiders before. She turned back to Derek, expecting him to wilt, but he was smiling too. Except his smile was a pleasant, relaxed-looking smile. "Amanda!" he said. "Try Lady Macbeth. Who else would serve rabbit on Easter Sunday?"

Willa stared at him. Elaine, raptly silent till now, made a sudden snorting sound. And then Willa's father said, "Now, folks; look now. Can't we sit down and talk this through?"

But Willa said, "Talk what through? I'm marrying him and that's that."

And she picked her suitcase up, and Derek slung his bag over his shoulder again, and they headed toward the front door.

Willa's mother did not accompany them to the airport. Elaine did, oddly enough, but it hardly mattered, because she didn't speak once during the whole trip; just slouched in the front seat, still in her pajamas and baggy sweater, and gazed out her side window. Although she did say, when they drew up in front of the terminal, "Bye, you guys." And then, with another of her snorting sounds, "Try not to get yourselves hijacked."

Derek chuckled, but Willa didn't.

She thought about the hijacker, though, after she and Derek had checked in for their flight. She wondered whether his gun had been real, and what his motive had been. Both questions that Derek had asked her himself, and she had been irritated with him at the time, but not now. Now she felt a sense of . . . more than gratitude—actual *dazzlement*, as she remembered how Derek had risen and bent to grip her upper arm and drawn her firmly to her feet and rescued her.

1997

WILLA AND Derek were out on the freeway, driving to a swim party in Coronado. A vice president at Sports Infinity had a house there with an Olympic-size pool. Turning down the invitation was not an option, according to Derek, but Willa could think of lots better things to do with her Sunday afternoon. She found Derek's business associates difficult to talk to. They all seemed to have this slick, smooth surface with no bumps that she could grab onto, she told Derek. (Derek said, "Huh?") Also, she didn't see swimming as a social activity. Here she'd given so much thought to her clothes—slim silk pants, peach-colored tunic, Mexican huaraches—and now she was supposed to struggle into a swimsuit in somebody's cramped cabana and dunk her carefully straightened pageboy in liquid chlorine.

More to the point, though, they were having a little crisis at home and she really felt she should be there. Ian, their sixteen-year-old, was insisting that he needed a year off from high school. Willa had occasionally heard of students taking a break between high school and college, but never *during* high school. And he didn't even have a plan! He just said he might like to hitchhike around the country getting to know "the people." He was also talking about camping in the desert so he could experience the Hale-Bopp comet in a meaningful way. It didn't inspire confidence that he frequently misspoke and called it the "Hale-Boggs" comet.

"One thing we might do," Willa told Derek now, "is get in touch with the college admissions counselor at the school. You know what a help she's been with Sean's applications. I realize this is not *about* college, but she might convince Ian that colleges take a very dim view of an applicant who's had a spotty attendance record in high school."

"You are such a pushover," Derek said. He was driving badly, as he always did when he was annoyed. He revved the SUV's engine as if it had personally provoked him. "The kid is breaking the law," he said, "pure and simple. You're not *allowed* to ditch high school. He could be hauled in by a truant officer."

"Even if he's sixteen?" Willa asked. "I thought people could drop out after they turned sixteen."

"Willa, why are you trying to *negotiate* with him? We're the parents. We say, 'No, goddammit, you stay in that school where we put you.' Lord knows we pay enough for it."

"I just think he seems so unhappy," Willa said. "Really, I don't feel the school has been such a good fit for him. It might have been fine for Sean, but Ian is more, I don't know—"

"More lazy," Derek finished for her.

Ian wasn't lazy, exactly, but Willa knew better than to argue. Another not-good fit was Ian with his father. They just didn't understand each other.

"Did you find out when that exit comes?" Derek asked her.

"Oh," she said, and she looked hastily at the map book on her lap.

"Don't tell me we've missed it."

"No, no . . ."

He honked at a sports car in front of them that wasn't doing anything wrong, as far as Willa could see.

She squinted at the map for a moment and then looked out the windshield again, so as not to feel carsick. It was a sunny, warm May afternoon, that unvaryingly perfect weather of southern California. Willa was tired of sunshine. She missed the seasons; she longed for a thunderstorm or even a nasty winter blizzard where everyone stayed inside curled up cozily with a book. But no, there was just this eternal blue sky, skin-temperature air, brassy yellow sheen bouncing off the freeway.

"That damn fool must be asleep," Derek said.

He meant the driver of the station wagon to their left. Willa couldn't see the man's face, but she noticed that his car was too close to theirs. Derek tapped his horn, and the station wagon nonchalantly moved away.

"What Ian needs is an aim in life," Derek said. "Why has he got no aim? He's so damn . . . limp. If only he'd gone out for a sport the way I kept telling him he should do—"

"Ian isn't the sporty type," Willa said.

"Well, why the hell not? I was crazy about sports at his age. So was Sean."

"Ian is not you," Willa said. "Ian is not Sean."

Ian didn't even look like Derek or Sean. He took after Willa's side of the family; he was slight and he wore glasses. Put him next to Derek—so square-jawed and solid—and you would think they were two different species.

"Fellow must be saying, 'I know what: why not grab a quick nap while I'm driving?' If 'driving' is what you want to call it."

Derek stepped on the gas to speed past the station wagon, but at that moment the station wagon started drifting into their lane again. "God *damn*," Derek said, leaning on his horn. He braked violently as the station wagon arrived in front of them. Willa reached for the dashboard, more as a protest than anything else, since she was safely fastened into her seat belt. "Did you see that?" Derek asked her.

"Yes, I saw. But now, don't you react, Derek."

Because she knew him all too well. He would treat this trip like a bumper-car game if he got riled enough.

"Write down his license number," Derek ordered.

"What good will that do?"

"He shouldn't be allowed on the road, I tell you. Write it down."

Willa sighed and bent for her purse. But while her head was lowered she felt the SUV gathering speed again, and she straightened to see that they were swerving to the left and roaring past the station wagon. Except *not* past it, actually, because the station wagon was gathering speed too. Now Willa was side by side with the driver and she could see that he was a thin, hawk-profiled man with his eyes trained on the road in front of him. She surprised herself with a sudden competitive urge. "Faster!" she wanted to tell Derek, although she stopped herself because that was the last thing he needed to hear. Luckily their own lane was clear for some distance ahead, so there was no real danger. But then Derek flicked his right-turn signal on. "Don't do it," Willa said.

He ignored her. He tucked the SUV into the space directly in front of the station wagon, with only an inch to spare. Or less than an inch. In fact, no room at all. She felt a scraping sensation. She heard a ghastly metallic shrieking sound, and then time began to slow down, stretching out so interminably that she fancied she saw the word "s-t-r-e-t-c-h-i-n-g" written letter by letter across the bottom of her mind. Each individual piece of damage seemed to happen in its own eon. Their right rear fender ripped. (But that was easily fixable.) Their right rear door buckled. (Oh, dear, slightly more serious.) Her own door was crushed inward. (What if she couldn't get out?) And then the whole car was slung sharply around so that it ended up perpendicular to the freeway and partly on the shoulder, its front end buried in tall, waving, sunshiny grasses.

She had a kind of crick in her neck from when they'd spun around, but otherwise she wasn't hurt. She wasn't even frightened. She seemed to be in a kind of bubble, sealed away on her own.

Entirely on her own. Because that very still form beside her, with its head resting on the steering wheel, was surely not a person.

He had been forty-three years old—too young to think of making funeral plans. So all of that was left to Willa, and Willa just wanted to huddle in the dark with her arms around her two boys. She felt her loss as a physical ache. She felt hollowed out, scooped away at the center. Also angry, to be honest. What had he been *thinking*? How could he have done this to her? Why was he not here to feel deeply ashamed and remorseful?

The anger invigorated her. She freely admitted to the police that the accident had been Derek's fault; he'd cut in too close after passing. She told her sons, "You know how he could get when he thought somebody was driving badly." They nodded, needing no elaboration. (Sean probably even approved.)

The only funeral she had overseen before now was her mother's, a dozen years ago, and that time she'd had her family around and her ex-neighbors and the church she'd grown up in. Here she had just

Derek's two brothers and their wives, whom she barely knew, and she didn't belong to a church. She was forced to rely on her woman friends—sympathetic, but lacking much experience with death—and a funeral director named Mr. Percival, a pale, fragile-looking young man without strong opinions. If she said, of some choice he offered, "Oh, I don't know; I just don't know," then he would say tentatively that many people liked to do such-and-such, and she would say, "Okay."

"But *you* may prefer—" he would venture.

"No, that's okay."

In fact her one firm directive was that Derek should be cremated, because the cemeteries she had seen in California didn't look anything like the little church graveyard back home. Oh, and she wanted just drinks and tidbits served in the funeral home's reception room after the service—no real food involved, and certainly no guests coming back with her to the house. She needed to be rid of everybody as soon as this was over.

School was still in session but Sean stopped going, which hardly mattered since he was a senior mere days from graduation. Ian, on the other hand, went on attending, even though he usually seized on any excuse to skip class. He was probably trying to escape the atmosphere in the house. He didn't talk about Derek at all and he avoided any contact with Willa or his brother, instead spending his evenings shut away in his room twiddling tunelessly on his guitar. Sean was the opposite: he followed Willa around pestering her for every detail of his father's death. Had Derek had a chance to realize they were crashing? Had he said any last words? And how about the other driver: had he been injured, did he speak to Willa afterward, did he apologize for his part in it?

"I don't know," Willa kept telling him. "I don't know; I don't remember."

"Because face it: the guy was not blameless," Sean said. Which was exactly what Derek would have said, if he had lived.

It took Willa two days to get hold of her father, although he was the first person she thought of calling. Now that he was retired he kept mostly to his basement workshop, where there wasn't a telephone. He'd told her once that he avoided the phone because it was generally some neighbor or other trying to make him come for a meal. And he didn't have an answering machine. But she persisted, calling early and late till she finally reached him on Tuesday evening. "Hello?" he asked, in that reluctant, dread-filled voice he always used when he answered the phone, his second syllable trailing away as if he were already preparing to hang up.

"Pop," she said.

But then she couldn't say the words. Her eyes glazed over with tears and her lips started trembling.

"Wills?"

"Pop, Derek is *dead*," she said, and Derek all at once filled the room—his rapid, confident stride; the way he would smooth a strand of her hair off her cheek before he kissed her; his habit of buttoning her top button after he'd helped her into her coat. Nobody would ever again focus his whole attention on her. Nobody would take on that watchful, appreciative look when she walked into a room.

"I don't understand," her father said.

She didn't, either, she wanted to say, but she made herself tell him, "He had a wreck on the freeway."

"Oh, honey."

"Can you come out?"

"Well, of course I'm coming. When's the funeral?"

"It's Thursday," she said. "Is that too soon to find a flight? I tried to reach you earlier, but—"

"I'll be there. Did you call your sister?"

"Yes," she said, because she had, by then. Elaine was almost as hard to reach as their father; she worked in a lab in Michigan and her hours were unpredictable. But she did answer her phone, finally, and right away she said that she would come to the funeral, although she showed no particular reaction to the news of Derek's death. "Thank you," Willa told her. The two of them had very little to do with each other these days, but she found herself looking forward to her sister's cool, sensible presence.

In fact, though, it turned out that Elaine was *so* cool and sensible that she arranged to arrive the night before the funeral and fly out right afterward. Willa wasn't happy about that. Still, she had to admit that her literal request had been for Elaine to come to the funeral, period. Oh, they were never going to be like the sisters in *Little Women*!

She used to feel hurt that after Elaine became so distant from their parents, seldom returning home once she started college, she hadn't thought to stay in touch with Willa, at least—to write or call her from time to time, or visit her and Derek during holidays. Wouldn't you think she would realize that of all people, Willa was the one who understood her side of things? But no, she basically resigned from the family, and on the rare occasions now when they saw each other, her conversation was like that obsessive rehashing you hear from the survivor of some natural disaster. "I was standing in front of my bureau," she said once. "It was early in the morning. I was wearing my footed pajamas. I was three years old and I had never gotten dressed on my own before but I thought I'd surprise Mom and try doing it that day. So I opened my underwear drawer and started hunting for my favorite underpants, the ones with the rhumba ruffle on the seat. And Mom walked in and said, 'I hope you're not messing up all those things I so carefully folded.' I said, 'Nope!' and quick-quick I tried to pat everything smooth again, but she came up close behind me and 'You did!' she said. 'You *did* mess them up!' And she had her hairbrush in her hand because I guess she'd been doing her hair and she started hitting me in the head with it, *slam* on one side of my head, *slam* on the other side, and I was ducking away and shielding my head—"

"Yes, well," Willa said, "it's true she could be—"

"You know what's the saddest thing about kids whose mothers are mean to them? It's that even so, their mothers are the ones they hold their arms out to afterward for comfort. Isn't that pathetic?"

"Elaine. Just move *on*," Willa said.

And then felt guilty that she had spoken so sharply.

She always did feel guilty about Elaine, for some reason. But what could she have done differently? And hadn't she had just as bewildering a childhood herself?

Maybe guilt was her natural state. She felt guilty about Derek's death, too, because she should have known better than to bring up the sensitive subject of Ian while Derek was driving. And she felt guilty about that jolt of competitiveness she'd experienced when they were overtaking the station wagon. Actually, it had been something a little stronger than competitiveness. You could almost call it rage. Yes, rage had flashed through her chest like a viper. Faster! she had thought. And Derek had gone faster.

She bent double in her chair and pressed the heels of her palms hard into her eye sockets. Then one of her sons walked into the room and rested a hand on her shoulder for a moment before he walked out. She assumed that it was Sean, but when she raised her head to watch him leave she saw it was Ian.

The owner of Sports Infinity came to the service, along with several of the vice presidents and their wives. Willa's friends came with their husbands, and a few of her sons' classmates came, which she found touching, and some random people like Derek's squash partner and his secretary and the woman who'd been the family's housekeeper when he was a little boy.

Willa sat in the front pew, which was made of blond wood—the whole chapel was blond wood—with her father on her right and Ian on her left. Elaine sat on her father's other side and Sean sat at the end, where he could get out easily, because he was going to make a speech. He was the only speaker from the immediate family, in fact. Willa couldn't have managed it.

She felt proud of her sons, both looking very responsible in their dark suits and crisp white shirts. How was it that they had become these *men*, who knew how to tie a tie and whose shoes were like long, shiny beetles? But she was concerned about her father. His form of aging seemed a kind of erasure, his scanty rim of hair not turning white but merely fading and his features growing blurry and less certain. And Elaine, she thought, could be any random stranger glimpsed in passing: a sensible-looking woman with a choppy brown bob, her face bare of makeup, her brown slacks and loose, wrinkled top so unflattering that they seemed a deliberate reproach to Willa in her stylish black suit.

While the guests were arriving the organist played something unfamiliar that seemed chosen for its blandness. Willa hated organs. She should have told Mr. Percival that. She murmured to her father, "It sounds like it's whimpering, doesn't it?"

He stirred and said, "What's that, honey?"

"The organ."

"Ah."

"Makes me wish for Bert Kane Presbyterian," she said. (Bert Kane Presbyterian had just an upright piano.)

"Well, we *could* have held it there," her father said dubiously.

"Be a little hard to explain why all these Californians should have to fly to Pennsylvania, though."

"Yes, well, and then there's the matter of my not belonging to Bert Kane anymore."

"You don't belong?" she asked, turning to look at him.

"I haven't for quite some time," he said. "I wrote to Reverend Sands and told him I was resigning on grounds of disbelief."

"Disbelief! What made you stop believing?" Willa asked.

"Well, I've never believed, actually."

"You haven't?"

"Reverend Sands came to call at the house and asked if I would reconsider. Not reconsider my disbelief, he said, but reconsider my resignation. He said, 'Many of your fellow members probably don't believe, either, but at least in church you put yourself in *position* for belief. Otherwise you reduce the possibility.'"

"Good point," Willa said thoughtfully.

"Yes, it was a good point. But I'd given it sixty-some years by then and I figured any further developments were unlikely."

Willa laughed, and then she laid her hand on his, but only for an instant. She was so grateful to have him there that she almost felt she should hold her breath so as not to scare him away.

Sean's speech was just what it should have been—affectionate and regretful, but not in the least mawkish. He welcomed the guests and thanked them for coming, and he offered up a memory of Derek's willingness to play catch with his sons whenever they requested. While Sean was talking, Ian looked at his knees. Maybe he was wishing now that he had agreed to speak too, although he had flatly declined when he was invited. (Not for the first time, Willa reflected that in some ways the relationship between her two sons echoed her own relationship with her sister. "Sean : Ian :: Me : Elaine" was how she envisioned it. But why was it that at this moment, Ian was the one she sympathized with?)

The owner of Sports Infinity spoke, resurrecting the image of the "bright young go-getter" whom he had hired right out of college. And one of Derek's brothers said a few words about what a good brother Derek had been. Then there were a couple of testimonies from old friends of his, mostly describing boyish misdeeds and practical jokes. Willa especially appreciated those; they were the only references that presented him as something other than the Saintly Late Departed. At the end the minister supplied by the funeral home delivered a short, generic prayer, and then everyone rose to sing "Abide with Me," and that was that.

Elaine's flight left at seven that evening, which was so close on the heels of the funeral reception that Willa arranged for a taxi to take her to the airport. This gave her another twinge of guilt. Back home, people drove their guests to the airport themselves and the whole family tagged along. But anyhow, she reasoned, their only car now was her little Toyota, which Willa (a nervous driver) never drove more than she had to. They'd have had trouble fitting everyone into it, even.

It would be something of a relief to send her sister packing, she was sorry to say. She had begun to feel the strain of Elaine's silent criticisms—or not so silent, on occasion. She'd asked Willa if there were some decree that women in California had to wear white slacks. She'd referred, supposedly teasing, to Willa's "cloned hairdo." And she was so distant with their father. Willa had asked her outright, finally, "Lainey, are you *mad* at Pop?"

"Mad at Mr. Good Guy? Me?" Elaine had asked sardonically, which Willa found mystifying, because he certainly *was* a good guy, and what was wrong with that?

So when the taxi honked out front, Willa was almost glad. She gave her sister a brief hug and said, "Bye, Elaine. Thanks for coming."

Although the instant the door closed behind her, Willa had a sense of missed chances.

But then she changed into her oldest, softest bathrobe, and her father took off his coat and tie and put his slippers on, and she reheated a few of her friends' casseroles and set them out on the kitchen table. First Ian and then Sean reappeared, wearing jeans now, to announce that they wouldn't be eating here themselves, but she didn't mind as much as she might have. She was so tired of talking, reacting, looking lively and appreciative. She and her father ate without speaking at all, in fact, until her father asked, at the end, "How about I fix us some cocoa?," and she said, "Okay." She didn't lift a finger to help, just sat passively while he hunted down the ingredients and a saucepan.

He had told her he would be here a few days, and almost super-stitiously she had refrained from asking exactly how many. She indulged in a daydream that he might stay forever. They could mosey along together very comfortably, she figured. She knew enough not to crowd him, to let him go his own quiet way. And he was so good with her boys.

When she was a child she used to imagine that her mother might painlessly die somehow and her father would marry a lovely, serene woman who would sit at Willa's bedside when she had a bad dream and lay a cool palm on her forehead. Willa had pictured this woman in layers of flowing white chiffon, for some reason. Her name would be something like Clara, or Claire. Something calm.

Well, okay, that had not happened. But now here was this alter-nate plan.

Her father set a mug of cocoa in front of her and then sat down across from her with his own mug. "It's going to be hard for a while," he told her.

"It's going to be unbearable," she said. Meaning "So can't you stay and help me through it?"

"When I lost your mother, I didn't see how I could even get up in the morning. One morning after another: I didn't see how I could manage it."

Willa watched him. She knew how devastated he'd been by her mother's death. (It had been totally unexpected—a catastrophic stroke.) Willa had flown home to find him mute and gray-faced, barely able to go through the motions. But then the next time she saw him, a few months later, he seemed to have recovered. She had not been especially surprised. He was a very self-reliant man.

But now he said, "I'd pick up my toothbrush and I'd think, Oh, what's the point? I'd open the fridge and think, Why bother?"

Willa knew that feeling. Applying her lipstick before the service today, she had stopped to gaze at her face in the mirror and realized that she had no earthly reason to care what she looked like any-more. But she couldn't quite tamp down the notion that her father's loss had been easier. Why, her mother had been such a handful! Her father, though, seemed unaware of that. Even now his eyes grew watery, and he looked down into his mug a while before he resumed speaking.

"I'll just tell you what I've learned that has helped me," he said. "Shall I?"

"Yes, tell me," she said, growing still.

"I broke my days into separate moments," he said. "See, it's true I didn't have any more to look forward to. But on the other hand, there were these individual moments that I could still appreciate. Like drinking that first cup of coffee in the morning. Working on something fine in my workshop. Watching a baseball game on TV."

She thought that over.

"But . . ." she said.

He waited.

"But . . . is that *enough*?" she asked him.

"Well, yes, it turns out that it is," he said.

He didn't stay forever, after all. He left the following Wednesday. She and the boys took him to the airport—Sean driving—but he wouldn't let them come in with him. So on the sidewalk in front of the terminal Willa hugged him goodbye and the boys shook his hand, and then he picked up his suitcase and went in alone.

Now she settled into the *dailiness* of grief—not that first piercing stab but the steady, persistent ache of it, the absence that feels like a presence. Sean graduated from high school, but Derek was not there to clap and cheer. Ian dropped all talk of taking a year off, but Derek would never know about it.

Out on a walk one afternoon, she came across a young woman kicking a soccer ball across a lawn with her three little boys. As Willa approached, a car pulled into the driveway and the woman turned toward it and her face lit up and she called, "Look who's here, guys!" Then a man got out of the car and the little boys ran toward him.

Willa could remember how that used to feel, that lifting of the spirits when your husband comes home from work.

She was asked to lunch by her friends, and to movies and dinner parties, and she did her best to hold up her end of the conversation. Some of her friends were uncomfortable with death and pretended it hadn't happened, which filled her with a perverse desire to mention Derek's name at every opportunity: "Derek always claimed . . ." and "Derek used to say . . ." Some were oversolicitous, telephoning too often and treating her like an invalid who needed dutiful tending. But she knew it was important to maintain her social connections. Or so she had been told.

Over the summer Sean worked as a lifeguard at the local pool, and Ian got a busboy job, and Willa took two courses at the college near her house. She was thinking she might finish her degree, which had been sidelined by her first pregnancy. Then maybe she could find a job teaching French or Spanish at some local school. Not that money was an issue, what with the trust fund Derek's grandfather had left him, but she was concerned about how she would fill her time once Ian, too, had graduated and moved out.

She wondered if her sons would keep in touch with her after they were gone. Would they remember their childhoods fondly, or were they storing up grudges against her? She had tried her best to be a good mother—which to her meant a *predictable* mother. She had promised herself that her children would never have to worry what sort of mood she was in; they would never peek into her bedroom in the morning to see how their day was going to go. She was the only woman she knew whose prime objective was to be taken for granted.

Sean had a serious girlfriend that summer and Ian joined a garage band, so they were almost never around in the evenings. When she went to bed she left a light on for them downstairs, and later she would wake to find the whole house dark and she would know they must have come home. Returning to sleep after that was the hard part. The word "insomnia" didn't do her condition justice, she felt; she was awake all the rest of the night. Where once she had despaired if she woke to find it was four a.m., and therefore too early to get up (five being her idea of the earliest possible hour to begin her day), now she was awake at two, and then at one, and sometimes even at midnight, when the boys hadn't yet returned. Maybe this was because for the first time in her life, she was sleeping alone. She'd gone straight from the room she shared with her sister to the room she shared with her college roommate to the room she shared with her husband. With a husband you could turn and fling an arm across him, set your cheek against his back, and nestle into sleep again.

Alone she could only reflect, and worry, and wince at something she had said yesterday and dread something she had to do tomorrow.

She often thought back to the moment she and Derek had met. It was at a party known as the Numbers Racket, which the sophomore boys threw every year to welcome the freshman girls. A boy drew a number from a fishbowl, and whichever girl held the matching number would be his date for the evening. Willa's number was 45. When Derek called it out, she was dismayed; he was so good-looking and so comfortable in his own skin that she felt sure he would find her a disappointment. But she held up her number, timidly, and he crossed the room at once. "It's you!" he said.

What he meant, it turned out, was that he had seen her before, studying in the library, and had asked someone who she was. This person had shrugged and said, "Haven't a clue." And then the very next evening there she stood, holding up number 45. But Willa, of course, didn't know any of this at the time. To her it sounded like "It's you, whom I have been looking for all my life!" And it might as well have been that, really, because from then on they were a couple.

Those things don't happen twice. She knew that. A well-meaning friend had told her that even if she couldn't imagine it right now, someday some man would love her again and she would love him back. Willa just gave her a blank look. She had trouble even processing the words.

Her father's suggestion about breaking her life into moments didn't work for her, it turned out. Although she did keep trying. But what helped more was to walk down a crowded sidewalk sometimes, or through a busy shopping mall, and reflect that almost everyone there had suffered some terrible loss. Sometimes more than one loss. Many had lost their dearest loves, but look at them: they were managing. They were putting one foot in front of the other. Some were even smiling.

It could be done.

One day when she was studying for a quiz her doorbell rang, and she answered to find a stranger in his early fifties or so, tall and dark-haired, with a sharp-boned face. "Mrs. MacIntyre?" he said.

"Yes?"

She could tell he wasn't a salesman because he was dressed too casually for that, in well-cut khakis and a polo shirt such as the men in her neighborhood wore. Still, there was something suspiciously hopeful about him, something he wanted of her.

"I'm Carl Dexter," he said.

"Yes?"

"The . . . I'm the driver of the . . ."

He was searching for words, but he didn't have to; she knew him now. Whole scenes came back to her out of some closed-off room in her mind: he was taking hold of her shoulder and saying, "Are you all right? Are you hurt? You have to come away from the car." He was standing on the grassy embankment talking to two policemen, and a bright thread of blood was trickling down the side of his face.

"Oh," she said.

"I got your address from your husband's firm. I hope you don't mind."

"No," she said, "I don't mind."

"I don't want to disturb you."

"You're not disturbing me," she said. "Won't you come in?"

Something about the way he stepped over the threshold gave her the impression that he was holding a hat in his hands, although of course he wasn't; it was just that he was so hesitant. She was about to take him to the living room, but on second thought she asked, "Could I offer you some coffee? Or tea?"

"Water," he said urgently. This surprised her, until she saw that his lips were noticeably dry and he seemed to be speaking with difficulty. It must have been due to nerves. "Please," he added, and then he cleared his throat and said, "If it isn't too much trouble."

"Not at all," she said, and she led him into the kitchen. "Have a seat, why don't you?" she asked, because it occurred to her that he might be more comfortable here. "Would you like ice in that?"

"Just straight is fine."

He pulled out a chair and sat down at the table. His bearing was so tense that his back didn't touch the chair back.

She poured him a glass of water from the bottle in the fridge and handed it to him, and then she drew out a chair herself and settled across from him. He drank till the glass was almost empty before he put it down.

"I never asked about *your* injuries," she said. "Or I don't think I asked. I can't remember much."

He merely turned one hand over on the table, dismissing the subject. "I needed to tell you I'm sorry," he said. "I mean, sorry for your loss."

"Thank you," she said.

In the early days she'd had to fight down the impulse to say "Oh, that's okay." But now she was more adept.

"I can't stop thinking about it," he told her. "Did I cause it, in some way? Was I responsible for it? It's true he cut me off, but did I play some part in it?"

He didn't seem to expect her to answer. He was gazing at some point to one side of her, as if replaying the scene in his mind.

"I knew I'd become a bad driver," he said. "Or a less good driver, at least. Distracted. I'd noticed that. I'd be traveling along and all at once I'd think, Whoa, look at how close that other car is! I'd pull into my garage and thank God I'd made it home without an accident."

"I do that every time I get behind the wheel," Willa said. She wasn't joking, but he must have imagined she was, because he lifted one corner of his mouth in a brief, unamused smile.

"Before then I'd been a fairly decent driver," he said. "I wasn't *always* distracted. But then I . . . see, this is not an excuse or anything, that's not how I mean it, but this past winter my wife left me."

"Oh, dear," Willa said.

"I'm not saying that to make you feel sorry for me or anything."

"No, of course not," Willa said.

"We'd been married twenty-eight years. I thought we were doing fine. No children, but . . . it always seemed to me we had a perfectly okay marriage. Then one day she says, 'I have to tell you something: I'm in love with somebody else.'"

Willa tilted her head and looked sympathetic.

"I wanted to argue with her, at first. 'Look,' I wanted to say, 'we all get crushes, for God's sake.' But I didn't, because, I don't know, I guess I thought I'd be giving myself away, right? But I did say, 'Maybe it will pass.' And she said, 'No, I want to marry him. I've already talked to a lawyer.'"

"Well, that is really, really hard," Willa said.

"Oh, God," he said. "I come here to say I feel bad about your husband, and listen to me, yakking about my own little troubles."

"I wouldn't call divorce a *little* trouble," Willa said.

He lifted his glass and drank the last of his water, and then he set the glass back on the table and stared down into it.

"Can I get you a refill?" she asked him.

"What I'm trying to say is, I thought I was doing okay but really I'm just going through the motions. Even now. Most of my meals nowadays are just cold cereal."

"Well, *that's* not good," she said.

"I forget to mail things and I drop things and spill things, and several times I've gotten lost when I'm driving somewhere I've driven to a million times before."

"That's how it is after a death, too," Willa told him. "I've been that way since my husband died. Sometimes I think I have Alzheimer's! I guess divorce is just another kind of bereavement, really."

"Except friends don't know what to say about it," he said.

"They don't know what to say about a death, either."

He said, "It used to irk me when people got divorced and they'd say, 'Oh, we just drifted apart,' or 'We just decided to go our separate ways.' 'Come *on!*' I wanted to tell them. 'How about saying she was so bossy you couldn't stand it, or he was sleeping around?'"

"Oh, I know!" Willa said. "Who's going to believe a couple would bother divorcing if they've only developed different hobbies or something?"

"So when friends ask me, I tell them straight out: 'She fell in love with another man.' I mean, they'll learn the truth sooner or later anyhow, am I right?"

"Yes, it always comes out in the end," Willa said.

"But then they look uneasy and they change the subject. Or a guy friend might say something like, 'Gee, what a slut.' Miriam isn't a slut."

"Of course not," Willa said.

He looked into her eyes now, maybe for the first time. "Did he know I was there?" he asked her.

"What . . . ?"

"Did he see me? My car, I mean? Or did he cut in front of me not knowing I was so close behind?"

"Oh," Willa said. "No, he saw you. But I think he was . . . annoyed with you."

"Annoyed! Oh, God, so I *did* cause it."

She'd liked it better when they were discussing his divorce. It had been so long since she'd had a conversation that didn't center on Derek's death—what a shock it was, how on earth it could have happened—that she was sick of the subject. She said, "Look. He was a short-tempered driver, that's all. He was the kind of driver who's always talking to other cars. 'Make up your mind now, right lane or left,' he'd say; 'you can't have both." Or 'Let's think about this: green light. What exactly might that signify, do you suppose?'"

Carl Dexter flicked one corner of his mouth again, but he didn't look any happier.

"Once when he was teaching our younger son how to drive he made him stop the car and get out and walk home. And they were *far* from home. Miles. He said Ian was letting every Tom, Dick, and Harry get in front of them."

"You're a very nice woman," Carl Dexter told her out of nowhere.

She said, "Well. Too nice, my sons always claim."

"No, I mean it. I would have understood if you'd said you couldn't bear the sight of me. 'If you'd been paying attention, everything would be different now,' you might have said."

"Well, you could say that about *any* situation," Willa told him.

Then she stood up, and Carl Dexter stood up too and held out his hand. "Thank you for seeing me," he said.

"Thank you for coming," she said.

In September she and Ian delivered Sean to UC Santa Barbara— Sean driving there and Ian driving back in her suddenly too-empty Toyota—and Ian started his junior year in high school and Willa signed up for a full load at her college. She packed Derek's clothes into cartons and donated them to a charity. She turned his study, where he'd mostly watched TV, into a place where Ian could hang out with his friends, and once he'd learned that she didn't mind having his band practice there, too, he actually did start staying home more than he used to.

At night she still woke up, she still mulled and worried and reflected and regretted, but after an hour or so now she would drift back into sleep, and by morning she felt well rested. She felt more or less normal, in fact.

She was reminded of rainy days in her childhood when she would resign herself to staying in, reading or watching daytime TV, and then in the afternoon the sun would break through unexpectedly and she would think, Oh. I guess I can go outside now. Isn't that . . . a good thing, I guess.

In October she and Ian flew east to visit her father, because he kept making excuses not to come to them. He seemed pleased enough to see them, in his muted way, and she enjoyed feeling useful—giving his house a good turning-out and stocking his freezer with individually wrapped meals. They went only for Columbus Day weekend, a three-day whirlwind of activity, and the Tuesday after they got back Willa was so jet-lagged that she fell asleep on the couch in the middle of the afternoon.

She dreamed about Derek, which she didn't usually do even though she kept hoping to. She dreamed he wasn't dead after all; there had been a misunderstanding. The doorbell rang and there he was, the same as always—his dear freckled face and the sun lines around his eyes. He was looking irritated, though. She knew that look. He said, "Really, Willa? You threw all my clothes out?"

"Oh, Derek!" she said. "I'm so sorry! I thought—"

"I turn my back for one minute and you throw away all I own?"

And meanwhile the doorbell kept ringing. She couldn't explain that.

She woke and the doorbell *was* ringing, for real. Blearily, she sat up and smoothed her hair. She struggled up from the couch and went out to the front hall and opened the door. Carl Dexter was standing on the stoop. "Oh," she said.

"Hello," he said.

"Hello."

"I hope I haven't caught you at a bad time."

"No."

She supposed she should invite him in, but she still hadn't quite surfaced from her dream. She blinked at him.

"I was wondering," he said. "Is there any chance you'd be interested in coming out to dinner with me? I mean, either this evening or some other time; you could choose the time."

Willa said, "Oh."

She considered a moment.

"Thank you," she said, "but I think not."

"Okay."

"I'm sorry."

"No, I understand."

He gave her an awkward little wave and turned and walked away.

Willa shut the door and went back to the living room. First she sat down on the couch, and then she stretched out and closed her eyes and tried to retrieve her dream—rewinding to it, so to speak. She summoned the jingling sound of Derek ringing the doorbell; she relived the act of getting up and going out to the hall to answer. But her mind stayed stubbornly awake, as alert as if she'd drunk a whole pot of coffee.

Even so, she kept trying. She crossed the hall. She opened the door. She saw Derek on the stoop, looking mad as hell. "For shit's sake, Willa," he said.

"It's you," she said, and she stepped out to throw her arms around him and rest her head on his chest.

PART II

2017

1

The phone call came on a Tuesday afternoon in mid-July. Willa happened to be sorting her headbands. She had laid them out across the bed in clumps of different colors, and now she was pressing them flat with her fingers and aligning them in the compartments of a fabric-covered storage box she'd bought especially for the purpose. Then all at once, *ring!*

She crossed to the phone and checked the caller ID: a Baltimore area code. Sean had a Baltimore area code. This wasn't Sean's number, though, so of course a little claw of anxiety clutched her chest. She lifted the receiver and said, "Hello?"

"Mrs. MacIntyre?" a woman asked.

Willa had not been Mrs. MacIntyre in over a decade, but she said, "Yes?"

"You don't know me," the woman said. (Not a reassuring beginning.) She had a flat-toned, carrying voice—an *overweight* voice, Willa thought—and a Baltimore accent that turned "know me" into "Naomi," very nearly. "My name is Callie Montgomery," she said. "I'm a neighbor of Denise's."

"Denise?"

"Denise, your daughter-in-law."

Willa didn't have any daughters-in-law, sad to say. However, Sean used to live with a Denise, so she went along with it. "*Oh*, yes," she said.

"And yesterday, she got shot."

"She what?"

"Got shot in the leg."

"Who *did* that?"

"Now, that I couldn't tell you," Callie said. She let out a breath of air that Willa mistook at first for laughter, till she realized Callie must be smoking. She had forgotten those whooshing pauses that happened during phone conversations with smokers. "It was just random, I guess," Callie said. "*You* know."

"Ah."

"So off she goes in the ambulance and out of the goodness of my heart I take her daughter back to my house, even though I don't know the kid from Adam, to tell the truth. I hardly even know Denise! I just moved here last Thanksgiving when I left my sorry excuse for a husband and had to rent a place in a hurry. Well, that's a whole nother story which wouldn't interest *you*, I don't suppose, but anyhow, I figured I'd be stuck with Cheryl for just a couple of hours, right? Since a bullet in the leg didn't sound all that serious. But then lo and behold, Denise had to have an operation, so a couple of hours turns into overnight and then this morning she calls and tells me they're keeping her in the hospital for who-knows-how-much-longer."

"Oh, dear . . ."

"And I'm a working woman! I work at the PNC Bank! I was

already dressed in my outfit when she called. Besides which, I am not used to dealing with children. This has been just about the longest day of my life, I tell you."

Willa had known that Denise was a single mother, although she'd forgotten how old the child was and she had only a vague recollection that the father was "long gone," whatever that was supposed to mean. Helplessly, she said, "Well . . . that does sound like a problem."

"Plus also there is Airplane who I think I might be allergic to."

"Excuse me?"

"So I go over to Denise's house and check the numbers on the list above her phone—doctors and veterinarian and whatnot—thinking I will call Sean if I have to although everybody knows Denise wouldn't even let him back in the house that time to pack his things, and what do I see but where she's written 'Sean's mom' so I say to myself, 'Okay, I'm just going to call Sean's mom and ask her to come get her grandchild.'"

Willa couldn't imagine why her number would be on Denise's phone list. She said, "Actually—"

"What state is this, anyhow?"

"Sorry?"

"What state is area code five-two-oh?"

"It's Arizona," Willa said.

"So, do you think you could find yourself a flight that gets in this evening? I mean, it must be afternoon for you still, right? And I am losing my *mind* here, I tell you. I cannot wait to set eyes on you. Me and Cheryl and Airplane all three—we'll have our noses pressed to the window watching out for you."

Willa said, "Actually, I'm not . . ."

But this time she stopped speaking on her own, and there was a little pause. Then Callie let out another whoosh of smoke and said, "I live two doors down from Denise. Three fourteen Dorcas Road."

"Three fourteen," Willa said faintly.

"You've got my number on your phone now, right? Let me know when you find out what time you're getting in."

"Wait!" Willa said.

But Callie had hung up by then.

Of course Willa wouldn't go. That would be crazy. She would have to call Callie back and confess she was not the child's grandmother. But first she spent an enjoyable moment pretending she might really do this.

The truth was that lately, she had not had quite enough happening in her life. She and her husband had moved this past fall to a golfing community outside of Tucson. (Peter was passionate about golf. Willa didn't even know how to play.) She had had to leave behind an ESL teaching job that she loved, and she was hoping to find another one, but she hadn't exactly looked into that yet. She seemed to be sort of paralyzed, in fact. And Peter was out for hours every day with his golf chums, and her sons lived far away—Sean managing the Towson, Maryland, branch of Sports Infinity, Ian doing something environmental in the Sierra Nevada mountains—and both of her parents were dead and she rarely laid eyes on her sister. She didn't even have any woman friends here, not close ones.

What would a person pack, she wondered, if this person were to contemplate making a trip to Baltimore? It would certainly not be a formal place. She tried to remember whether that A-line dress she liked to travel in was back from the cleaners yet. She went to her closet to check.

By the time her husband returned from his game, she had a seat on the first available flight the next day.

"I don't understand," Peter said.

He was watching from the bedroom doorway as Willa packed the suitcase that lay open on their bed.

"I've never heard you so much as mention a Denise," he said.

"Oh, I've mentioned her a million times! Sean and she lived together for a couple of years, remember?"

"Well, still, who is she to *you*? Why would she ask you to come?"

"Have you not been listening?" Willa said. "Her neighbor asked me. Callie. Denise is in the hospital, and her little girl is—"

"But it isn't *Sean's* little girl."

"Well, no."

"How old is this child, anyhow?"

"I'm not sure," Willa said.

Peter shut his mouth and looked at her, patiently waiting for her to realize how illogical all this was.

He was eleven years Willa's senior, a tanned, trim, serious-looking man with a crisply etched face and close-cut silver hair, and sometimes he could make her feel sort of naïve and inexperienced. He often addressed her as "little one," for instance. He did it now. "Little one," he said. "I know you've been at loose ends since the move. And I know you wish you had more of a connection with your boys. But this just doesn't make sense. You've never even met this woman!"

"Well . . . I've talked to her," she said.

"You have?"

"I talked to her on the phone a couple times, when I called to speak to Sean."

He gave her that patient look again.

"Oh, Peter," she said, "can't you see my side of this? I haven't felt useful in . . . forever! And here are these people who say they need me, Callie and Cheryl and Airplane with their noses pressed to the window! Surely you can understand that!"

"Airplane?" Peter asked.

"Airplane the dog," she said, taking a guess.

There was a pause.

"Okay," he said finally, "I'm coming too."

"Coming to Baltimore?"

"How long has it been since you traveled alone, hmm? When have you *ever* traveled alone? And someone needs to make sure these people don't take advantage of you."

This was where she should tell him that for goodness' sake, she was sixty-one years old and she still had all her faculties. Also, she *had* traveled alone, several times in her life. Although not recently, she had to admit. And it was such an enormous comfort to think he'd be along to look after her. So she just said, weakly, "But we don't even know if you can get a seat."

"Of course I can," he said. "These things can always be arranged."

And he went off to take care of it.

She waited till later, when he was watching the evening news, before she called Sean. She dialed from the phone in their bedroom and then walked through the French doors to the terrace overlooking the golf greens. It was beginning to get a bit cooler out, thank heaven. One thing she was never going to adjust to was how you needed constant air conditioning here. People were dependent upon it in the same way that space travelers were dependent upon their oxygen tanks. It seemed possible that if the electricity went off, they could actually die. When Willa thought about that too long, it made her feel kind of panicky.

Sean answered his phone on the third ring. "Mom?"

"Hi, honey. I hope I'm not calling too late."

"Nah, I'm good," he said. He had his father's casual, sauntering style of speech. It always made her sad.

"I just wanted to tell you I'm coming to Baltimore tomorrow," she said.

"You are? What for?"

"Well, you remember Denise," she said.

"Denise. Denise. My Denise?"

"Right. So she got . . . I don't suppose anyone's told you, but she got shot in the leg and I said I would—"

"Shot!"

"It seems it was something random. I don't know the details. But anyhow, I said I'd come tend her daughter until she gets out of the hospital."

"What?"

"Her daughter. Cheryl. And . . . is Airplane a dog?"

"What? Who's Airplane?"

"That's what I'm asking you."

"Mom," he said, "why are you doing this?"

She sighed. "I knew you wouldn't understand," she said.

"How did she even get in touch with you?"

"Her neighbor got in touch with me. Callie."

"Callie What's-Her-Name? The fat one?"

"She telephoned," Willa said.

She stepped off the terrace into the yard—or what they called a yard, hereabouts: carefully sculptured gravel paths winding between clumps of succulents. She was feeling a bit tense; she tightened her hold on the phone because now Sean was asking, "Why *you*? And how did she know your number?"

"It was on Denise's phone list."

"Why would it be there?"

"Well, I'm not exactly sure," she said.

"This is kind of cockeyed," he said, and she knew he would be raking his fingers through his hair the way Derek used to do.

"So anyhow," she said in a rush, "we should get together while I'm in Baltimore!"

"Yes, okay," he said.

"We're flying in tomorrow afternoon."

"Peter's coming too?"

"Right. I'll phone you once I'm settled and we can all go out to dinner someplace."

"Okay," he said again. "Sure. You can meet Elissa."

"Who's Elissa?"

"This woman I've been seeing."

"Oh. Of course," she said. "I'll look forward to it."

It was tiring, keeping track of his girlfriends. But sooner or later he was bound to find one he could stick with. Then Willa could start hoping for grandchildren. She longed for grandchildren.

After she got off the phone with Sean she didn't go back inside immediately. She walked over to where a giant saguaro cactus towered, easily triple her height, its two symmetrically placed arms reaching up toward the darkening sky. Willa loved saguaros. She loved their dignity, their endurance. They were the only things in Arizona she felt a deep attachment to. The first time she saw one—a whole assemblage of them, actually, looming outside the airport last summer when she and Peter came to house-hunt—it was like meeting some mythical race. She had told Peter then and there that whatever house they bought should have a saguaro in the yard. Peter had been amused. He had viewed it as some sort of feminine thing—women and their gardens! But Willa had never taken much interest in gardening. She just loved saguaros, was all. She laid a palm on this one's trunk, on a bare space between its bristles. It felt like a cucumber, cool and smooth and sturdy. It seemed aware of her. She could almost believe it was steadying itself to receive the pressure of her hand.

Peter stepped out on the terrace and called, "Little one?"

"Coming," she said, and she gave the saguaro a final pat and turned to go inside.

2

"The first time I ever flew on a plane, a man stuck a gun in my ribs," Willa said.

Peter said, "Say again?"

They were seated across the aisle from each other, but he had probably heard her just fine and so she merely smiled at him.

"A gun?" he asked her.

"At least he claimed it was a gun. I didn't actually see it."

"What'd you do?"

Oh, dear, now she remembered why she never told this story: it made her look so passive. "Um . . . nothing?" she said.

"Nothing?"

"It was complicated."

He stared at her. A flight attendant came between them, wheeling the drinks cart back to the galley, and Peter briefly vanished from sight, but when he reappeared he was still staring.

"He said he'd shoot me if I made a move, and so I didn't move and he didn't shoot," Willa said.

"But what was he trying to accomplish?"

"I don't know what he was trying to accomplish."

"And how did it end?"

"Oh, I was traveling with Derek—this was when we were just dating—and Derek took it into his head that we should trade seats and that was that."

Peter sat back and considered for a moment.

The reason this incident had come to Willa's mind was that Peter had been grumbling about the security line. He tended to get into arguments with TSA agents. "So you see," she told him now, "I think security's a good idea. If we'd had TSA agents back then, that man would not have pointed a gun at me."

"But you weren't sure there really was a gun, you said."

"Well, no."

"TSA couldn't have prevented him from *pretending* he had a gun."

"No, but . . . well, I would have known he *was* pretending, though, if he had been screened beforehand."

"I can't imagine what makes you say that," Peter said. "Once you realize all TSA agents are idiots, why would you have any faith in them?"

Then he leaned out into the aisle and raised his empty glass toward the flight attendant.

It was the lawyer in him; he loved a good debate.

Another reason he'd been grumbling was that he'd tried earlier to switch seats with someone so he and Willa could sit together, but no one had been willing. Everybody seemed to feel very strongly about it. The boy next to Peter—still in his teens, by the look of him—had claimed he wanted to see out the window. Peter had grimaced at Willa. (She had refused to ask her own seatmate. She didn't like to discommode people.)

"What's a mere kid doing in first class, anyhow?" Peter had said to her in an undertone.

"Oh, is there an age requirement?" Willa had asked, all fake innocence.

Peter wasn't amused.

Then it turned out that Peter's seatmate and Willa's seatmate knew each other, because once they were airborne Peter's seatmate leaned forward and called across, "Dude! Are you going to order a drink?" and Willa's seatmate leaned forward too and called, "Yeah, I figured why not, right?"

Peter cocked an eyebrow at Willa. These two were friends? And yet had turned down a chance to sit together?

"Like, a *drink* drink, right?" Peter's seatmate was asking.

"Right."

Till then, Willa had avoided looking at the person next to her so as not to get trapped in a conversation, but now she saw that he was no older than the other boy, with an effortful little blond silk mustache and a Wildcats T-shirt. (Not a chance on earth he'd try to talk to a woman with a flowered chiffon scarf knotted perkily at her throat.)

"Don't they card people on airplanes?" Peter asked her, a little too loudly.

She gave him a prim smile and pulled a paperback from her purse.

All last night and then this morning, she'd had a feeling like Christmas Eve. She didn't know what to expect of this trip. She was simultaneously thrilled and scared and hopeful—such a flurry of emotions all at the same time. And then every now and then she would ask herself what on earth she thought she was doing. Also, she was grateful that Peter had decided to come along, but she worried too that he wouldn't enjoy himself, and that this would dampen her own enjoyment of her ... well, not her grandchild, of course, but ...

"Dude!" Peter's seatmate called. He was leaning forward again; he was holding up an in-flight magazine. "There's a free magazine in the seat pocket!"

"Oh, yeah?" the boy next to her asked.

"With a crossword puzzle in it!"

"Yeah?"

Peter was working on his laptop now; he still kept his hand in at the firm. He drew back a bit to make way for the boys' conversation, but he went on typing. Meanwhile, Willa's seatmate located his own magazine and flipped through it. He stopped at the crossword puzzle, folded the magazine open, and bent to root through the knapsack at his feet. When he straightened, his face was flushed; he was one of those people with nearly transparent skin. "Could I please borrow a pen?" he asked Willa.

"Certainly," she said. She fished a ballpoint from her purse and handed it over.

"Thanks."

He began studying the puzzle. He started to enter a word, changed his mind, and went on studying. After a while he wrote something, and then something more. Willa slid her eyes sideways but she couldn't see the letters. He had little nubbins of warts on a couple of his fingers the way Ian used to have when he was that age.

She randomly turned a page of her book—a detective story that she didn't find very interesting.

"I got one!" Peter's seatmate called.

"Yeah? What'd you get?"

"'Detroit baseball team.'"

"Oh, I got that."

"You did? Bummer."

In fact, the boy next to Willa seemed to be making considerable progress. He had a way of holding his breath while he was trying to think and then letting it out in a little explosion when an answer came to him. "Yesss!" he said once, in a whisper.

"Dude?" Peter's seatmate called.

Peter drew back again. He had his chin tucked in and he held himself ostentatiously rigid.

"'To be in Paris,'" Peter's seatmate called. "Five down."

"Oh, yeah, I can't figure that one."

"I mean, what? Is it, like, 'heaven'? Or 'romantic'? Do you think it's a line from a song?"

"'Être,'" Willa called to him.

"Pardon?"

"'Être.' 'To be,' if you were in Paris."

"Oh, yes."

He bent over his magazine. The boy next to Willa started writing too, and Peter tipped his head and gave Willa a look: Really? She smiled at him.

"Then, ma'am? How about 'needle holder'?" Peter's seatmate called. "It's got to begin with an e: four letters."

"'Etui,'" Willa called back. This must be a very fusty puzzle.

"Et what?"

"'Etui.' E-T-U-I."

"Thanks."

Peter said, "For God's sake, Willa."

"Would you like to borrow some earplugs?" Willa asked him. "I have some in my purse."

He just sighed and went on typing.

Willa noticed that another emotion she was experiencing was happiness.

When they landed the sun was setting, and by the time they were outside the terminal hailing a cab the air had cooled to a pleasant temperature. Their driver, who wore a turban, spent the whole ride talking on his hands-free phone in some musical, curly language without any cognates that Willa could identify. He did seem familiar with Baltimore, though. He sped toward the city's outskirts, where the warehouse roofs and factory smokestacks were suffused with a leftover, pale-yellow glow that made them look eerily beautiful. He rounded the harbor and threaded past clusters of brightly dressed people ambling toward the ballpark with babies and diaper bags and seat cushions and homemade posters. The cab left downtown behind and finally, after a long trek north, they entered a neighborhood of small, dingy white houses with squat front porches, some of them posted with signs for insurance agencies or podiatry offices. Peter gazed out his window without comment. Willa lifted a hand testingly to her hair. It worried her that Cheryl was probably old enough to know that Willa and Peter were not her grandparents. "These are, *who* did you say?" she would ask Callie. "I've never laid eyes on these people!"

The cab drew up in front of a house like all the others. "Here?" the driver asked.

"I guess so," Willa said. Numerals reading 314 slanted down one porch pillar.

Peter paid the fare, and the driver got out to lift their suitcases from the trunk. Willa's was the largest size allowed as carry-on—she liked to dress nicely when she traveled—and as she wheeled it up the little front walk it seemed *pathetically* large. She looked like some refugee, she thought, arriving on a stranger's doorstep with all her worldly belongings. By now it was dusk but the porch light was not lit, and after Peter pressed the doorbell she had a moment of anxiety until she heard footsteps from inside.

Callie turned out to be just as Willa had imagined—an extremely heavy blonde in her early fifties, packed into tight stretch pants from which tiny, dainty feet emerged in little ballet flats. "Finally!" she said, raising her pillowy pink-and-white face in gratitude toward the heavens. "You made it!"

She meant that she had been on duty too long, of course, but Willa chose to believe that she was glad to see them for their own sakes. "It's good to be here," she said, stepping into the house. A smallish white-and-tan dog emerged from behind Callie's calves, its comically oversized ears flaring out like, yes, airplane wings, and its tail wagging. And in the background now Willa saw a child lurking, some eight or nine years old, with chin-length, taffy-colored hair. She had a pudgy face and a keg-shaped tummy that strained her T-shirt, and her legs were so plump that the inseams of her shorts had worked their way up to her crotch. Willa had imagined someone a bit thinner and cuter, to be honest. She tamped that thought down guiltily. Surely a *real* grandmother would not have allowed it to cross her mind. She said, "Hello, Cheryl."

"Hi."

"I'm Willa."

"I know."

"And this is Peter, my husband."

"Hi," Cheryl said again.

"Hello there," Peter said. His own suitcase was smaller and hung by a strap from his shoulder. He looked less supplicating than Willa—more like a regular tourist just casually passing through.

"Listen. I feel so, so silly," Callie said. "I phoned Denise last night to let her know you were coming and she said, 'Who?' Said, 'What in the world!' Said, 'Oh, my lord, I can't believe you did that! Sean's mother is no relation to Cheryl!' Well, how would I know, right? I mean, onliest thing I know is she's got 'Sean's mother' on her phone list."

"Well, of course," Willa said soothingly.

"Denise said to call you right back and tell you not to come, but you know: by then it was so late and all . . ."

Callie hadn't wanted to say goodbye to her one chance of rescue, was what she meant.

"And I was *beat*!" she added, proving the point. "And had already had to miss a day of work as it was. Today was my second sick day! Besides, I figured if you didn't want to come you would have said so, isn't that right?"

"Absolutely," Willa said. "We were happy to come. How *is* Denise?"

"Well, she's still in a heap of pain, she says. I've only talked to her on the phone, but Ben our neighbor took Cheryl in to visit today, and he said she's doing real well considering what she's been through."

"How did she get shot?" Peter asked.

"Oh, that was the durndest thing! Cheryl, go fetch your stuff," she said. Cheryl, who had been fixing Willa and Peter with a steady, measuring gaze, turned away reluctantly to climb the stairs behind her. The dog wheeled around and followed her.

"She's a nice enough kid, I guess," Callie murmured confidentially, "but she's a *kid*, know what I mean? Lord, I am worn to a frazzle. Anyhow!" she said, switching to normal volume. "We had all stepped outside, late Tuesday, just about everyone on the block, because this unbelievable noise had started up across the street. This rackety engine noise, fit to bust your eardrums. First we didn't know *what* it was, but when we got outside we saw this big old rusty truck, 'Pressure-Plus Power-Washing' painted on its door. Did you know people power-wash? These folks straight across the street have some kind of added-on deck, stupidest thing you ever saw—deck about as big as their whole house that you never see them using, and they were having it power-washed at six o'clock in the evening. Well! Of course we were all like 'Oh-la-la,' we're telling each other. 'Don't you wish *you* had a deck that needed a bath?' Then all at once there's this extra-loud slam of noise like a truck backfiring, and Denise sits down on the ground. Just sits plunk down on the ground like she's been shot. And we start laughing. 'That Denise, she's such a card,' we were saying. Till we saw that her shin was bleeding and we said, 'Wait! She *has* been shot! She's been shot, I tell you!' And Cheryl runs up screaming 'Mama?' and Denise is looking like, 'What? Hold on a minute: what?' We were just flummoxed."

"But who would do that?" Willa asked.

It was Cheryl who answered. She was coming back down the stairs with a green plastic trash bag hoisted high in both fists and smacking against her legs with each step, the dog so close to her ankles it was a wonder he didn't trip her. "Some criminal, I bet," she told Willa.

"Cuz we've got this private-detective guy, Dave, right on our same block; keeps a sign in his window for all to see *saying* he's a detective. Doesn't even try to hide it. Some criminal he was closing in on must've shot off his gun and accidentally hit Mama."

"Now, you don't know that," Callie said. "She doesn't know the first thing about it," she told Willa. "Dave wasn't even home at the time."

"The criminal could've *thought* he was home, though," Cheryl said.

"Well, of course he could!" Willa caroled. "I couldn't agree more!"

Oh, dear, exactly what she had resolved earlier not to do: put on that chirpy false speaking-to-children voice that she hated. (It was only because she'd been so pleased that Cheryl was talking to her.) And Cheryl didn't let it go unnoticed. She narrowed her eyes at Willa a moment and then shifted her gaze to Peter, who told her, "He must not have been much of a criminal, I'd say, if he couldn't handle his gun any better than that."

He didn't use a chirpy voice. Cheryl sent him an approving glance and said, "Nope, and that's how come Dave was closing in on him, I bet. It's not like Dave is all that hotshot of a detective."

"Good point," Peter said.

They smiled at each other.

Children loved Peter. Which was so ironic, when you considered that Willa was the one who'd had children of her own while Peter and his first wife had deliberately chosen not to.

"Well, I don't buy that," Callie said. "I'm thinking it was Sir Joe, is more likely."

"Sir Joe would *never*!" Cheryl protested.

Willa asked, "Sir Joe?"

"He lives next door to me," Callie told her. "Him with his noisy Harley and his cigarette pack rolled in his T-shirt sleeve all *Rebel Without a Cause*."

"He would never in a million years," Cheryl said staunchly.

"And a barbwire tattoo around his biceps, to boot. Don't forget your dog stuff, Cheryl."

Cheryl dropped the trash bag on the floor at the foot of the stairs and headed toward the rear of the house, first sending a scowl in Callie's direction.

"Can't wait to get all that mess out of here," Callie said to Willa, and then she lowered her voice and asked, "What's the story, anyhow? Sean and Denise weren't married? I never knew! Though I have to say, this does put a whole different slant on him leaving her. Not his *method* of leaving, I don't mean, but, you know . . ."

Willa had no idea what method Callie was talking about. She was dying to ask—Sean had merely announced that he'd moved to a new place and so Willa shouldn't phone him at Denise's anymore—but a significant throat-clearing sound from Peter warned her not to. Men were so priggish about gossip. (Or sensible, Peter himself would claim.) So she just said, "Oh, well, *couples*. Who can ever tell from outside what might be going on with them?" Then Cheryl came back with a big sack of kibble and two plastic dog bowls, and Peter stepped forward to take them and they said good night to Callie. She was busy lighting a cigarette, though, and merely trilled her fingers at them as she took her first drag.

It was the dog who led the way to Denise's house, bustling up the sidewalk purposefully. Cheryl followed with her trash bag, and

Willa wheeled her suitcase just behind while Peter brought up the rear.

"Does Airplane not need a leash?" Willa asked, and Cheryl said, "Nah, he's okay just in the neighborhood."

"He never runs into the street?"

"Nope. Mama says he must have belonged to a *guy's* guy, once upon a time. One of those guys that takes it for granted dogs will do what he tells them to, and so they do. We got him from a shelter. Mama let me pick out any dog I wanted, so as to make me feel better after Sean left."

Willa hadn't stopped to consider that Cheryl might have minded Sean's leaving. She felt a twinge of something like shame for him, although of course she didn't know his side of things.

The dark was that halfhearted kind that happens on summer evenings, so that even with all the lights off at Denise's house Willa could make out its shabby condition—the flaking paint on the porch pillars, the rust stains trickling from the black metal numerals next to the front door. The welcome mat was so frayed that long, ropy strands of it straggled across the porch floorboards.

Cheryl drew a key from the chain that hung inside her T-shirt, and she unlocked the door and stepped in to snap the overhead light on. A foyer sprang into view, with a staircase on the right and an archway on the left opening into the living room. Somehow the place managed to seem both cluttered and bare at the same time. A sheaf of mail lay strewn across the rug just inside the front door. The one piece of furniture in the foyer was a gateleg table bearing an old-fashioned black corded phone and a box of Ritz crackers.

Peter set down his suitcase and asked, "Where do you want the dog things?"

"In the kitchen," Cheryl said, and she led them to the rear of the house, to a kitchen with Mondrian-patterned linoleum from the 1950s and elderly, oversized appliances. This was how kitchens had looked back home, Willa reflected. She gazed around appreciatively, and then she walked over to the sheet of paper Scotch-taped above the wall phone.

Nowhere in the printed column of names did she find "Sean's mom." For that she had to look in the right-hand margin, where it slanted upward like an afterthought—a handwritten scrawl above another scrawl noting the number for Prince of Pizza.

Peter set the dog supplies on the table. Airplane curled himself onto a nest of plaid flannel beside the back door and gave a contented groan.

"Have you had supper?" Willa asked Cheryl.

"Kind of," Cheryl said.

"Kind of?"

"I had some Chinese takeout I found in Callie's fridge."

"Do you want me to fix you something?"

"I'm okay."

"Peter, how about you?"

"Oh, I couldn't eat another bite after that sumptuous feast on the plane," he said.

He was talking about the snack they'd been served shortly before landing—cheese and crackers. Willa said, "Very funny." Then she asked Cheryl, "Is there a guest room?"

"Sure. I'll show you."

Cheryl led them back out to the foyer, where Willa and Peter retrieved their bags, and up to the second floor. The guest room opened off the hall to the rear, next to the bathroom. Twin beds nearly filled it, with a low bureau between them. No other furniture could have been squeezed in. The wallpaper was pink with white daisies.

Peter made a comically mournful face at Willa. "Great: separate beds," he told her.

She gave him a consoling pat and asked Cheryl, "Do we need to find sheets?"

"They're already on," Cheryl said, and she lifted one spread to prove it. "Mama says you should always have your guest room set to go in case, like, your neighbors' house burns down in the middle of the night and they need a place to sleep."

"Does that happen often?" Peter asked.

"Not so far," Cheryl said.

Willa liked it that Cheryl was so fond of quoting her mother. It implied that Denise was involved and invested, not some chilly absentee parent.

Cheryl opened the door to a tiny closet. "Hangers," she said, gesturing grandly. "Shoe bag."

"Perfect," Willa said.

She lifted her suitcase onto one of the beds and opened it flat. Peter asked Cheryl, "Do you people have a TV?"

"Sure, downstairs in the living room."

"Does it get CNN?"

"I don't know."

"I'll go check it out," he said, and he left the room.

Willa and Cheryl looked at each other.

Up close, it emerged that Cheryl had soft, tawny skin, unfortunately pouching a bit below her jaw, and opalescent gray eyes. She must have been making an assessment of her own, meanwhile, because she suddenly asked, "Do you wear lip liner?"

"Um, yes," Willa said.

"I thought so."

Willa had to fight down the urge to ask her if that was all right.

When Willa was Cheryl's age, she had found older women intimidating. Scary, almost. She used to flinch inwardly when she met up with one, sliding her eyes sideways. Once, in a supermarket, she had *not* flinched—had bravely faced the elderly clerk who accused her of "pawing the pears"—and later realized it was because she'd been wearing big sunglasses at the time, so that her eyes were shielded. Now that she was older herself, she worried that she, too, might frighten children. She took it as a kind of miracle when Cheryl peered into Willa's suitcase without trying to hide her curiosity. "How come you pack your clothes in Kleenex?" she asked.

Tissue paper, she meant. Willa said, "Oh, that's just something women do when they have too much time on their hands."

Cheryl said "Huh?" and Willa laughed.

Coming here had not been a mistake. Willa couldn't say exactly how she knew that, but she did.

"Northeast Baltimore woman shot by unknown assailant," Willa read. It was the headline of a newspaper clipping she'd picked up from the rug along with the supermarket flyers and the electric bill. Actually there were three clippings, but all of them were the same. Various neighbors must have slipped them through the mail slot.

In yet another Baltimore shooting incident, police report that a 31-year-old woman was shot in the leg around 5:45 Tuesday evening while standing in her front yard on the 300 block of Dorcas Road.

The victim was hospitalized but is expected to make a full recovery. No suspect was apprehended.

"It's getting so you can't step out of the house no more to watch a simple power-washing event," one resident opined. "How much longer can this go on?"

Anyone having possible knowledge of the incident is asked to contact the police.

Willa placed the clippings with the mail on the foyer table, where she and Cheryl were collecting items to take to Denise the next morning. So far, they had a pair of terry-cloth slippers, a book of word-search puzzles, and a list of phone messages in Cheryl's painstaking print: "Mrs. Mitten called to see how you are," "Dentist called it's time for our checkup," "Howl called."

Howl?

Cheryl hurtled down the stairs pell-mell, flip-flops slapping, and stopped short at the bottom to ask, "Can we watch *Space Junk*?"

"What's *Space Junk*?"

"You don't know what *Space Junk* is?"

"I must have missed it."

"Oh, you would love it, Willa. It's, like, only the best program in the world. Sit and watch it with me! Please?"

"What time is it on?"

"Um!" Cheryl said. "It's recorded, silly."

Willa could have taken offense, but she found it heartening that Cheryl had progressed so quickly to the eye-rolling stage. She said, "Let's just see if Peter's finished watching the news," and they went into the living room.

Peter still had CNN on, but he wasn't watching it. He was frowning at his cell phone, his feet propped on the coffee table. When they walked in, he glanced up and asked Cheryl, "Does this place have Wi-Fi, by any chance?"

"Sure."

"I don't suppose you know the password."

"Cheryl two thousand eight," she said. "Want to watch *Space Junk* with us?"

"No, thanks." He stood up, still focusing on his phone, and moved to the armchair in the corner. Cheryl plopped herself on the couch and patted the cushion next to her. "Sit! Sit!" she told Willa.

The couch was brown corduroy, and it was dotted with crumbs and stains. The flowered brown armchair Peter was sitting on more or less matched it, and there was also a rocking chair and an oval brown-and-green braided rug, everything faded and hand-me-down-looking. But the TV was fairly new—flat-screen, at least—standing on a wheeled cart with a jumble of electronic equipment on the shelf beneath. From the coffee table, Cheryl picked up a remote control lying beside a yellowing philodendron plant and expertly stabbed at the buttons. A silver flying saucer appeared against a deep-blue background while eerie space-age music started up, *woo-hoo, woo-hoo*. As if summoned, Airplane trotted into the room and hopped onto the couch to settle between Cheryl and Willa. "This is his favorite show," Cheryl said. It was true that his eyes were fixed on the screen and his ears were straight out; but then, his ears were always straight out.

"Bob Graham's wife had a stroke," Peter said, looking up from his phone.

"Oh, what a pity," Willa said. She tried to remember who Bob Graham was.

"So let me just catch you up on what is going on here," Cheryl told her. "There's this bunch of total strangers, see, eating lunch in a hamburger joint. All these different people on their lunch break. And these space aliens come and kidnap them and take them off to study them, because they believe these people are a family. See? They want to learn how families work and that's what they think these customers are. Get it?"

"Got it," Willa said.

On the screen an alien who looked very much like an earthling, if you didn't count the antenna sprouting from his forehead, was listening to a middle-aged black woman in a business suit and an olive-skinned man in striped coveralls, both talking at once. The man in coveralls was speaking Spanish.

The telephone rang in the foyer. "Shoot," Cheryl said. Her eyes stayed on the screen.

The phone rang again. Willa said, "Should we answer that?"

Cheryl gave a loud sigh and punched the Hold button and got up. Airplane stayed where he was, watching the frozen screen intently as if he hoped to will it into moving again.

"Ron says they need me back in San Diego for a client meeting in August," Peter told Willa, looking up again from his phone.

In the foyer, Cheryl said, "Carlyle residence." Then "Hi, Mama."

And "Yeah, she's here. And him too . . . Huh? . . . Him, her husband. Peter. My grandpa."

Denise must have corrected her, because next she said, "Yeah, I know, but he's *like* a grandpa . . . Huh? . . . Yeah, I did, and I showed her the sheets were on and all."

Willa waited to be summoned—wouldn't Denise want to confer with her?—but the next thing Cheryl said was, "Okay, I'll tell her. Bye." And Willa heard the clunk of the receiver against the cradle.

"Mama says her car keys are on the hook beside the kitchen door," Cheryl said, returning to the living room. "She says we can come visit her tomorrow after ten."

"How's she doing?" Willa asked.

"She didn't say." Cheryl wriggled back into position on the couch and pressed the Play button. "Isn't this a great show?"

"Yes, it is," Willa said.

Although now a teenage boy in a white apron had appeared, and most of what he said was four-letter words. But Cheryl didn't bat an eye, and neither did Airplane.

Cheryl said she didn't have a regular bedtime, but when Willa suggested at nine o'clock that she might want to go up, she didn't argue. "Airplane needs to pee, though," she said. "Mama always takes him outside before he comes to sleep with me."

"Oh, okay, why don't I do that while you're getting into your pajamas," Willa said.

Peter glanced up from his laptop, which he was working on now. "Have you lost your mind?" he asked her.

"What?"

"You're going to walk the dog alone in the dark where somebody just got shot?"

Cheryl, halfway out of the room, turned back to say, "The shooter wouldn't still be there, you know."

"I'm coming with you," Peter told Willa. And he set aside his laptop and stood up.

Willa wasn't sure how he planned to protect her from random gunfire, but she appreciated the fact that he wanted to.

Outside, the air was warm and heavy and some kind of locusts were scritching away in the distance. "I don't know how people put up with this humidity," Peter said.

"Well, I did notice an air conditioner in our bedroom window," Willa told him. "We can turn it on, if you like."

"No ifs about it."

Willa was carrying a plastic bag that Cheryl had given her for dog poop. She hoped she wouldn't need to use it, though. Also, it seemed odd to walk a dog without a leash. What if he didn't consider her a person of authority? What if he ran away?

But Airplane walked docilely a few feet in front of them, pausing once or twice to investigate something invisible. Out by the curb he encountered a cat—just a shadow floating by in the twilight—but he barely glanced in its direction and the cat paid him no attention. In front of Callie's house he stopped and lifted a leg, after which he turned and looked up at Willa. Evidently that was that, so she said, "Good boy," and they headed back toward the house.

"How long do you think before Denise gets out of the hospital?" Peter asked.

"Maybe she'll tell us tomorrow when we visit."

"I don't have a whole lot to do here, you know."

"Well, Peter?" Willa said.

She hadn't *asked* him to come, she was going to say. But that would have sounded ungracious, so she tucked her arm in his and said, "I'm sure it won't be long."

Then they went back inside, and Peter returned to his laptop while Willa and Airplane climbed the stairs to Cheryl's room. It was very neat, for a child's room. The only clutter, if you could call it that, was a lined-up array of horse statues on the bureau. Cheryl was sitting against her headboard, playing some sort of game on a hand-held device. She wore pink pajamas with cap sleeves that showed her upper arms, which were wide and soft and squishy like a grown woman's arms. Willa felt guilty all over again for noticing such a thing.

"Willa," Cheryl said, "you know how you are Sean's mom."

"Yes?"

"Well, so, now that you're in Baltimore, do you think he'll come here to visit you?"

"Oh. I'm not sure, honey," Willa said. Although inwardly, she felt an urge to make any number of promises.

Airplane hopped delicately onto the foot of the bed, and Willa wished them both a good night and went back downstairs.

3

Denise said, "This is so embarrassing. What was Callie *thinking,* to call you?"

She was sitting up in her hospital bed, looking perfectly healthy except for the thick white cast encasing one leg from the knee down. Seeing her gave Willa a whole different slant on Cheryl, because this was probably how Cheryl was going to turn out when she was grown: no longer plump but just enticingly rounded, at that perfect point where one more pound would have been one too many but you wouldn't want her weighing any less. Denise's hair was a streaky dark-blond color, hanging straight to just above the neckline of her hospital gown, and the fact that her part was slightly crooked added to her air of naturalness—that and her total lack of makeup.

"I was delighted she called me," Willa said. She sat down in a molded plastic chair, making a production of it to hide the fact that Peter was not chiming in to agree with her. He had taken a stance beside the door as if he might leave at any moment, while Cheryl settled on the foot of her mother's bed. There was another bed, but it was unoccupied, for now. All in all the room was fairly pleasant—

small but airy, with plenty of sunlight coming in through a long plate-glass window that overlooked a parking lot.

"What I was wondering, though," Willa said, "is how come you had my number."

"I had no idea I had it! When Callie told me, I said, 'What in—?' Then I remembered that time after you moved to Tucson, when you called to give Sean your new number and I was the only one home to write it down."

"She wrote it on her emergency list," Cheryl explained to Willa. "Doctor, dentist, Poison Control . . . like I would be the type to go and swallow Mama's allergy pills."

She seemed different in the presence of her mother. She looked relaxed and expansive, loosely clasping one ankle and resting her chin on her bare knee. Side by side, the two of them were strikingly alike—their skin the same tawny gold and their eyes the same pearly gray, although Cheryl's mouth, which was softer and more curved, must have been a contribution from her father, whoever he was.

"I don't know why Callie made such a big deal about keeping an eye on one puny child," Denise was saying. "Cheryl is no trouble! Lots of times she stays home by herself, even. Callie could've just called to check on her during the day and then had her over to spend the nights."

"Or I could've gone to Sir Joe's!" Cheryl said, lifting her head.

"Get real," Denise told her.

Cheryl subsided.

"Well, in any case," Willa said, "here we are. Peter, where are those things we brought?"

He stepped forward to hand her a paper lunch bag. "Puzzles," Willa said, hauling out the word-search book, "slippers . . ."

"One slipper would've been enough," Denise told her. She wriggled her toes, which were the only part of her left foot not covered by the cast.

"Well, I wondered," Willa said, "but Cheryl couldn't remember which leg it was that got shot." She reached into the bag again. "Mail, such as it is . . ."

"Who did it, do you think?" Peter asked Denise.

"Pardon?"

"Who do you think shot you?"

"Oh. I don't know. Took me a while to realize I *was* shot, even. First I was all 'Funny, my leg's not holding me up anymore.' So I sat down. And it didn't hurt one bit, can you believe it? Not at first. But later, *hoo* boy. Bone pain: nothing like it." She turned suddenly to Cheryl. "Wouldn't that make a good song title? 'Bone Pain,' by the So-and-Sos. Number one on the charts."

Cheryl giggled.

"But seriously," Peter persisted. "Was it someone you know, do you think?"

"You can ask all you want," Denise told him, "but I can't give you the answer. In this town, you don't expect to identify every single person that fires a gun off."

Peter slumped into silence.

Denise started riffling through her mail. "Most of this stuff I don't even need to open," she said. She came to the list of phone messages. "Hal called?" she asked Cheryl.

"Mm-hmm."

"Oh, *Hal!*" Willa said.

They both looked at her.

"That's what 'Howl' meant," she explained. Cheryl's misspelling all at once made sense, in light of how Baltimoreans turned "towel" into "tal."

"What did he want?" Denise asked Cheryl.

"He didn't say."

"Well, I am just not up to that right now," Denise said. She slapped the list down on her stack of mail.

"Hal is, like, our neighbor," Cheryl told Willa. "He's real mopey and bitter."

"What is he bitter about?" Willa asked.

"What isn't he bitter about?" Denise said. "See, Hal's wife and me were friends, once upon a time. At least I was trying to be friends, because no other gal my age lived on our block. I was tickled to death when her and Hal moved in. Not that he is such a prize . . . But anyhow, a few times I had her over for a glass of chardonnay after work, and when Sean came home I'd say, 'Look who's here, hon!,' but he'd just be all 'So I see' and ask when supper was. So anyhow—do you not know this story?"

"What? No," Willa said.

"Okay: So, one day I tell Sean, I say, 'Look. I don't get why you have to act so grumpy with my girlfriend. What's she ever done to you?' I ask. 'And we don't have a single pair of couple friends,' I tell him, 'so Saturday I am having she and her husband to dinner and I'm counting on you to be nice to her, hear?' And he says, 'Okay, whatever.' And Saturday night they come over and he's polite as can be all evening. And Sunday morning he walks out, and him and her move in together."

"What?" Willa said, and Peter seemed to come to attention. "I'm sorry, who did he move in with?" she asked.

"Elissa."

"Wait, you mean Hal's wife was Elissa?"

"Oh. You know her."

"No, no, I only just learned there *was* an Elissa. So, let me understand this . . ."

"It's like he was saying, 'Nice to her? I'll show you nice!' And elopes with her. Well, of course it wasn't really like that. Now I see they must have been carrying on for some time, and he was acting all cold just to cover it up. But wouldn't you think he could have been more straightforward about it? Men are so bad at these things! And now I'm minus the both of them. I've got nobody left."

"You've got *me*, Mama," Cheryl said.

"So that's what Hal is bitter about," Denise told Willa flatly.

"Oh, my heavens," Willa said.

"I'm going to look for a *New York Times*," Peter said all at once, and he walked out. It was true: men were bad at these things. Willa pivoted in her chair to watch him leave, and when she turned back Denise was furtively blotting her eyes on a corner of her sheet.

Willa fished a Kleenex from her purse and silently handed it over.

"Stupid, stupid, stupid," Denise said. She blew her nose. "I'm not crying because I'm sad," she said. "It's more that I'm mad, is what it is." She seemed to be addressing Cheryl, who was giving little pats to the ankle of her mother's cast.

"Well," Willa said. "I am just horrified."

This was awkward, to say the least. She didn't even have the right to apologize on Sean's behalf, although that was what she felt the urge to do. She looked helplessly at Cheryl. Cheryl said, "There, there, Mama. He'll come back; just you watch."

"Oh, for God's sake, I don't want him back!" Denise said. "Are you kidding? I wouldn't have him back on a silver platter! Sorry," she added to Willa.

"No, that's all right. Sean was never very . . . forthright, I have to say . . ."

"What's this?" a nurse asked, wheeling a machine in. A huge, trudging woman with a wide black face, wearing a uniform resembling pajamas printed all over with teddy bears. "Things getting to you, hon?"

"I'm just having a nervous breakdown, is all," Denise said into her Kleenex.

"She's reliving sad memories," Cheryl told the nurse.

"Sad memories, huh? Can't have *that*," the nurse said. She stuck a digital thermometer into Denise's mouth. "You ought to be thanking your stars! You could be a whole lot worse off than what you are. Could have been shot in the spine; could have been paralyzed. You know how many quadriplegic young folks I have seen?"

Denise shook her head, mouth clamping the thermometer.

"Young brothers shot on the street," the nurse said, "and so accustomed to how it goes down that they're brought to the emergency room already telling you what kind of high-tech, name-brand wheelchair they have in mind that is just like their cousin's wheelchair and their brother's and their best friend's."

Willa made a sound of distress, and the nurse transferred her gaze to her. "It's not often we get a *Caucasian* shooting victim," she said. She pronounced "Caucasian" with careful delicacy, the way Willa might have pronounced . . . well, the way Willa might have pronounced "African-American."

The thermometer chirped and the nurse drew it from Denise's mouth, giving it barely a glance before she shucked the sheath into the waste can and jammed the thermometer into a vase of other ther-mometers. "What level's your pain at?" she asked Denise. "From one to ten."

"Eleven," Denise said.

"No, it's not," the nurse said. "I can see by the look of you it's not. I am *not* upping your meds, I tell you."

"I'm not asking you to up my meds. They don't even work, and anyhow, they make me puke."

The nurse shook her head and got busy with her machine, adjust-ing a couple of dials and pressing buttons.

"I don't even want to know what all this is going to cost," Denise told Willa.

"Do you have insurance?"

"Well, kind of."

Willa decided not to ask what "kind of" meant.

"And it's true it's summertime, but even in the summer I need to check into work every so often."

Why had it not occurred to Willa that Denise must work? Of course she did; she was a single mother. "What do you do?" she asked.

"I'm an office assistant at Linchpin Elementary. Same school Cheryl goes to."

"Oh, that's convenient."

"Yeah, they're nice about letting her hang around till I get off every day. And Mrs. Anderson, that's the principal, she phoned this morning and said not to sweat it if I need to stay out for a while. But I should be helping them get ready for fall!"

"At least you've *got* a job," the nurse told her, winding an electri-cal cord.

"Will you stop with the Pollyanna talk?" Denise said. The nurse tsked and wheeled the machine out of the room.

"A cop has been going all round the neighborhood, Mama," Cheryl said. "He knocks on doors and asks people did they see you get shot."

"Yeah, he came here too," Denise said. "Heavyset fellow, acting like he couldn't be more bored," she told Willa. "Wanted to know if I owed anybody money. 'Are you for real?' I said. 'You think it was my dealer, don't you, collecting on my cocaine debt or something.' 'Ma'am,' the cop says, 'I am only asking what they tell me to ask. Don't get yourself in a tizzy.'"

"Oh, dear," Willa said.

"I hate when they call you 'ma'am.'"

In the pause the followed, Willa heard a woman out in the hall saying, "Well, I wasn't overwhelmed, to tell the truth. Or underwhelmed, either one. I was just . . . whelmed, I guess you could say."

"It could have been worse," Willa told Denise. "It could have been 'lady.'"

"Ick!" Denise said.

But this seemed to lift her spirits. She asked Cheryl, "You been behaving yourself, missy?"

"Yep."

"She's been very helpful," Willa put in.

"Oh, and guess what, Mama! Willa made me this thing for breakfast this morning called Bubble Eggs."

"She did, did she," Denise said.

"She boiled up this huge bunch of butter in the skillet and then she broke an egg into it and spooned the hot butter over it the whole time it was cooking and it bubbled up like a . . . balloon! It was the best thing I've ever eaten."

"Well, lucky you; you seem to be having a fine time," Denise said. "I ought to get shot more often."

Willa stirred and started to speak (it seemed something really should be said to this), but Cheryl only laughed. "*Silly* Mama," she said, and she tapped her mother's cast affectionately.

She was an admirably well-balanced child, Willa thought.

Peter walked in with a newspaper and a little plastic pot. "Look what I found in the gift shop," he told Willa, and he held out the pot. Inside was a saguaro cactus barely three inches tall, its one stubby arm no bigger than a thumb.

"Oh!" Willa said, and she took it from him. Evidently when saguaros were this tiny their barbs were much closer together, because this one was positively bristly, like a little old white-whiskered man. She held it up to show Denise. "Have you ever seen a saguaro?"

"Not in real life."

"Ordinarily they're huge. Twenty or thirty feet tall, at least."

She said this protectively, almost defensively. She felt the same kind of pity that she would feel for a caged tiger. Saguaros were not supposed to be *cute*! There was nothing cute about them! Saguaros were calm and forbearing; they had stoically weathered everything from Apache arrows to strip malls. But Peter was looking so pleased with his purchase that she had to tell him, "Thank you, sweetheart."

"You're welcome," he said. Then he slapped his newspaper against his thigh and said, "So! Denise! When they going to let you go home?"

"Couple of days or so, I guess."

"Couple of days! Couple of days after this one?"

"I guess."

He looked over at Willa. "And here they're always talking about hospitals kicking their patients out too soon," he said. "So much for *that* idea."

"Well, I did just undergo surgery," Denise told him. "What did you expect?"

"Does Cheryl have any *real* grandparents?" Peter asked her.

Willa could have killed him. He was going to ruin things! But Denise just said, "Oh, yes, there's my mom. She's got Parkinson's, though, so she lives with my brother and sister-in-law in Rhode Island."

Not even Peter was brash enough to inquire about the grandparents on Cheryl's father's side. He just sent Willa a look. She knew what he was thinking: this was all her fault. They were trapped. She gave him her blandest, brightest smile and asked Denise if there was anything else they could bring her the next time they came to visit.

4

Airplane had the most appealing face. His eyes were a deep, thought-ful brown, topped by tufted black eyebrows that gave him a look of concern. His muzzle was a velvety caramel color, the whiskers sprouting from precisely placed dots that reminded Willa of the stippled scalp of a "real hair" doll that she had owned in her child-hood.

And then there were his signature ears, which stood out so lev-elly that they might have been held up by scaffolding. Yet there was nothing stiff about them. When Willa ran one between her fingers, it was almost too soft to register against her skin.

She stroked his other ear as well, for symmetry's sake, and then set the tip of her nose to his and asked, "What do you have to say for yourself, Airplane?"

He answered with an enthusiastic puff of meaty-smelling breath that made her sit up straight again on the couch.

In her left hand she held her cell phone, which she rarely used for actual calls, but she needed to dial Sean from her contacts list. She had the phone pressed to her ear and she was listening to it ring. It was late afternoon—a likelier time to reach him than in the evening, she had learned, when he often seemed to be unavailable. Maybe she'd miscalculated, though, because he wasn't answering.

But then he picked up. "Mom," he said.

"Hi, honey. I'm sorry to call you at work, but I thought we should connect so we can make a date for supper."

"You're in Baltimore?"

"Right."

"How's Denise?"

"She seems okay," Willa said. She was glad he had thought to ask; you couldn't always count on that with Sean. "She's still in the hospital, though, so we're staying here with Cheryl."

He didn't ask how Cheryl was. "So, supper," he said briskly. "We're kind of tied up over the weekend, but how about Monday?"

"Oh," Willa said. Monday was five days away. She wasn't even sure they'd still be here. "Is that the earliest you can manage?" she asked him.

"It's not like you gave us a lot of warning, you know."

"No, well . . . fine, then. Monday," she said.

"I'll call someplace and make a reservation," he said. "For four of us, right? Is Peter coming?"

"Yes, of course, and then also . . . well, we might have to bring Cheryl, if Denise is not home by then."

"Cheryl!" he said. "Can't she stay by herself for a couple hours?"

This made Willa sad. "I get the impression she might like to see you," she told him.

"That would be kind of awkward, Mom."

"Oh."

"And I can guarantee you that Denise wouldn't go for it."

She could see his point. She said, "Sorry. I guess I wasn't thinking."

"What's wrong with leaving her on her own? She watches out for herself all the time, ordinarily."

"At night? She's just a child!" Willa said.

"So? We'll eat early. You can be back before dark."

Willa said, "All right, Sean. We'll think of something. I'll wait to hear from you, then."

"Talk to you later," he said. He hung up.

Willa clicked her phone off and put it down on the couch beside her. She set her nose to the dog's nose again. "Oh, Airplane," she said.

Airplane gave a little whimper, and Willa laid her cheek on top of his silky warm head and hugged him closer against her.

Over the day she had gained a better sense of this household, and therefore of its inhabitants. Cheryl turned out to be a tidy child, with staid, old-ladyish habits. (She preferred to do her own laundry, she said, because her mother let things sit in the dryer so long that they got all crinkled.) Denise was the helter-skelter type—her bed unmade, her room a sea of tossed-off clothing and *People* magazines and Diet Pepsi cans. The kitchen was equipped for only rudimentary cooking, with a few basic pots and some mismatched dishes and glassware, but there was an electric mixer and a large supply of cake pans and pie tins and cookie sheets because Cheryl, it emerged, loved to bake. She told Willa that when she grew up she might want to open a birthday-cake shop.

It was, in fact, a bare-bones kind of house, its small rooms furnished sparsely with pieces that seemed to have led full lives in other houses long before this one. The only two pictures in the living room were a framed print of a van Gogh *Sunflowers* and a Ramones poster. The only books in the bookcase were children's books—some of them for very young children and others (mostly having to do with horses) for older children. Willa should have felt pity for the meagerness of it all, but in fact her main emotion was envy. She drifted idly through the rooms, relishing the hollow sound of her heels on the worn wooden floors. She gazed out a rear window at the scrubby backyard, where Peter sat with his laptop at a wrought-iron table scabbed with rust. She eavesdropped on Cheryl's phone conversation in the foyer—a call from her mother, the third one this afternoon. "Yes, Mama, we're *fine*. Me and Peter and Willa went to the Giant and bought all these groceries. For supper we're having pork chops." Denise had told them not to bother making a second visit today, but now Willa wondered if maybe they should have gone anyhow. Evidently Denise was just lying there fretting in her hospital bed.

In the front yard, which was also scrubby and no more than a dozen feet deep, Willa caught sight of a teenage boy clipping the low boxwood hedge that bordered the walk leading to the street. Even from here, it was obvious that he was not your standard gardener. For one thing, he looked like an elf. He was thin as a green bean, and he wore stovepipe jeans and a blue-and-white-striped jersey and a pointy red-and-white-striped knit hat from which a tangle of golden corkscrews exploded almost horizontally, long enough to touch his shoulders if his hair hadn't been so gravity-defying. Also, he didn't seem to know what he was doing. He was clumsily gripping a large pair of hedge shears and snipping a tiny sprig here, a tiny sprig there, with lengthy pauses in between. Snip, think a while;

snip, think a while. From time to time he glanced toward the house as if he were hoping to be noticed.

Willa opened the screen door and stepped out onto the porch. "Hello?" she said.

"Oh, hi!" he told her. His perky tone sounded artificial.

"So, are you . . . you're doing some pruning, are you?" Willa asked.

"Yes, ma'am," he said. His chin was as pointy as his hat, which made his whole head a sort of diamond shape. He couldn't be more than fifteen or so, in Willa's estimation. "I just wanted to help Denise out, you know?" he said. "I live next door." And he cocked a thumb toward the house on Willa's right.

"That's very kind of you," Willa said.

It was true, she saw, that the hedge needed trimming—it was sending off random shoots in all directions—although she didn't have much confidence in his landscaping skills. "I'll have to tell Denise," she said. "She'll be grateful."

"Is she coming home soon?"

"Maybe in a couple of days."

"First I was thinking I would mow her grass, but it's like she doesn't *have* any grass. Not so's you would notice."

"No, I guess that won't be—"

"Erland?" Cheryl called. She came bursting out of the house, letting the screen door slam behind her. "What're you up to?"

"I'm cutting your hedge; what's it look like?"

"You don't have to do that."

"I wanted to help out."

She hurtled down the porch steps, bypassing Willa, and came to stand in front of him, both hands on her hips. "What have you two been talking about?" she demanded.

"Nothing! I was just telling her I wanted to do something for your mom."

"Who says she needs anything done?"

Willa said, "I think she'll be very pleased."

"We don't know that! Maybe she's trying to grow the hedge taller," Cheryl said.

She sounded like some jealous little sister, Willa thought; but before she could come to the boy's defense, someone called, "Hello, everybody!"

They all turned toward the yard on Willa's left, where a stooped old woman in a housecoat was hanging on to a walker. A basset hound stood next to her, its leash looped around the walker's crossbar. "Erland Erikson, aren't you the sweetest thing," she said. "Denise is going to be thrilled!"

"I just thought I should help out," Erland said.

"And people claim teenagers are self-centered!" the woman told Willa. "I'm Lucinda Minton, by the way."

"I'm Willa Brendan," Willa said. "I'm staying with Cheryl while her mother's in the hospital."

"See? Everyone's being so nice," Mrs. Minton told Cheryl. "Aren't you blessed! I would have offered myself, you know, except I don't get around well enough."

"We're okay," Cheryl said. Then she said to Erland, "We're *okay*. Really."

"Well, if that's how you want it," he said. He lowered his hedge shears. He looked disappointed.

"When is Denise getting out?" Mrs. Minton asked Willa.

"We're not sure yet. Maybe in a couple of days."

"I was standing right here, you know, with my dog. I saw the whole thing happen. Well, not literally—I mean, not a one of us saw the gunman—but I was standing right here in this yard and I saw that poor girl drop to the ground. 'I'm shot!' she says."

"She didn't say 'I'm shot,'" Cheryl told her.

"She didn't?"

"She didn't say a thing. She didn't *know* she was shot, at the start."

"I could have sworn she said 'I'm shot.'"

"Well, she didn't."

"In any case," Willa said. "I guess it's time to start working on supper, Cheryl."

"Oh, okay," Cheryl said. "We're having pork chops," she told Mrs. Minton.

"Lucky!" Mrs. Minton said.

"I'm going to make the biscuits. Peter found a recipe on his computer and Willa wrote it out for me."

"See? Aren't people nice?" Mrs. Minton asked Erland.

Then they all turned and went into their separate houses.

Peter was the one who'd suggested pork chops, because that morning he had spotted a gas grill in the backyard and he prided himself on his grilled pork chops. "That's a *wonderful* idea!" Willa had said, almost singing. (It made her happy to see him involving himself in a project.) Cheryl, it turned out, had never eaten pork chops, or at least she couldn't remember eating them. Willa added this information to the other clues she'd gathered; she suspected Denise of specializing in SpaghettiOs and frozen fish sticks.

While Peter was tinkering with the grill, Cheryl set to work on the biscuits. First she studied the recipe with almost comical absorption, collecting each ingredient one by one as she read. Willa, reading over her shoulder, pointed out that if they added an extra quarter-cup of milk to the batter they could make drop biscuits— much easier than rolling and cutting them. But Cheryl said, "I *like* rolling and cutting," and took a very professional-looking white-marble rolling pin from a drawer.

So Willa left her to it and started cleaning up after Peter. Peter believed in brining, and everything he had used for the brine was still on the kitchen counter: an uncapped bottle of vinegar, an open box of brown sugar, a container of salt . . . "I can't believe she doesn't have kosher salt!" he had fumed. "I knew I'd have to buy juniper berries, but it never occurred to me I should get kosher salt too, for God's sake."

The silverware—stainless steel—was stored in a wooden divider tray in a drawer, and each compartment had a thread of crumbs and grit and dried parsley flakes lining its seams. Willa felt a great urge to empty out the tray and scrub it down, but she worried that might offend Denise. Then she decided Denise would most likely not even notice, so she went ahead and did it. Cheryl, meanwhile, was efficiently chopping the butter into the flour. She hadn't put an apron on, and the front of her T-shirt was dusted with white where her belly mounded out.

"How come Erland wears a knit hat on such a hot day?" Willa asked her.

Cheryl said, "Cuz he's a dork, I guess."

"What are his parents like?"

"He doesn't have any parents. He just has Sir Joe."

"*Who*," Willa asked, "is Sir Joe?" She had been wondering this for a while now.

Cheryl said, "Erland's half-brother, maybe? Or whatever you call it when the man and the woman each have a kid of their own and then they get married to each other."

"Stepbrother," Willa said.

"Right, and then they died somehow and Sir Joe got stuck with Erland. Sir Joe has a motorcycle," Cheryl added. There was something worshipful in her tone. "Everything he wears is black leather, even his pants."

"He wears leather pants in the summer? Gee, it must run in the family."

Willa was teasing, but Cheryl sent her an unamused look and then dumped her batter onto the counter and reached for her rolling pin. Clearly Sir Joe was a whole different order from his stepbrother.

Peter came in through the back door, wiping his hands together briskly. "Does your mom own a grill brush?" he asked Cheryl.

"She did once upon a time, but I don't know where it got to."

"Whole thing is a mass of soot and spiderwebs," Peter told Willa. "Must not have been used in months."

"Sean was the one who grilled," Cheryl said. "Mama's scared of gas."

Peter gave a derisive "Tch!" but Cheryl was oblivious. She had started cutting her biscuits out. The recipe had said she could use the rim of a drinking glass, but she took an actual biscuit cutter from the drawer. "You're very well equipped," Willa said admiringly.

"I've got muffin tins too, and mini-muffin tins."

"My goodness!"

"I always ask for baking equipment for Christmases and birthdays."

Peter had been rummaging through the clutter under the sink, no doubt still hoping to find a grill brush, but now he sat back on his heels and stared at Cheryl. "Don't you have any friends?" he asked her.

"Sure," she said, unruffled. "Lots of them, when school is in session."

"I mean, here in the neighborhood?"

"Well, not on Dorcas Road. But Patty and Laurie Dumont, over on Briscoe, we hang out all the time, except they're away at their cousins' right now."

She was setting the biscuits on a cookie sheet, each spaced a precise half-inch from the last in a perfectly straight line.

"Dorcas Road is all grownups, except for me and Erland," she said. "But I'm not *that* much of a kid. I'm way more grown-up than I seem."

"So you think now," Peter told her. "Just wait till you look back on this time."

But Willa knew what she meant. She had felt that way during her own childhood; she'd felt like a watchful, wary adult housed in a little girl's body.

And yet nowadays, paradoxically, it often seemed to her that from behind her adult face a child about eleven years old was still gazing out at the world.

The neighbor who lived on the other side of Mrs. Minton's house stopped by after supper, while Willa and Cheryl and Airplane were watching *Space Junk*. Peter was supposedly watching too—"Please?" Cheryl had begged him, and Willa had said, "Oh, try it, Peter"—but his heart wasn't in it, you could tell; he kept checking his phone. So when the doorbell rang he said, "I'll get it!," and stood up from the couch looking relieved. Cheryl pressed the Hold button, and two aliens froze in mid-conversation while Peter went out to the foyer, followed by Airplane. He returned with a man in his sixties or so, white-haired and lanky and ruddy-faced, wearing a faded plaid shirt with the sleeves rolled up and a pair of loose-kneed gray pants. "Evening," he said in a gravelly voice. "Hi there, Cheryl."

"Hey, Ben!" Cheryl said.

He walked over to offer Willa his hand, and she stood up to shake it. "I'm Ben Gold," he told her. "And you're the woman who came all the way from Arizona to tend this young lady here."

"Willa," she said. Ben Gold had narrow, saggy-lidded blue eyes that almost disappeared when he smiled at her, and his glasses were the type that certain boys in her grade school used to wear, with transparent pinkish frames and smudged lenses.

"I've been visiting Denise," he said, "and I promised her I'd look in on you all and see how you're doing."

"We're doing fine, thanks. How was Denise?"

"Good, good . . . she's in good hands. I went to medical school with her surgeon, about a million years ago. He's got no bedside manner but he does know what he's up to."

"You're a doctor?" Willa asked. She would have said he didn't look like one, except that all at once she saw that he did. He had that humorously resigned air about him.

"In my humble way," he said, and Cheryl chimed in with, "His house has got this teeny doctor office added on to the back."

"So I'm the one to come to if Denise has any problems once she's home," he told Willa. "Not that I expect her to."

"Can I offer you a drink?" Peter asked him suddenly.

Willa wasn't sure what he planned to offer, since Denise's liquor supply seemed limited to a cardboard box of chardonnay in the fridge, but Ben said, "No, thanks, I'd better get back and fix myself some supper. I seem to be running late all day, as usual."

"We had pork chops!" Cheryl told him.

"Well, I'm having a can of chili," he said, and then he told Willa, "I'm just over at three-oh-six; call on me any time."

"Thank you, that's good to know," Willa said.

Peter was the one who saw him out—Peter and Airplane—while Willa and Cheryl sat back down on the couch and Cheryl restarted *Space Junk*. One of the aliens was telling another that earthlings appeared strangely averse to engaging with the opposite sex. "We put the white-haired female wearing tall-heeled shoes and the pink-faced male wearing an apron in a room together for a week, and they did not once mate," he said. This struck Cheryl as hilarious; she was squawking with laughter, although by her own admission she had seen the episode half a dozen times. "You missed it!" she told Peter when he came back into the room. "You missed the best part!"

"I'll try to contain my disappointment," he said.

Airplane jumped onto the couch next to Cheryl, but Peter didn't sit back down. "You want me to play it again?" Cheryl asked him.

"No, that's okay."

Then his cell phone gave a tweet-tweet, and he took it from his pocket and walked over to the lamp to read his message.

"He's never going to get the point of this if he keeps doing other things," Cheryl told Willa.

"Oh, I bet he can catch up," Willa said.

"This one's finished, though! That was the end of the episode."

Cheryl slumped back in her seat and let the remote drop into her lap. The TV screen rolled the credits and then offered the next episode—how many *were* there?—but Cheryl made no move to start it. "I hate when people get texts," she told Willa.

"Me too," Willa said. She barely knew *how* to text, herself; she didn't even e-mail people unless she had something specific to say.

"Mama gets texts all the time," Cheryl said. "Only hers make a dinging sound."

"I kind of like Peter's tweet-tweet," Willa said. "It reminds me of how my father used to wake me in the mornings. He'd whistle those same two notes—these cheerful, birdy notes. Like the first two notes of 'Dixie,' I always thought."

Cheryl considered for a moment. "Or of 'Hey Jude,'" she suggested.

"Oh, you're right. Except 'Hey Jude' hadn't been invented yet."

"Texting hadn't, either," Cheryl said.

"Well, *that's* for sure," Willa said.

And subtly, she leaned closer to take a deep, pleasurable breath of the buttered-popcorn smell of Cheryl's hair.

It must have been the mention of her father's wake-up whistle that made her think of him that night when she was trying to get to sleep. *Tweet*-tweet! she heard again, and there he was: his dear, mild face and his kindly smile and the way he'd stand at her bedroom door with his knees slightly bent and his head at a tilt like some awkward, long-legged shore bird.

For the whole of her childhood his death had been what she'd feared most, but now that it had finally happened she had trouble wrapping her mind around it. (He had collapsed in his driveway while getting out of his car—not alone in his basement, thank heaven.) In fact, his death had been more of a shock than Derek's, in some ways. It used to be that the world had rested entirely on her father's shoulders. He was the steady one, the safe one—the person she could depend on when her mother was in a state.

But even the thought of her mother, now, gave her a tugging feeling of loss, and she often found herself missing that shy look her mother used to send from under her eyebrows when she hoped to be forgiven for something, and her lighthearted, girlish laugh, and her floating soprano voice singing "Write me a letter, send it by mail . . ."

Oh, sounds were what brought the past alive most clearly! "Take my hand," she heard the back-of-the-room boys crooning, "I'm a strange-looking parasite . . ." And then other, more anonymous voices, blurred and staticky like those ancient radio waves rumored to be traveling endlessly out into space. "One potato, two potato, three potato, four," and "He-e-ere's Johnny!" and "Instinctively, the arthritis sufferer rubs the afflicted area."

From his bed across the room Peter gave a sudden sharp sigh, and Willa started. It took her a second to remember who he was.

5

They skipped their hospital visit on Friday morning, because Denise telephoned during breakfast and said she'd be having a physical therapy session. "She's going to learn how to use crutches," Cheryl announced when she had hung up. "We're supposed to come in the afternoon instead."

"In the afternoon I've got a conference call," Peter told Willa. "You two will have to go without me."

Willa said, "Oh, can't you come too? I wouldn't know how to get there."

"Then it's high time you figured it out," he said.

To him it was a cinch, figuring out directions, but Willa seemed to be lacking that particular part of her brain. And the GPS on her phone was no help, because it didn't let her see more than two inches ahead; and anyhow she hated driving, and she especially hated driving a car that wasn't familiar to her.

But instead of reminding him of all this, Willa just made her voice go soft and said, "Well. All right, sweetheart."

"The call's been scheduled for weeks now," he said in a defensive tone.

"That's okay. I know I've been a pest," she told him.

"I didn't say you were a *pest*; I just said I'd be tied up."

"I understand."

There was a brief silence. Peter took a sip of coffee. Then he said, "Well, I suppose I could take you after I'm finished. If you don't object to waiting."

"Oh, we don't object in the least!" she said. "Do we, Cheryl?"

Cheryl said, "Um, no."

"Thank you, sweetheart," Willa told Peter.

"Whatever," he said, looking resigned. But she could tell he wasn't all that put out about it.

Marriage was often a matter of dexterity, in Willa's experience.

After breakfast, she and Cheryl took Airplane on an extra-long walk. They hooked him to a leash, for once, because Cheryl said he got nervous when he had to cross through traffic.

The air had a watery feeling today, although no rain had been forecast, and the breeze seemed loaded with promise. Willa wore sandals and a cotton shift. Cheryl, of course, was in shorts. For some reason she had a crab decal stuck to her right cheek.

They walked past Mrs. Minton's house, its lowered paper shades giving it a blank-faced look. Mrs. Minton never got up till noon, Cheryl confided, and then she fixed herself one big meal for the whole day because it was so hard to cook leaning on that walker of hers. "How does she get her groceries?" Willa asked, and Cheryl said, "Ben does that. Mrs. Minton gives him a list every Friday evening." ("Mrs. Mitten," she pronounced it.)

They walked past Ben's house with its peeling white wooden sign suspended from a post: "Benj. Gold, M.D. Walk-ins welcome." An ancient couple was creeping toward the rear where his office was, the wife clinging with both hands to her husband's elbow. "Arthritis, I bet," Cheryl said knowledgeably. "Cortisone shot will fix *that*."

In the window of the house next door to Ben's was another sign: "Raeburn Investigations," with "Domestic Adultery a Specialty" in smaller letters beneath it. "That's where the private detective lives. Dave," Cheryl said. Willa wondered if there was some type of adultery that wasn't domestic. (And had Dave known about Sean's secret trysts with Elissa?)

They passed the last house on the block, where blue hydrangeas billowed in abundance. "Barry and Richard," Cheryl said. "They're both gay, but-that's-all-right!"—these last words running together in a reflexive little chant. On the corner they waited for a police car to streak by, its lights flashing but no siren sounding, and then they started up the next block. The signboards multiplied: picture framing, computer repair, clothing alterations. All those hopeful little enterprises squeezed into front rooms or glassed-in porches.

After that the houses gave way to actual shops—delis and dry cleaners—and Willa and Cheryl took a right to get back to a more residential area. "Over there is Briscoe Road, where Patty and Laurie live," Cheryl said when they paused for a stoplight. "They're so lucky! Their grandma has a swimming pool in her apartment building."

"That does sound lucky," Willa said.

"Also, both of them get their nails professionally manicured. Would you ever take me for a manicure?"

"Oh, honey, I wouldn't even know where to go," Willa said.

"*Their* grandma takes *them*," Cheryl said.

The way she stressed the word "their" made it sound as if Willa were *her* grandma. Willa couldn't help feeling pleased by that. All at once she could imagine tracking down a manicurist for Cheryl.

"Mama says we don't have the money for manicures," Cheryl said as they resumed walking. "We just do our own nails."

"Me too," Willa told her.

"Mama cuts our own hair, even."

"Well, she does a good job," Willa said.

"How about you?" Cheryl asked her.

"Me?"

"Do you cut *your* own hair?"

"No, somebody does it for me," Willa said. She almost felt she should apologize.

"Do they dye it, too?"

"Well, they touch it up."

Cheryl squinted at it.

"It's not gray but it's starting to fade, kind of," Willa told her.

"That's okay," Cheryl said. Then she said, "You're really pretty, for an old person."

"Well, thank you."

"Were you pretty when you were nine?"

"When I was nine? Oh, goodness, no."

Cheryl smiled at her.

They took a second right; they were heading toward home now. Airplane met another dog, a tiny gray dust mop who bounced straight up off the sidewalk in excitement and yapped frantically, but Airplane just gave an aloof sniff and turned away. The other dog's owner was a hunched old lady in a droopy black dress. It seemed to be the time of day for the old people to be out, Willa noticed. Everyone else had work to do.

When Willa and Cheryl reached their own block again, Willa asked, "Do you know the neighbors across the street, too?"

"Nope. None of us do," Cheryl said. "Across the street is real snooty; they think they're so diverse and all because they've got an African-American family. And the boys who live in the house where they power-washed the deck go to private school and they never say boo to Erland even though they're his same age."

Willa clucked.

They had traveled in a circle, so that they were returning from the opposite direction. They passed a house that Cheryl identified as Hal's, where a red sticker reading "Your Friendly SafeHome Insurance Agent" was plastered to the front window, and then Callie's house and then Erland's. A man perhaps still in his twenties strode down Erland's front walk frowning at his cell phone—a short, dark, muscular man with thick black hair that seemed all of a piece. "Sir Joe!" Cheryl said in a thrilled voice. He glanced up, and his forehead cleared. "Well, hey," he said.

Sir Joe wasn't the hoodlum that Willa had been led to expect. His pants were not leather but denim, and the vehicle parked at his curb was not a motorcycle but a white panel truck with "Season-All HVAC" painted on its side. "Sergio Lopez," he told her, tucking his phone into his rear pocket.

"Oh, *Sergio*," Willa said, finally understanding.

She must have sounded like some sort of groupie—like Cheryl, in fact—because he favored her with a slow, gratified smile. "That's me, gorgeous," he said.

"Willa," Cheryl corrected him sternly.

"How's your mom?" he asked her.

"She's okay. She's learning how to use crutches today."

"Terrible thing," he said. He turned back to Willa and gave her a cocky salute with two fingers tipped to his temple. "See you around," he told her, and then he sauntered off toward his truck, his crumpled leather boots clopping heavily and a loop of steel chain clanking from his belt.

Willa was amused. Cheryl stood gazing after him with a rapt expression, her lips slightly parted. Even Airplane was gazing after him.

"Shall we get on home?" Willa asked.

Cheryl sighed and said, "I guess."

After lunch Peter went upstairs to wait for his conference call, and Willa and Cheryl baked a batch of peanut-butter cookies to take to Denise. It didn't surprise Willa that Cheryl owned a dedicated Tupperware cookie bin, into which she carefully layered the cookies once they had cooled. Meanwhile Willa checked her e-mail: nothing but spam and one birth announcement from an old San Diego friend's daughter. She'd been hoping to hear from Ian. Well, maybe over the weekend. Occasionally he drove to some little town on weekends where his phone could pick up a signal. She typed a brief e-mail just to let him know where she was in case he tried to call her at home—not that there was much chance he would. Then she sent almost the same message to her sister. Elaine wouldn't notice if they were gone for months on end, but Willa liked to keep up some illusion of connection. She had only the one sister, as she often told

Peter when he asked why on earth she bothered. He had met Elaine a single time, when she passed through San Diego several years before, and he said later he couldn't believe that she and Willa came from the same family. "Charmless" was the word he used for her.

Something went wrong with his conference call; it appeared they forgot to include him. Eventually this was straightened out, but it put him in one of his "harrumph" moods, as Willa thought of them, and he had to mutter and grumble a while and complain about the incompetent girl in the office who had caused the mix-up. It was almost four o'clock before he agreed to head to the hospital. Four o'clock on a Friday: people were taking off from work already, and when the three of them walked into Denise's room they found a little party going on. Two young women were filling plastic tumblers of wine while an older, managerial-looking black woman stood at the bureau spreading Brie on crackers. "Oh, look, everybody!" Denise sang out. "It's Peter and Willa! Sean's mom. So, this here is Ginny, from school, and that's Sharon, and over there is Mrs. Anderson, our principal." The younger women just smiled and murmured their hellos, but Mrs. Anderson turned with a cracker poised between her thumb and index finger and said, "Oh, I always like meeting the grandparents. We consider them a resource. Do you-all have any skills you might want to share with our students?"

"We're not actually from Baltimore," Willa told her, gliding right past the grandparent reference. "We live in Arizona." Just like that, she and Peter fell off Mrs. Anderson's radar. Ginny handed each of them a glass of wine, and Cheryl passed around her cookies, and Mrs. Anderson proposed a toast to Denise. Peter didn't take so much as a sip, though; Willa hoped nobody noticed. He set his glass down untouched and told her, "I'm going to go buy a paper."

"I'll come with you," she said. Maybe she could smooth his feathers a bit on the way.

She set her own glass down and they stepped out into the corridor, which seemed very wide and peaceful compared to Denise's room. As they walked toward the elevators, Peter said, "Wouldn't you think one of *them* could have taken Cheryl?"

"They have jobs, Peter. They work at Cheryl's school."

"Still," he said, unreasonably. He pressed the elevator button.

The gift shop was a disorganized alcove off the downstairs lobby. It offered newspapers and celebrity magazines, a bucket of cellophane-swaddled bouquets, a cluster of coffee mugs printed with jokey slogans . . . On a ledge behind the register stood a row of tiny, whiskery saguaros identical to the one Peter had brought her. They were nowhere near any sunlight, not even under a grow light. Willa felt an absurd urge to buy them all and set them free.

While Peter was paying for his paper, a very pregnant woman walked in wearing a pink flannel bathrobe, her hair straggling down limply on either side of her face. She started drifting around the shop, gazing at various items in a distracted, unhappy way. The cashier—a young man barely past his teens—called out, "Can I help you?"

She turned and glared at him. "Why are you asking me that?" she demanded.

"Ma'am?"

"What makes you think I need help?"

"Ma'am, I was just wondering if there was anything you were looking for."

"Don't you think I can find it for myself?" she said.

The cashier turned to Peter and Willa with a baffled expression.

Willa raised her eyebrows sympathetically, but Peter said, "Let's get out of here," and he seized her by the upper arm and propelled her toward the door.

In the lobby, which was a sea of chairs and couches in little conversational groupings, he didn't head for the elevators but let go of her arm and collapsed onto a green vinyl couch. "I hate this city," he said.

Willa sat down next to him in a gingerly, unobtrusive way, barely entrusting her weight to the seat cushion. "Was it that woman back there?" she asked him.

He didn't answer.

"I don't understand," she said.

"It's everything. I hate the heat; I hate the humidity; the accent is atrocious . . . I don't know what we're *doing* here."

"Well, sweetheart? We're just helping Denise for a few days."

"We don't even know Denise!"

She couldn't think what was upsetting him so. She cast her mind back over everything that had happened since their arrival. She felt she had missed some important clue. "Is it something to do with the firm?" she asked. "With the person who messed up your conference call?"

"What do *you* care about the firm?"

She grew still.

"Willa," he said. "I think you're going to pieces."

"What?"

He didn't repeat it.

"I was just wondering if *you* were the one going to pieces," she said finally.

He let out a puff of a breath. Then he gave his knee a brisk slap with his folded paper and said, "Well, back to the funhouse," and stood up and started for the elevators.

Willa rose and followed him. She had a heavy feeling in her stomach.

In the elevator, they didn't speak. They rode upward in a humming silence and glided to a stop at the second floor and stepped off. Even from here, she could hear the rising swell of merriment coming from Denise's room.

6

On Saturday she was awakened by the ringing of the telephone. It was unlikely anyone would be calling her, but the fact that the ringing went on and on still managed to make her feel anxious. Even when it stopped she couldn't relax, because the air conditioner was running full blast in the window and she didn't know whether Cheryl had answered or the caller had merely given up. She lay squinting at the ceiling, straining to hear. No sounds at all made it through that infernal droning.

It was almost nine, according to the elderly electric clock on the bureau. Peter's bed was empty, his covers tossed back and his pajamas in a heap at the foot. The light from the windows was a mellow gold, not the early-morning paleness she was accustomed to.

She sat up and smoothed her hair down and slid her feet into her slippers. As she was reaching for her kimono, Peter opened the bedroom door and stuck his head in. "You're awake," he said.

"I don't know why I slept so late," she told him.

"Denise just called. They're saying she can come home today."

"Oh, good!"

"She told Cheryl she'll be ready to leave once her doctor's stopped by. Ten or so."

Willa stood up and tied her kimono sash. "So, will you . . . are you going to drive us?" she asked.

"I should, I guess. You'll need my help loading her into the car."

Willa felt relieved, but she didn't show it.

"And then as soon as Rona's office opens," he said, "I'm going to give her a call."

Oh. Rona was their travel agent. Willa said, "Well, maybe we should wait on that. We're not sure yet when Denise will be able to manage without us."

"Manage what?" Peter asked. "She's got Cheryl; got her neighbors; it's only a broken leg, for God's sake."

"Yes, but—"

"In fact I might just go online and book the tickets myself," he said.

"Oh, let Rona do that, why don't you," Willa said. "You always tell me she's so good at finding upgrades."

"Well, you're right, I guess. I'll wait. God *damn* all these time zones!"

Peter sometimes claimed—jokingly, she assumed—that the whole country should keep its clocks set to the same hour, even though that meant that some states would have to conduct their business in the dark.

Willa wasn't at all sure that Denise could make it up the stairs, but even so, she and Cheryl changed the sheets in her room and tidied a bit after breakfast. Cheryl turned bossy, first deciding that Denise would need an extra pillow and then clearing every bit of clutter off her vanity—even things that could have stayed there, like a hairbrush and a bottle of perfume. "Mama's *such* a slob," she said affectionately. The crab decal on her cheek had faded to little orange dots by now. She was wearing majorette boots today—white, with tassels—along with her usual bunchy-crotched shorts and a crop top that exposed the globe of her tummy. Willa found herself admiring the child's lack of self-consciousness.

As the three of them were heading to the car they saw Callie crossing her yard to her own car, tripping along on her little hoof feet. She waved to them and called, "How's Denise?"

"We're on our way now to bring her home," Willa said.

"Well, tell her I said hey, hear? Does she need anything from the Giant?"

"I don't think so, thanks."

Callie trilled her fingers and got into her car. Cheryl said, "We ought to buy Callie a plant for taking care of me."

"Oh, what a nice thought," Willa said.

"I told Mama that and she said, 'Right,' but I'm worried she'll forget."

"We could do that for her," Willa said. "Can't we, Peter?"

Peter just said "Mmph" and unlocked the car doors; Denise's car was old enough to require an actual key. When Willa was settled in front and Cheryl in the rear, Cheryl leaned forward to say, "Callie didn't *like* taking care of me, though, so I think it should be a not very expensive plant."

"In fact it should be a *more* expensive plant," Peter said as he slid behind the wheel. "If taking care of you had been something she liked, we'd let her do it for free, like Willa here."

Willa turned to gauge Cheryl's reaction to this and found herself practically nose to nose with the child, who was studying her from beneath her lashes with an expression that seemed oddly bashful. "He's right," Willa told her. "I would pay *you* for the privilege."

Cheryl gave a little giggle and sat back to fasten her seat belt.

The trip to the hospital was vaguely familiar by now—the stream of shabby front porches, the kiddie pools and Big Wheels littering the yards, the signs for Tamaqua's House of Hair Weaves and Fix-It Fred. It was already getting hot, and after a mile or two Peter sought out Cheryl's face in the rearview mirror and asked her to crank her window up because he had the AC on. She obeyed without interrupting herself; she was talking about this idea she had for starting a pet library. "You know how people can't always own an animal," she said. "Like, they're traveling salesmen or something and they have to be away from home a lot. So they would come to the pet library and borrow a nice cozy dog or cat for a couple days at a time."

"Well, good luck with that," Peter told her. "Think of the liability issues."

"Huh?"

"What if a dog bites someone? That's a lawsuit waiting to happen."

"I'd make people sign something first. They'd have to promise not to sue."

"A waiver," Peter said.

"Right."

Willa said, "I'm more concerned about the pets' side of things. How do you know the borrowers will treat them well?"

"They would have to give us three references," Cheryl said promptly. "And if someone tells us, 'Well, I don't know, this guy's a little bit of a loser,' we would turn the guy down."

"Losers wouldn't worry me," Willa said. "Sometimes it's the losers who need a pet the most, and would be nicest to them."

"Pay no attention to Willa," Peter told Cheryl. "She's one of your bleeding-heart types."

"Well, I know that," Cheryl said.

Willa laughed. For a moment, she felt she was back in the days when her sons were still chatterboxes, many years ago.

The hospital lot was fuller this time, perhaps because it was the weekend, and Peter would have had to park in the auxiliary lot at the rear. He said, "I'll just let you two out in front and wait for you to bring her down."

"You're not coming in?" Willa asked. "It could be a while, you know."

"That's okay. I'll catch up on my e-mail."

She decided not to push it. She was being extra tactful since yesterday. "Just don't blame us if Denise's doctor hasn't stopped by yet," she told him as she got out.

But the doctor had come and gone, as it happened. Denise was waiting for them in a wheelchair, wearing street clothes—a white denim miniskirt and a halter top that tied at the back of her neck—and one wedge-heeled sandal. Her injured leg was stretched out on the wheelchair's elevated footrest, and a pair of crutches stood propped behind her back, the short metal kind with arm cuffs. "What kept you?" she asked immediately, although it was not much past ten. "I've been waiting forever!" She reached over to press the call button dangling from a cord at the head of her bed, and a few seconds later a voice said, "Yes?"

"My ride's here," Denise shouted. She dropped the call button and turned to Cheryl. "Did you bring that tote?"

"Oh," Cheryl said.

"Cheryl! Honestly." She told Willa, "I asked her to bring a tote bag for my stuff."

She meant the pile on the foot of her bed—magazines and puzzle books, the cookie bin, her slippers and her other shoe, a beige vinyl purse. Willa said, "Oh, I'm sorry. I should have thought of that myself. We'll ask the nurse for one."

"It's not like the ambulance guys waited while I packed a suitcase," Denise said.

Cheryl was opening drawers now and slamming them shut, then opening a skinny closet. On the closet floor was a turquoise plastic bedpan in a transparent plastic bag, and she stripped the bag off efficiently and took it over to the bed, where she started filling it with Denise's belongings. Willa was impressed, but all Denise said was, "I reckon I could take the bedpan too, if I really, really wanted. They told me they throw everything out once a patient leaves here."

"Well! How wasteful," Willa said.

"Yeah, that's the modern world for you. There you are!" she said to the nurse who was walking in.

"Leaving us so soon?" the nurse asked. She was a rosy-faced little redhead in lavender scrubs that clashed violently with her coloring. "Did they give you all your prescriptions?"

"Just the one; it's in my purse," Denise said. She told Willa, "They wanted me to take pain pills but I said, 'I can't take pain pills! I'd barf.'"

The nurse clucked and bent to release the wheelchair brakes. "Where's your car parked?" she asked Willa.

"It's waiting at the main entrance."

They set off down the hall, Cheryl swinging her bag with a crackling sound. At the elevators, the nurse punched a button. "Get a load of what they gave me to walk with," Denise told Cheryl. She jerked her head toward the crutches. "Aren't they awful? They make me feel like an old lady. I wanted the long, classy wooden kind, so people would think I'd been skiing."

"In the summertime?" Cheryl asked.

"It can happen."

Their elevator arrived, and the nurse pivoted Denise's wheelchair and hauled it in backward. The only other occupant was an old man in a hospital gown that didn't cover his knees. He studied Cheryl for a moment and then asked, "How you doing, young lady?"

"I'm good," Cheryl told him.

"Got your hands full, I see," he said, nodding toward Denise.

"I'll say."

Denise glared at her, and Cheryl gave her a smirk.

When they reached the main floor, the nurse pushed the wheelchair across the lobby and out the automatic doors. Peter emerged from the car and came around to help her load Denise into the rear, while Willa put the crutches and Cheryl's bag in the trunk. The whole time that Denise was maneuvering into the back seat, she was saying "Ack!" and "*Damn*, that hurts" and "Watch it!" She landed with an explosive breath, and the nurse held her injured leg out straight while she slid backward until she was occupying the length of the back seat. Then Cheryl climbed in after her and lifted Denise's feet and settled them in her lap. "Thank you," Willa told the nurse before she got into the front, and the nurse said, "Good luck!" Willa wondered if she said that to everyone, or only to people with crabby relatives.

As Peter started the car, Denise said, "God only knows how long before I can drive myself again."

"Well, it's your left leg," Peter said, "and this is an automatic transmission, so you could start right away, I should think."

"Right away! Not a chance! I've got this big huge cast on! I've got no place to put it! How do you figure *that*?"

No one answered her.

Denise's arrival on Dorcas Road was quite a production. She had to rely on her crutches for the trip from the car to the house, and she kept staggering and wobbling and collapsing against Peter, who was struggling gamely to hold her up. Willa tried to help, but she only got in the way and at one point nearly knocked one of Denise's crutches out from under her. "Durn!" Denise said, panting. "That durn physical therapist! I saw him *one* time, *once*. How do they think I'll work these things?"

They had progressed only a few feet when Erland appeared, wearing his elf hat and a T-shirt riddled with holes, but all he seemed capable of was hovering around the edges wringing his hands and saying, "Oh, crap . . . oh, crap . . ."

"Stop that," Denise told him, and he said, "Sorry, Denise . . ." and then someone else called, "Need any help?"

It was a fortyish man in khakis, crossing from the yard just beyond Callie's. Denise told Willa, "Great. Hal," in a flat tone of voice, and Willa glanced at him curiously, because this must be Elissa's jilted husband.

"I've got this," he announced reassuringly. Denise sent Willa a wry little grimace. He took hold of Denise's free arm, and he and

Peter between them managed to keep her upright as she made her way toward the house. But when they reached the porch steps, she gave a groan.

"I don't think I can make it," she said.

Peter said, "Well, let's think, now . . ."

"Wait up," someone commanded from behind them.

Cheryl said, "Sir Joe!"

Willa turned to watch him approach. Today he did have leather pants on, maybe because it wasn't a workday. "Stand aside," he ordered Peter and Hal, and he strode forward and scooped Denise into his arms and carried her easily up the steps, leaving the two men holding a crutch apiece. Denise looked back at the others over his shoulder, her expression comically startled.

"Door," he said.

Cheryl sprang to unlock the door for him, and Airplane popped out like a jack-in-the-box but then, catching sight of Denise, wheeled and raced back inside and watched intently as Sir Joe carried her in. Sir Joe clopped through the foyer in his heavy boots, turned left and went into the living room and deposited her on the couch. Denise said "Oof!" and Sir Joe stepped back and dusted off his hands in a businesslike way.

Cheryl said, "How's she going to get to her bedroom every night?"

She was still in the living-room doorway, hugging Denise's plastic bag to her chest. The others had gathered around—Peter and Hal, Willa, Erland, and now Ben Gold, shambling up behind them to say, "She's not. There's no way she can safely manage that flight of stairs."

"Well, I was wondering," Willa said.

"But where am I going to sleep?" Denise wailed.

She was sitting on the couch with both legs extended in front of her, Airplane sniffing her cast inquisitively. When Ben came forward to pick up her feet and swing them around so that she could lie down, she said "Ow!" and Ben said, "Cheryl, go fetch your mom a couple of pillows."

Cheryl raced off, still clutching the plastic bag. Ben told Denise, "We've got to rent you a hospital bed."

Denise said, "I am *not* having a hospital bed."

"It's nothing to be ashamed of, you know. Plenty of people rent hospital beds."

"I don't care; it would still depress me," Denise said.

"Even if we put it out of sight in the dining room?"

"You're not going to change my mind about this."

"Also," Ben said, "we should think about a commode."

"Ick!"

"Just for a couple of weeks or so, till you get a walking cast."

"A couple of *weeks!*" Peter said, looking distressed.

Denise said, "I am sleeping here on the couch, and I am making do with the powder room."

"Or," Sir Joe said, "I'll come over every night and carry you up the stairs."

"Absolutely not," Ben said.

"Why can't he?" Cheryl asked. "He could do it, easy!" She was back in the living room now, hugging a pillow under each arm and gazing adoringly at Sir Joe.

But Ben said, "The last thing we need is to drop her and break her other leg."

Sir Joe shrugged. Then he turned his attention to Peter. "Hey there," he said. "Sergio Lopez."

"Peter Brendan," Peter said. "And this is my wife, Willa."

"Her I know," Sir Joe said, cocking an appreciative eyebrow at her.

"If we put the hospital bed in the dining room," Ben was continuing doggedly, "people coming to visit wouldn't even see it."

"I would see it," Denise said. "It would make me feel like an invalid."

"You *are* an invalid," Cheryl told her. "Deal with it."

Denise scowled at her. "The way this kid acts," she told Ben, "you'd think mothers get shot all the time."

"They do, actually," Ben said. He sighed. "Okay, have it your way."

"Gal knows her own mind," Sir Joe told him. He winked at Willa.

Meanwhile, Hal turned to Peter. "You're Sean's dad?" he asked.

Willa stiffened. Peter said, "Stepdad, actually."

"I'm Hal Adams. Happens Sean ran off with my wife."

"Pleased to meet you," Peter said pleasantly.

Willa followed suit; she held out her hand and told Hal, "I'm Sean's mother."

Hal hesitated, but then he shook her hand. He had sunken eyes and a long-chinned, morose face not unlike the face of Mrs. Minton's basset hound. It looked as if it had been clamped between two sliding doors at some point.

Denise was letting herself relax, finally, her head resting on one pillow and her injured leg on the other. "One good thing," she told the ceiling, "is there's no PA system here. No 'Dr. Smith, *please* come resuscitate this dead guy.' I feel like I could maybe actually sleep. So, yeah!"

This seemed to be the cue for her neighbors to start taking their leave. They trickled one by one into the foyer, Hal hanging back a moment to give Denise a tentative pat on her bare toes. (Denise jerked away irritably.) "You just phone if you need me, now," he told her. "Night or day! I can be over in a jiff." And from the foyer Erland said, "Me too, Denise!"

Denise just said "Huh."

Ben asked Willa, "Did they give her any prescriptions to fill?"

"One," Willa said. "I'm going to send Peter for that."

"Let's see what they've got her on; maybe I have samples."

Willa looked around for Denise's purse, and then she asked Cheryl, "Where's that bag you brought in?"

Cheryl was trailing Sir Joe and Erland to the front door. She glanced back distractedly and said, "Oh, um, maybe upstairs?" So Willa went to fetch it herself. "Are you going to visit again?" Cheryl asked Sir Joe. Willa didn't catch his answer.

As she crossed the upstairs hall, she heard Peter talking in the guest room. She hadn't noticed that he'd left the living room. "Let's try for Monday morning," he was saying. "Anything nonstop, although we'll take what we can get."

She went to the doorway and said, "Peter?" He was pacing between the two beds, holding his cell phone to his ear. "Not Monday!" she said in a piercing whisper. "We're having dinner with Sean on Monday."

"What? Wait a sec, Rona." He lowered his phone and frowned at Willa.

"And Denise will still be needing us, I'm almost sure of it," she told him.

"If she needs us, we'll just reschedule," he said. He didn't address the Sean issue.

"But then why even make the reservation yet?" she asked.

Although she knew this was the wrong strategy. She should never go at him head-on. He said, "Willa, I'm on the phone. We can discuss this later." He put the phone back to his ear. "Sorry, Rona. You were saying?"

Willa went on standing there, but he didn't look her way again and so finally she turned and continued to Denise's room. The plastic bag lay at the foot of the bed; she rummaged through it for Denise's purse. As she crossed back through the hall Peter was saying, "Right, let's go for that one."

Ben was waiting at the bottom of the stairs. Willa took the prescription from Denise's purse and handed it to him. "Good," he said, adjusting his glasses to study it. "Just your everyday antibiotic. We can save Peter a trip to the pharmacy."

"Well, thank you," she said.

Right then, though, she didn't feel like doing Peter any favors at all.

7

Denise said, "Doesn't it seem to you like Cheryl is acting kind of coldhearted about my injury?"

"No, not at all," Willa told her. "I don't think that's true in the least."

She was remaking the bed on the couch, smoothing the sheets that Denise had rumpled during the night while Denise, newly returned from an arduous trip with Willa through the foyer to the powder room, sat in the armchair with her crutches propped beside her.

"Okay: she's standing out in the yard," Denise said, "and she hears this big loud bang. She looks over and her mother's sitting flat on the ground with her leg bleeding. How is that not traumatic? But *oh*, no. *Oh*, no. Cheryl is just like, 'So can I spend the night at Sir Joe's, then?'"

"She's sensible, is all," Willa told her. "She could see you were going to be fine, and so she took it in stride."

Denise didn't look convinced.

Privately, Willa felt there were other things that should worry Denise more. Look at that crush Cheryl had on Sir Joe, for instance;

look at how she missed Sean. This was a child who felt the lack of a man in her life. And there were times when she seemed to lack a mother as well, because surely the average mother would not expect a nine-year-old to fend for herself as much as Denise did. But Denise was saying, "Most kids would be having nightmares right now. They'd be asking if their mom was okay. They'd be upset that she was suffering instead of rolling their eyes any time she made the least little complaint."

Willa couldn't help smiling at that. It was true that Cheryl showed no patience with Denise's moaning and groaning.

"And I'm all she's got!" Denise said. "Who would Cheryl have gone to if I'd been shot dead, I'd like to know!"

Willa said, "How about, well, her father?"

"Oh, him," Denise said airily. "Her father doesn't know she exists."

"Oh," Willa said.

"Too many Amstel Lights one night, my sophomore year in college."

"You were in college?" Willa asked.

"Towson University. You sound surprised."

"No, no, I just meant . . . that must have been hard."

"You're durn right it was hard."

Willa folded back the top sheet, and then she went over to the armchair to help Denise stand. Since yesterday they'd developed a system: Willa faced her and held out both hands, and Denise took a firm grip of them and heaved herself upright. Then Willa backed toward the couch with her—a distance of only a few steps, so they didn't bother with the crutches.

"I've always been a little disorganized," Denise said once she had dropped onto the couch. "So I didn't catch on I was pregnant until I was five months along, and by then it was too late to do anything about it."

In Willa's opinion, this was more than just a little disorganized, but she bent silently to lift Denise's feet and help her swing them onto the couch. Denise lay back with a sigh and pulled the top sheet over her. She was wearing a pair of voluminous shorts and an over-sized T-shirt—her one outfit for both night and day. She and Willa had settled on it the previous evening when they were getting her ready for bed.

"What I thought: I'd have the baby and then finish school," Denise told the ceiling. "But that didn't actually work out."

"I did that, too," Willa said. "I quit college when I got pregnant with Sean; thought I'd go back as soon as he was born. But I ended up staying home till both boys were in their teens."

"Well, that's a lot different," Denise said.

Because Willa hadn't needed to support herself, she meant. And because she'd had the money to go back once she had decided to. There was really no comparison, was what Denise was saying.

Peter and Cheryl were off buying lunch things, their third errand this morning. Peter seemed glad to have something to do, and Cheryl liked to tag along with him. (Yet another man to shadow.)

He'd gone ahead with the Monday plane reservation, it turned out, even though it meant they'd have to transfer in Denver. That was how desperate he was to leave. Never mind that Denise still needed help, and Cheryl was too young to be the only one in charge, and none of the neighbors seemed able to take full responsibility.

Besides which, when Denise phoned her family after breakfast she hadn't so much as mentioned her situation. "Oh, things are good here," she had assured them. "Going great!" Clearly these weren't people she felt she should call upon.

Now Willa said, "I wish we weren't leaving tomorrow. I'm worried how you'll manage."

"I wish you weren't, too," Denise said. "But hey: you've got lives of your own, I guess."

"Not really," Willa said. "I don't. And Peter's supposed to be retired, or all but retired. But you know how it is: he just can't quite let go yet."

"Well, he's a guy," Denise said.

"Right."

Sometimes Willa felt she'd spent half her life apologizing for some man's behavior. More than half her life, actually. First Derek and then Peter, forever charging ahead while Willa trailed behind picking up the pieces and excusing and explaining.

"Durn, I meant to put ice cream on the list," Denise said suddenly.

"You want me to phone them?"

"Nah, who needs the calories, right?"

"I'll just phone them," Willa said. She went to the foyer for her purse.

"Tell them mint chocolate chip, but not the green kind, hear? I like the white. None of that artificial coloring."

"White mint chocolate chip," Willa said. She took out her phone and tapped Peter's number.

"Yes?" he said. She heard voices behind him, and the beep of a scanner.

"Denise was wondering if you could buy ice cream," she told him. "Mint chocolate chip, the white kind."

"White chocolate?"

"White ice cream."

"Okay," he said. "We're already in line, but that's okay."

"Sorry."

"That's okay."

He was being extra accommodating because he felt bad about making her leave so soon. Willa could read him like a book.

"Cheryl will know the brand," Denise said after Willa had hung up. "That is no Chuck E. Cheese child, I tell you."

"Chuck E. . . . ?"

"Nor McDonald's child, nor Burger King. Cheryl's a Red Lobster child, through and through."

"Ah," Willa said.

"I don't know where she gets it from."

"Well, look at *you*: you're the one who doesn't want artificial coloring."

"Only for fear of cancer."

"Even so, though," Willa said.

"I shouldn't have ice cream anyway. It's not like I'm getting much exercise just laying here."

"Oh, I always think tension and pain and anxiety burn more calories than exercise," Willa said. She slipped her phone back into her purse.

Denise said, "Yeah, but then you're so tiny and petite and got those bitsy little bones and all. You have a whole nother metabolism. Plus, you're already married and you can relax now. I am still hunting."

"Really? You'd like to be married?" Willa asked her.

"Of course I would. Are you kidding? People are *supposed* to be married. Supposed to go through this world two by two."

Wasn't that a line from *Our Town*? Willa remembered something of the sort from when her mother had played the Stage Manager. She remembered absorbing its truth even as a child.

As delicately as possible, she asked, "Did . . . you and Sean ever think about getting married?"

She had been wondering that since she and Denise first met. Denise was such a change from Sean's usual type of girlfriend, the cheerleaders in high school and the sorority girls in college, all so prim and pert that Willa had had no clue what their true feelings were.

"I thought about it," Denise said. "Can't say as Sean ever did."

"Oh," Willa said sadly.

Well, it was probably just as well.

In the afternoon, Callie stopped by with a canned ham. "Sorry, but I'm not a cook," she told Willa as she handed it over. She was wearing a dressy dress and a lot of jewelry, and as soon as she entered the living room she announced that she'd gone to church that morning. "I put forth your name during the offering-up of prayers," she told Denise. "I said, 'My neighbor Denise has been shot, and her with a daughter who is still a dependent child.'" She made her way to the armchair and sank into it with a thud.

"Actually, I'm more a preteen than a child," Cheryl said. She was sitting on the rug tailor-fashion, petting Airplane.

"You don't *look* like a preteen," Callie told her.

"Come January I'll have two digits. Plus also, I'm not dependent."

"Well, have it your way," Callie said without interest. In broad daylight, Willa saw, her hair was that overblonded kind that made her face seem much older than she probably was. She kept plucking at stray curls with her fingertips, as if she sensed that they were unsatisfactory somehow. "How you feeling?" she asked Denise.

"I'm going crazy," Denise said.

"Turn on the TV, then. I don't get why you don't have the TV on."

"I've watched TV till my eyes are crossed."

"Could I offer you a glass of iced tea?" Willa asked Callie. She was looking for an excuse to leave them on their own, but Callie said, "No, thanks. So, where's that handsome husband of yours?"

"Oh, somewhere around," Willa said. He was shut away in the guest room with the air conditioner running, but she didn't want to admit it. She said, "I'll just . . ." and pointedly raised the ham she was holding and made her escape to the kitchen.

After she set the ham on the counter, she checked the soil around her little saguaro on the windowsill. Then she shifted her gaze to the backyard next door, where Erland was aimlessly bouncing a shuttle-cock up and down on a racquet. In the yard on the other side, Mrs. Minton stood holding her walker one-handed while she painstakingly, ineptly draped a petticoat over a clothesline.

Cheryl walked into the kitchen and said, "Willa, are you-all really leaving tomorrow?"

Willa turned away from the window. "We're supposed to," she said.

"I don't think I'm strong enough to get Mama to the powder room on my own."

Willa studied her. "I don't think you are, either," she said.

"And I'll have to buy groceries and all, and fix the meals."

"Well," Willa said, "maybe I should ask Peter if he can change our reservation."

This should have been enough, but Cheryl went on watching her expectantly and so finally Willa added, "I'll just go do that now, why don't I." She wasn't looking forward to it.

As she left the kitchen she heard Callie telling Denise, "You're better off without him, in my opinion. When I got rid of Darwin it was like a weight lifted off my chest. Freedom! Fresh air! In my opinion, men are overrated."

Willa paused to hear what Denise's answer would be, but there wasn't one—just a whooshing sound as Callie exhaled. She must be smoking. Willa could smell it, in fact. She glanced into the living room as she passed and caught Callie in the act of tapping her ash into the philodendron plant.

Climbing the stairs was like climbing into different weather, steadily warmer and warmer. But when she opened the guest-room door a rush of cold air hit her, and the roar of the air conditioner filled her ears. Peter was propped against his headboard with his shoes off, reading the Sunday *Times* magazine. He looked up and asked, "How're things going down there?"

"Callie's here for a visit," she told him.

"Great," he said, and went back to his magazine.

"Peter," she said, "I'm thinking we shouldn't leave yet."

At first it seemed he wasn't going to answer, because he went on reading. But then, with his eyes still on the page, he said, "I disagree, in point of fact."

"But I don't know how the two of them are going to manage on their own," she said.

"They're *not* on their own. They have neighbors. They have Denise's coworkers."

"That's not enough," she told him.

Now he looked at her. "Here's a thought," he said.

She perked up. But what he said next was, "Denise could call one of those agencies. Hire somebody to help out."

"You know she can't afford that."

"So? Maybe you could chip in on it, if it's only for a week or so."

"Okay," she said, "but . . ."

She wasn't happy with that. She knew it might be more practical, but somehow it just filled her with unhappiness.

"Little one," he said finally. "Listen to me a minute."

She forced herself to meet his gaze, meanwhile twisting her wrist-watch band.

"You realize what's going on here," he said. "Both of your sons are grown and gone, and anyhow they've turned out to be something of a disappointment—"

"Disappointment!" she cried. She stopped twisting her watch band. "They're not a disappointment!"

"Well, they don't have much to do with you; let's put it that way."

"Yes, they do! We're supposed to have supper with Sean tomorrow night!"

"Willa. Haven't you canceled that yet?"

She was silent.

He said, "And supper was *your* idea, not his. As for Ian: well, face it, Ian is almost never in touch."

"Because Ian doesn't have cell-phone coverage, that's why! He *does* call any time he gets back to civilization. Oh, you're just saying this because you've never had children," she told him. "Kids grow up. They're *supposed* to grow up. And besides, these are boys. You can't expect boys to be all chatty and confiding, you know."

"In any case," he said, "isn't it just that you miss being a mother?

I can understand that. But look at it this way: now you've got me. The two of us are free now to enjoy our golden years."

He was using the term ironically, but Willa didn't smile.

"For instance," he said. "I've suggested several times that you should take up golf."

"I tried that," she said. She'd had a couple of lessons, even, and bought herself an array of sporty little drip-dry skirts and white cotton socks with bobbles on the backs.

"But then you gave it up," he said.

"Because I never got the hang of it! It isn't my fault I'm not athletic! Anyhow," she said, because she felt she was being sidetracked, here, "if you really insist on leaving tomorrow, maybe I'll just stay on by myself."

She paused, but he didn't say anything.

"Just let you go home without me," she said, "and stay till Denise can get around better. Ben says she'll have a walking cast soon. Then she'll be able to—"

"Ben who?" Peter asked.

"Ben her *neighbor*, Peter. The doctor, remember? A walking cast would let her go up and down stairs and such, and then I'd feel okay leaving her."

Unfortunately, she just at that moment recalled that Ben had said the walking cast would happen in a couple of weeks or so. But she decided not to remind Peter of that.

Peter said, "All right, Willa. If that's how you want it."

And he went back to his magazine.

She stood there a moment. She had a slightly stunned feeling. He was really going to make her do this on her own?

Finally she said, "So could you please cancel my plane reservation?"

He just nodded and turned a page.

She stepped out of the room and shut the door behind her. Heat slapped her face like a warm washcloth, but as she descended it grew cooler.

In the living room, Denise was sliding a straightened wire coat hanger down inside her cast. "My surgeon says I'm lucky," she was telling Callie as she scratched an itch. "He says it could have been that kind of bullet that ricochets around inside of you. I said, 'Lucky!' I said, 'Is that what you call this?'"

And Callie was doing that smoker's thing of turning aside to exhale and then ineffectually flapping a hand to clear the air. "Typical," she said, but whether of surgeons or of men in general, Willa couldn't say.

Callie had barely taken her leave when Ben Gold rang the doorbell with Mrs. Minton in tow. Willa opened the screen for them and stood back to let Mrs. Minton shuffle in, Ben following close behind in case she tottered. She'd left her walker at the bottom of the porch steps; evidently she used it just for balance. She kept telling herself, "Careful, now. Careful, now." Her skirt was unbecomingly short, barely knee-length, so that her blue-white mottled shins showed, and her sleeveless blouse exposed her stringy arms. It was the first time Willa had seen her out of her housecoat.

When she reached the living room, she halted to examine Denise. "Why, you look very healthy," she said.

"I *am* healthy," Denise told her, "except for this damn leg. Cheryl, scoot out of that chair and let Mrs. Minton sit down."

"What did it feel like, getting shot?" Mrs. Minton asked. She was inching toward the armchair now, Ben still shepherding her. "I've always wondered."

"Felt like nothing, at first. Like a jolt. But now it's giving me fits. Seems like the pain is subject to gravity; stand up and it swoops clear down my leg and slams into my heel."

Mrs. Minton said "Tsk!" She gripped Ben's hand as she lowered herself into the armchair. "I trust you're being a help to your mother," she told Cheryl, tugging her skirt down.

Cheryl said "Yup." She was kneeling beside Airplane now, tickling him behind the ears.

"Who would like iced tea?" Willa asked, but Mrs. Minton said, "Oh, no, thank you, dear," and Ben said, "None for me, thanks." He settled in the rocker.

"Where's that husband of yours?" Mrs. Minton asked Willa.

"I think he's upstairs packing," Willa said. "He has to go back tomorrow morning."

Cheryl and Denise both looked at her. Denise said, "You're not going with him?"

"I thought I might stay on a few days, if that's all right with you."

Cheryl whispered "Yes!" on a long outward breath, and Denise said, "Well, gosh. I know I should be arguing, but gosh. Thanks, Willa."

"Oh, that's okay," Willa said. "It's not as if I have anything urgent waiting at home."

"You don't want to neglect your husband, though," Mrs. Minton told her severely.

"It's only for a few days."

"You want to *cherish* him."

"Oh, I do," Willa assured her.

"Take it from me: I lost my husband many years ago, but not a day goes by that I don't wish I'd paid him more attention. He died at Gettysburg."

Willa was startled. "At the . . . Civil War Gettysburg?" she asked.

"That's the one. He liked to put on a rebel uniform and take part in famous battles, and this one time when he was supposed to be slain he didn't get up afterward and they found he'd had a heart attack and died."

"A re-enactor," Ben murmured to Willa.

"Well, goodness," she said.

"It was how he'd have wanted to go, though; I do take comfort in that," Mrs. Minton said.

"But still," Willa said.

"And now I'm rattling around in that house without a husband. This whole side of the street is rattling around; we all of us seem to be loners here."

"Except for me and Mama," Cheryl said. "And Sir Joe and—"

"No married people, though," Mrs. Minton reminded her. She started ticking off on her fingers. "Hal's wife has left him, Callie's divorced, Dave is divorced, Ben here's wife has passed . . . wait, are Barry and Richard married?"

"Not as I know of," Denise said. "Barry and Richard are gay," she told Willa, "which-is-fine!"

"So whenever I see somebody with a husband," Mrs. Minton said, "I say, 'Appreciate him, hear? Appreciate him while you have him!'"

Willa said, "I lost a husband myself, once."

Denise would already have known that, Willa supposed, but everyone else looked interested. She told them, "Sean's father was killed in a car wreck just before Sean left for college."

"Well, then," Mrs. Minton said, with a satisfied nod. "I don't have to tell *you*, then."

"Right."

"You get up some mornings and lay out the breakfast things and then you say, 'Oh, dear, I seem to have set the table for two.'"

"Right," Willa said. Although in fact she had never done that. But she knew what Mrs. Minton meant.

"You're sitting around in the evening and you say, 'Isn't it bedtime yet?' And then you look at the clock and it's not even seven thirty."

"And you talk to yourself," Ben put in from his rocker. "You say, 'So! Guess I should think about fixing something to eat.' And your voice sounds kind of rusty because it's been so long since you've used it."

Willa looked over at him. He shrugged apologetically, as if the words had popped out by accident. "Lizzy's been dead for seventeen years," he told her, "and my only kid's off in Uganda. Why do you think I still run that damn-fool paperwork factory I call a medical practice? I need to see another human being from time to time."

"His son is a Doctor Without Borders," Mrs. Minton told Willa.

"Oh, that's wonderful," Willa said.

"Except it means he's on the other side of the world," Ben said.

"Well," Willa said. Then she said, "My father told me once that after my mother died, he started breaking his days into moments. Like, not worrying how to get through the whole rest of his life but just enjoying the baseball game he was watching right then on TV."

"That's nice if it works," Mrs. Minton said.

"Yes, *if* it works. I don't know; for me it didn't seem to. I think I'm not a natural-born enjoyer of the moment," Willa said. "Even now: I'm the type who goes on vacation and spends the whole time wondering if I remembered to turn the oven off, and whether we can manage that tight connection when we fly home."

Denise laughed. She said, "Hoo, boy, all I would wonder is how to stretch the trip out as long as possible."

"See there?" Willa said. "You just naturally know how to do that."

Then Mrs. Minton said, "I have to be going, Ben. I need to water my African violets." And Ben slapped his thighs and stood up to help her out of her chair.

There had been talk of Peter's making his grilled chicken for supper, but when he failed to come downstairs at the proper time to preheat the grill Willa just went ahead and roasted the chicken in the oven. He didn't comment when she called everyone to the table; merely took his seat with a grim expression and spread his napkin across his lap. And he allowed her to do the carving, which ordinarily he claimed as his own special skill. Clearly he was in one of his har-rumph moods.

Now that there were four of them, they were eating in the dining room. Ben had brought over a wheeled typist's chair that morning for Denise to sit in, so that even Cheryl was able to push her from the couch to the dining-room table or to the little desk in the corner where she kept her computer. According to Ben, the chair's sturdy arms were a safety feature, but during supper Denise complained that they were a hindrance. "Like, when I try to shift from the couch to the chair they hamper me, know what I'm saying?" she asked. "So I'm thinking there has got to be a way to take them off."

She looked at Peter. She waited. "Unscrew them or something?" she suggested finally.

"I wouldn't know," he said. He forked up a morsel of chicken and started chewing it.

Denise looked at Willa.

"Why don't I try and figure it out after supper," Willa told her.

Peter forked up another morsel of chicken.

Mainly it was Cheryl who kept the conversation going. She was excited because Patty and Laurie were coming home tomorrow. "I can't wait," she said. "Patty always has the best ideas for things to do! Me and Laurie will be lolling around just bored out of our minds and then Patty says, 'I know what!' and she shows us some new card trick she's learned or some new app she just got on her phone. When she grows up she wants to be a game-show hostess."

"That child is entirely too old for her years, if you ask me," Denise told her. "I couldn't believe what she was wearing that time she came to the movies with us."

"It was a *super* outfit!"

"It made her look like a hooker."

Peter gazed meaningfully at the ceiling.

"Sleazy nylon top," Denise told Willa, "with only one shoulder. What is it with the one-shoulder look? Like, 'Whoops, imagine that: someone just tried to rip my clothes off.' And cutoff shorts so short the pockets are hanging out at the bottoms, and patent-leather shoes with heels. Heels! On an eleven-year-old! Going to the movies!"

"Those were tap shoes, for your information," Cheryl told her. "They're for dancing in."

"Oh, my mistake; I beg your humble pardon. Since it's common knowledge everyone has to dance at a Pixar movie."

"Who would like more chicken?" Willa asked.

No one answered.

Willa was starting to get a headache.

After she and Cheryl had done the dishes, she took a look at the typist's chair and decided it would be possible to take the arms off. "Do you have a Phillips screwdriver?" she asked Denise.

Denise said, "Well, if I do it would be in the odds-and-ends drawer, I'm just about certain."

This didn't sound promising, but Willa went out to the kitchen to rummage through the tangle of tools and duct tape and picture wire in the odds-and-ends drawer. Unexpectedly, a memory rose up from times her parents used to visit after the boys were born. Her father would come to her, shaking his head sorrowfully. "Think you've got a leak in your guest-room toilet," he would say. "But I can probably fix it for you." Or "I don't know if you realize your pantry door is hanging aslant. Mind if I take care of it?" It was his way of showing he loved her, she knew. Even as she'd sighed inwardly to hear of yet another flaw in her household, she had felt touched by how hard he was trying.

And now it was she who was shaking her head, deploring the state of the odds-and-ends drawer but coming up with a Phillips screwdriver, finally, and kneeling beside the typist's chair to set the world to rights.

Peter went up to bed immediately after 60 *Minutes*, saying he had a taxi coming at five o'clock the next morning. He did tell Denise goodbye and wish her a speedy recovery, and he told Cheryl to take care of her mother. Denise said, "Well, thanks for letting us borrow that wife of yours, hear?"

Peter didn't say she was welcome.

Then Denise and Cheryl and Willa played a few rounds of I Doubt It—Denise propped on the couch, Cheryl on the floor, and Willa in the rocker she had dragged closer to the coffee table. It turned out that nowadays people didn't say "I doubt it"; they said "Bullshit." The first time Willa tried to bluff and Cheryl shouted "Bullshit!" Willa was so startled that her mouth dropped open. She glanced over at Denise, but Denise just blew a giant pink bubble of gum and went on studying her cards. So Willa adjusted, although when she herself suspected a bluff she just said "Ahem." Cheryl and Denise thought this was hilarious.

After that, Cheryl went upstairs to bed and Willa took Airplane out. Then she settled Denise on the couch and wished her a good night, and at long last climbed the stairs herself.

First she stopped to wash up in the bathroom before she tiptoed into the guest room, although it turned out she could have made as much noise as she liked, because the air conditioner was running full blast. All the lights were off and Peter was either asleep or pretending to sleep; she wasn't sure which. She had half expected that he would suggest she squeeze in next to him on their last night together, but okay. She undressed in the dark and settled in her own bed, pulling her blanket up tight against the refrigerated air.

She had worried she would sleep badly, but the tensions of the day must have exhausted her, because the next time she opened her eyes, Peter was moving about in the dimness collecting his belongings. Then he slipped out of the room, his bag brushing the doorframe as he exited. She lay awake imagining him shaving and dressing in the bathroom; she imagined him heading down the stairs and out to the street to wait for his cab, but of course she was only guessing, because she couldn't hear a thing with the air conditioner running. She might as well be shut in a box, she thought—sealed away, airless. She began to have a slight feeling of panic. What am I doing here? she thought. Where, even, *am* I?

Eventually, she pulled herself together and got up to switch the air conditioner off. It gave a shudder and died. She crossed the room to open the other window and then climbed back into bed. Locust scritches floated into the room, along with a faraway ambulance siren. A few minutes later she heard a car pulling up. Two men briefly spoke, and a car door opened and shut and the car drove off.

Then all she heard were the locusts. Their scritches were back-and-forth scraping sounds like someone sanding a piece of wood, then stopping for a moment, and then sanding once again.

8

Willa had an e-mail from Sean saying, "Hi mom how about cafe antoine 6 tonite."

"Fine," she wrote back, "but I should let you know it will be only me." She was hoping this would prompt him to offer her a ride. She wrote him after breakfast, and then she and Cheryl took Airplane for his walk. Maybe by the time they got back, Sean would have answered.

It was a beautiful morning, and several of the neighbors were outside—Mrs. Minton in her walker urging her dog to do his business, and Sir Joe hosing down his truck but pausing to send Willa a seductive smile, and Dave the detective scowling at his crabgrass. Dave was a saggy, paunchy man in a rumpled sweat suit; Willa had met him the day before when he'd brought Denise a giant bag of Utz potato chips. Now she gave him a little wave, but he stayed sunk in his own shoulders like a bird puffed up in a rainstorm. "He's having a bad mood," Cheryl told her. "He's always in a bad mood on Mondays."

"What's wrong with Mondays?" Willa asked.

"His phone doesn't ring anymore on account of Facebook."

"Facebook?" Willa said.

"People don't need him to track anybody down now."

Willa laughed.

"What's so funny?" Cheryl asked.

"Oh, I don't know," Willa said.

She was feeling very lighthearted today. Of course it seemed strange without Peter, but at least she could stay out as long as she liked without worrying she was neglecting him.

When they got back to the house she checked her e-mail, but there was nothing more from Sean. Elaine had sent something, though—a photograph of a spectacularly sharp mountain peak poking through a smoke ring of clouds. This was just like her. Elaine thought people wanted to see the places she traveled to; it never occurred to her that they might want to see *her*. She hadn't even included a message; just "Mt. Alana" in the subject line.

Willa Googled Café Antoine's address in case she really did have to drive there. It was in Towson, she saw. All she knew about Towson was that it lay just north of Baltimore. She went to the dining room, where Denise sat playing solitaire on her computer. "Do you think I could borrow your car for my dinner with Sean tonight?" she asked.

No point keeping it a secret; it was only natural that she would want to see her own son.

Without taking her eyes from the screen, Denise said, "Be my guest."

She had maneuvered from the couch to the typist's chair on her own while Willa and Cheryl were out on their walk. She had propelled herself into the dining room with just the heel of her good foot, she announced, fending off walls and random pieces of furniture with her hands. Clearly she was making progress.

"We're supposed to meet at this place in Towson," Willa told her. "I was wondering if I could check the route on your computer once you're through there. I hate looking at maps on my little phone screen."

Now Denise did look at her. "What place in Towson?" she asked.

"Café Antoine?"

Denise made a face. "That is so, so typical," she said. "He didn't know Café Antoine existed before I took him there."

"Oh, dear," Willa said helplessly.

"And watch what he orders. I bet it's the crab fluff. I was the one who ordered that first, and I gave him a taste when it came and he just about ate the whole thing."

"How annoying," Willa said. It *would* be annoying. She felt a familiar flash of embarrassment for him.

"But anyhow," Denise said, and she clicked a few keys on her computer and then pointed to a spot on the screen. "Here's the map; take a look."

Willa bent to peer over Denise's shoulder. Even she could see that the route was fairly straightforward. Go west a ways and then north a ways. But Towson itself was a maze of small streets, not easily sorted out.

Denise's hair had the bruised-fruit smell of her shampoo, which Willa had helped her suds up last night at the kitchen sink. Ordinarily Willa disliked that smell, but on Denise it seemed oddly pleasant.

"It may be that Sean will offer me a ride," she said, "but I thought I should be prepared in case he doesn't."

"Why not just ask him?" Denise said.

"Oh . . ."

"Will *she* be coming?"

Willa didn't bother pretending she didn't know whom Denise meant. She said, "I believe she may be."

"Well, tell her I hope she's satisfied," Denise said.

The thought of doing that made Willa laugh, and Denise sent a sharp look at her but then grudgingly smiled and said, "Or don't, if it doesn't happen to come up on its own."

All morning long, a part of Willa was mentally flying west with Peter. By now he was crossing the plains; by now he was landing in Denver. She knew he would have a wait before he boarded the plane to Tucson, and she wondered if he would phone her then, but she didn't really expect him to.

Cheryl's friends Patty and Laurie came to play. The three girls walked to DuWayne's Deli and brought back sandwiches for lunch—roast beef for the grownups and subs for themselves—and they took theirs out to the patio table while Willa and Denise ate in the kitchen. From where she sat Willa could hear Patty and Laurie's high-pitched voices competing to describe a slumber party with their crazy cousins, and a scary movie they'd seen, and the mall their aunt had taken them to for earrings. She didn't hear much from Cheryl. She would have thought there'd be some discussion of Denise's shooting, but it didn't come up, and when they brought their empty plates back in and Denise said, "*Watch* it!" wincing as Patty stumbled over her outstretched cast, Patty just murmured "Sorry" and kept going. She was the older of the two, and while it was true that she was wearing the skimpiest of outfits—a shirred bandeau across her flat chest, with the cutoffs Denise had complained about—she and her sister were such wiry little blond scraps of things that Willa didn't see the harm.

After lunch the three of them went upstairs to Cheryl's room. From the sound of it, they *fell* up the stairs rather than climbing them, and there was a series of thumps and scrapes overhead as if they were rearranging furniture. Then they played a game that involved a lot of arguing and revising the rules, and after that some sort of music started up. "That must be Patty's cell phone," Denise said, making one of her faces. "Can you believe anybody would give an eleven-year-old her own phone?"

Willa said, "They seem to be having fun, though." She cocked her head to listen. "Isn't it interesting how children all sound the same from a distance? I bet even in Africa, they use that nyah-nyah tone when they're teasing and their voices get all thin and cracked when they say 'No fair!'"

"What do you want to bet Patty is teaching the others to strip-tease," Denise said. But she allowed herself a tucked-in smile when Willa laughed.

Later, crossing the upstairs hall with a basket of laundry, Willa glanced into Cheryl's room to see what they were up to. Patty stood facing her, both arms extended from her sides, with Laurie and Cheryl directly behind her. All that showed of Laurie and Cheryl were their own arms, extended too so that Patty seemed to possess six arms, all six moving in stiff, stop-and-start arcs in time to the clicking sounds that Willa could hear now punctuating the music. "It's a clock dance!" Cheryl shouted, briefly peeking out from the tail end. "Can you tell?"

Of course: those clicks were tick-tocks. Those arms were clock hands, jerking in time to the tick-tocks like the hands of those stuttery clocks on the walls of grade-school classrooms.

Willa smiled at the girls and said, "Yes, I can," and when she went back downstairs she told Denise, "I wish you could see this darling dance they're doing."

"I'm beginning to think I'll never get upstairs again," Denise said glumly.

Willa said, "Oh, it will happen."

Then she checked her watch. It was 3:45. Peter would be on the second leg of his flight by now, so she had no hope of his calling.

Using the map on Denise's computer screen, she drew a detailed diagram of the route to Café Antoine. She wrote in not only the name of each street she should turn on but the street before it as well, so that she would have ample warning. Denise, who was watching, found this comical. "It's just Towson!" she kept saying. "Plain little old Towson!"

"You don't know what it's like," Willa told her. "People who have a good sense of direction can't imagine."

"I still don't get why you can't ask Sean for a ride."

"I was hoping he'd think to offer," Willa said.

"But why just hope? Why pussyfoot around? Why do you go at things so *slantwise*?"

She was right. Willa knew it. She glanced down at her diagram in silence.

"Or maybe you're worried I'll feel bad if he comes by the house," Denise said.

"No, no . . ."

"Because it wouldn't bother me a bit if he came by, I swear it! That was just momentary, what happened when he came for his things. I'm totally over that now. So, yeah!"

"I wasn't even thinking about that," Willa said. (Not that she knew what had happened when he came for his things, but she could guess.)

"He's the one who's going to feel bad, by and by, stuck with that prissy Elissa. Just wait till you meet her. So *ladylike.* The type who keeps a fresh Kleenex tucked inside her sleeve. She's probably driving him crazy already, what do you want to bet. He's probably gnashing his hair."

"Teeth," Willa said. She laughed.

Denise said, "Whatever."

"Gnashing his hair and tearing his teeth," Willa said, and then they both got to laughing.

Willa didn't point out that sometimes, when she wore something without pockets, she tucked a Kleenex inside her own sleeve.

Why *did* she go at things so slantwise? By late afternoon, when she knew Peter must be home now but still he wasn't calling, why didn't she just call *him* and ask, "Are you back yet?" And "How was your trip?"

But maybe he was napping, she told herself, because he'd had to get up so early in the morning. She would hate to wake him.

She knew this was just an excuse.

She had planned to wear her A-line dress to dinner, but she saw now that it was too hot for that. She would have to make do with the plain cotton shift she'd already worn several times over. She ironed out the wrinkles on Denise's dining-room table, for lack of an actual ironing board. Oh, already she was feeling the limitations of living out of a suitcase. (And yet Peter always claimed she overpacked!) This afternoon she'd been forced to run a washerload of blouses and underwear, and her travel-size bottle of foundation wasn't going to last her much longer. She applied it sparingly, frowning into the bathroom mirror. Then she smoothed her hair with both hands. Back home she went to a place that chemically tamed the frizz, and she was just about due for a treatment.

Cheryl hung around for a while watching her preparations, but when the doorbell rang she said "I'll get it!" and scampered off. Barry and Richard would be babysitting, as they put it—a term that made Cheryl snort indignantly. Earlier in the day they had stopped by with a basket of fruit, and they had been horrified that Cheryl and Denise were going to be left on their own that evening. When Willa came downstairs she found them unpacking pizzas in the dining room— two comically mismatched men, Barry tubby and blond and bearded in wrinkled drawstring pants and Richard tall and dark and elegant, still dressed in his office clothes. (He was a real-estate agent. Barry was a carpenter.) They'd brought their Scrabble board for afterward, but Denise was telling them she was no good at Scrabble. "All's I ever come up with is three- and four-letter words," she said. Cheryl said, "Never mind, Mama; I'll help you," but Denise shook her head.

"I bet Willa's *great* at Scrabble," Richard said.

"Actually, I'm not," Willa said, "but I do like playing it."

Then she declined the slice of pizza Barry offered her (black olive and mushroom; it looked delicious) and picked up her purse to leave. "Have fun, everybody!" she told them. Half of her wished she could just stay here.

It was still daylight out, which would make the drive easier. She took her time settling into the car, sliding the seat forward and adjusting all the mirrors before she started the engine. The radio came on—NPR, Peter's choice—and she searched for the button and turned it off so she wouldn't be distracted. She opened her window a crack to lighten the musty smell, and then she inched away from the curb.

It turned out that the actual drive was less daunting than she had feared. On Dorcas Road she met only one car, and she was familiar with Reuben Road because of the stuffed rabbit that had been sitting at the corner for the past two days holding a cardboard sign that asked "Did You Lose Me?" Before she knew it, she was inching through the left turn onto Northern Parkway, and after that she had clear sailing for a while. True, there was some traffic, but just enough so she didn't have to worry she was slowing down other drivers. She headed steadily west and then turned north onto York Road—this time a right turn, so it wasn't a problem. After that she relaxed a bit. She drove past a clutter of shops and fast-food places, then rows of modest houses, and finally a commercial district that must be Towson. There she had to check street signs, but the traffic was so stop-and-start that she could take her time reading them. Yes, here was the last street before the next turn, here the turn itself . . . She took a left and almost immediately spotted the café, its name spelled out in neon script across a mullioned window. But there was no free space in front; oh, dear. She took an impulsive right at the next cross street and by some miracle spotted a metered parking lot. Thank God. She didn't even have to do the back-and-forth thing; she could pull into a space head-on.

She shut the engine off and sat there breathing deeply for a moment. Then she gathered herself together, reached for her purse, and stepped out of the car. She even remembered to feed the meter.

Heading back toward the café, she had the oddest experience. She noticed a man walking toward her in the distance, a fair-haired man in a short-sleeved shirt and khakis, and at first she merely registered his approach, but then some jaunty quality in his gait tugged at her and she stopped short. It was Sean. It was dear, familiar Sean, thirty-eight years old now and completely at home in a strange town, accompanied by a very thin blonde in a polka-dot sundress. When he saw Willa he just grinned and raised a hand; he wasn't struck motionless the way she was. He arrived in front of her and said, "Hi, Mom," and bent to kiss her cheek. "This is Elissa," he said, nodding toward the woman at his side.

Elissa offered Willa her hand. "How do you do, Mrs. Brendan," she said.

"Willa, for goodness' sake," Willa said. Elissa's fingers were long and cool and slim. She seemed younger than Sean—perhaps in her late twenties—and although her sundress allowed her no place to tuck a Kleenex, she did wear a cardigan draped just so across her shoulders, which in Willa's opinion gave almost the same effect.

"Shall we?" Sean asked, and he shepherded them both through the glass door and into a small room where already most of the tables were occupied. "MacIntyre, for six o'clock," he told the hostess. Even this gave Willa an odd sensation—that reminder of the days when she too had been a MacIntyre.

They were seated at a corner table—Sean next to Elissa, and Willa across from the two of them. Willa set her purse on the empty chair beside her and clasped her hands in her lap. "So!" she said. "It wasn't as bad a drive as I had expected."

"Well, no," Sean said. He told Elissa, "Mom is not a big fan of driving."

Elissa gave a sympathetic cluck.

"In fact, some of her oldest friends are surprised when they hear she has a license," Sean said.

"Oh, stop," Willa said. "He's making that up," she told Elissa. Already she was back in that hapless, dithery-mom role she'd been assigned when her sons reached their teens. She asked Elissa, "Are you a Baltimorean?"

"Oh, no, I moved here just a few years ago," Elissa said. "I'm from New York originally."

Though she didn't have what Willa would consider a New York accent. She spoke very crisply, enunciating each word. Her mouth was small and bright red and precisely outlined. (Cheryl would have asked if she wore lip liner.) And her cardigan sleeves were not so much knotted together as tidily flattened over each other, so that she had to be careful how she moved her shoulders.

Willa started missing Denise.

Their waitress brought them menus, slightly stained cream-colored menus with tassels. Sean told Willa, "I recommend the crab fluff."

"Oh, yes, the crab fluff," Willa said.

"Will you be having wine, Mom?"

"I guess I shouldn't if I'm driving. Maybe a glass of iced tea," she said.

"And we two would like a bottle of pinot grigio," Sean told the waitress.

Elissa asked Willa, "Have you been enjoying your visit?"

Willa was experiencing one of those rapt moments that often

overcame her in the presence of her sons. She was admiring Sean's profile as he discussed wines with the waitress; he had the finest, straightest nose, and charmingly stubby blond eyelashes. But she turned her attention to Elissa and said, "Yes, I have, thank you."

"I can't believe Denise was *shot*," Elissa said. "Have they found out who did it?"

"No, I think they've given up trying," Willa said.

It surprised her that Elissa could talk about Denise so comfortably. She started wondering how the two of them could have been friends—tightly wound Elissa and affable Denise.

Sean had finished with the waitress now. He told Elissa, "I can believe it. Bear in mind that that is not the fanciest part of town."

"It does feel perfectly safe, though," Willa said. "I don't worry in the least about taking a walk late at night."

"Well, you might want to reconsider," Sean told her. "Look at the neighbors. A motorcycle hoodlum, a seedy private eye, a has-been doctor with a pack of Medicaid patients . . ."

He was viewing them from the wrong slant, Willa thought. They weren't like that. Or they were, but there was more to them besides. But she didn't want to argue. She said, "How is your work, honey? Are things going well?"

"What? Yeah, sure," Sean said.

Willa didn't know what he did at work, exactly, but then she hadn't known what his father did, either. She said, "Do you think you'll be based here permanently?"

"I suppose so," Sean said. He started studying the menu.

"And Elissa, do *you* work?" Willa asked.

"Yes, I'm a representative for a window-treatment firm," Elissa said.

"Oh, how interesting!"

"It does take a bit of color sense and style sense," Elissa said. "Not to mention tact. You wouldn't believe what some people want on their windows."

"Oh, I can imagine," Willa said.

Their waitress arrived with their drinks then, and they had to place their orders. Sean and Willa ordered the crab fluff—Sean's with french fries, Willa's with slaw—and Elissa ordered the skinless chicken breast rémoulade without the rémoulade and a salad with the dressing on the side. Willa had been hoping they would have a first course too, just to stretch the occasion out longer, but the other two both said no.

When their waitress left there was a lengthy pause in the conversation, during which they all turned to watch a toddler fling himself on his back beneath a neighboring table and clamp both arms obstinately across his chest. "Georgie?" his mother kept asking. "Georgie, sweetheart? Now, Georgie . . ."

"I'm sorry Peter couldn't join us," Willa said finally.

"Oh, me too," Elissa said. "It would have been nice to meet him."

"He felt he should be getting back," Willa said. "You know how it is," she told Sean.

"I thought he'd retired," Sean said.

"Well, he did, but . . . he still keeps in touch with the office, though."

"I'll bet he does," Sean said. He told Elissa, "My brother and I call Peter the gift that keeps on giving."

Elissa made a hissing sound of amusement, but Willa was puzzled. "What does that mean?" she asked him.

"Oh, you know: he's always such a rich topic of conversation. His latest huffs and puffs and quibbles."

Willa said, "I don't know what you're talking about!"

"Like, say he *had* joined us tonight," Sean said. He turned to Elissa. "Peter never, ever accepts the first table he's shown to. He always has to request another, and sometimes one more instead of that one. Then there's the wine. They pour him a taste and he sort of sieves it through his teeth and gargles it and then sits there frowning while everyone waits for his verdict."

"Oh, Sean, he's not that bad," Willa said.

"And if you think *that's* a production, watch him order his meal. The waitress stands there, stands there, stands there, pen and pad at the ready—"

"He's exaggerating," Willa told Elissa.

"Finally she says, 'I'll just come back in a few minutes, why don't I,' but Peter says 'No, no . . .' and he makes her stand there a while longer. Then he says, 'Is your asparagus from your own garden? Was it picked while the dew was still on it?'"

"Sean is completely making that up," Willa told Elissa. "Peter is a very nice man. And he's funny, too; he's got this very . . . sardonic style of humor."

"How did the two of you meet?" Elissa asked.

"Oh!" Willa said gratefully. "Well, so I was in line at the post office, and I happened to have a bottle of water with me. And Peter leaned over from behind and asked, 'Shouldn't your Sherpa be carrying that for you?'"

She laughed, remembering. Elissa looked confused, and Sean told her, "You see what I mean."

"*What?*" Willa demanded. "What was wrong with that?"

Their food arrived and was set silently before them. The waitress seemed to sense that this was not the moment to ask if they had everything they needed.

"He's the type who likes to grandstand," Sean told Elissa. "He likes to *hold forth.* Remember, Mom, the time he got so exercised about the cracker box? He was studying the back of a cracker box," he told Elissa, "where they pictured one of those 'serving suggestions.' Panini, they were suggesting. Except they said 'paninis.' Which was their term for cracker sandwiches made with about a three-inch stack of cheese and peppers and zucchini slices and whatnot. And Peter said, 'Paninis! They call these *paninis!* What do you suppose they imagine the singular is? And how do they think people will get their mouths around them, for God's sake? They don't trouble themselves about *that* little detail, now, do they.'"

"Heavens," Elissa said.

"He's what's known as 'a difficult man,'" Sean told her. He chomped down on a forkful of crab fluff, looking fairly difficult himself.

Willa said, "Now you're being unfair, Sean. Everybody's entitled to an opinion from time to time."

Sean just stabbed another forkful of crab fluff.

Elissa made a delicate throat-clearing sound. She hadn't yet touched her own meal. "I'm so sorry I couldn't have met Sean's dad," she told Willa.

"Oh, I am too," Willa said. She welcomed the change of subject. "You would have liked him, I know. He was such a good father! He was with me in the delivery room when Sean was born, and he got so excited he said, 'It's a *baby!*' He meant to say 'It's a boy,' you see, but he got so—"

"He died in a road-rage incident," Sean told Elissa.

"Yes, you've mentioned," Elissa murmured.

Willa ducked her head over her plate and took a bite of her crab fluff. It tasted like deep-fried pancake batter.

"Is everything to your liking?" their waitress asked.

"It's great," Sean told her.

In spite of herself, Willa recalled that Peter had a special contempt for the phrase "to your liking."

"Well, let me know if there's anything more you need," the waitress said. She left.

Clinking of forks, rattling of ice cubes. Elissa was eating now, dabbing her lips daintily with her napkin after each bite. Sean had finished his crab fluff and was starting on his french fries. He had proceeded that way since childhood—tackling his meal systematically, one food at a time.

Willa said, "Now, have you two known each other long?"

The question was carefully worded. (She couldn't ask how they had met, because they must realize Denise would have told her.) There was a moment of silence before Elissa answered for the two of them. "Oh," she said, "a year or so, I guess. But I mean, not *dating* a year or so. We didn't start dating till . . . a little while ago."

"Ah."

"I'm not a bad person, you know."

This was so unexpected that Willa took a second to react. Then she said, "Oh! Of course not."

"I had every intention of sticking it out with my husband, believe me. It's just that, well, then Sean came along."

This made sense to Willa. Sean was infinitely superior to Hal, if she did say so herself.

"I kept seeing Sean in the gym I joined after we moved to Dorcas Road," Elissa was saying. "For a while I had no idea he lived on my block. And *Denise* never went to the gym. Or Hal, either. It was only me and Sean, side by side on the treadmills."

Now Willa remembered what a boon these young women could be: offering privileged glimpses into her sons' private lives. She nodded brightly; she was trying not to say anything that would cause Elissa to stop talking. But Sean no doubt wished she *would* stop talking, because he said, "At any rate—"

"For instance," Elissa told Willa. "I bet you didn't realize I still go to my in-laws' for supper every Sunday evening."

She must be returning to the topic of how she was not a bad person. Willa said, "No, I didn't realize that."

"I do it as a kindness to Hal. He doesn't want them to know."

"To know . . . ?"

"His parents think we're still together. His mother says to me, 'Tell me, dear, do you ever use that tablecloth I gave you?' and I say, 'Oh, I use it all the time. I used it just the other evening when we invited my boss and his wife.' I'm not sure what I'll do at Thanksgiving. Up till now Hal's folks have always come to *our* house for Thanksgiving."

"Well, by then you'll have broken the news," Sean told her.

"Why should I have to break the news? They're Hal's parents."

"Yes, but you're the one who walked out," Sean reminded her.

"I didn't walk out!" She told Willa, "We were originally going to announce it to Hal and Denise together, over dinner. Denise invited us to dinner, see, and I said to Sean, 'This is when we should tell them, jointly. Calm and civilized.' But then Denise burned the beef bourguignon."

Willa nodded again, encouragingly.

"All the chunks of beef were glommed to the bottom of the pan. She was trying to dish them out for us but they wouldn't come. She had to wedge the serving spoon under them and hit the handle of the spoon with her fist, and then a chunk would give way finally and fly clear out of the pan sometimes, or the pan would even skid a few inches across the table. And Denise's face was getting red and she was saying 'Goddammit...' and even when we got the beef on our plates it was just hard black shreddy bricks, you know, nothing we could stick a fork into, so I gave Sean a nudge with my foot and frowned at him because we couldn't tell her *then*. It would have been adding insult to injury. It would be, first the main dish is a flop and then her husband abandons her, all in the same evening. Right?"

"Wrong," Sean told her. He told Willa, "The one thing had nothing to do with the other. I did get why Elissa was nudging me— kicking me, is more like it. I knew what she was trying to say. So I held my tongue, but honestly? It just meant putting it off, is all. It just meant I had to get up the next morning and tell Denise, 'Don't fix any breakfast for *me*; I'm moving out,' and then go over to Elissa's house and the two of us tell Hal."

"Oh, my," Willa said.

She couldn't help picturing this scene from Denise's perspective. Or even from Hal's, unappealing though Hal was.

"I suppose I could go ahead with Thanksgiving as usual," Elissa was saying reflectively. "Give Hal the grocery list early in the week; get over there at crack of dawn Thanksgiving day—"

"Oh, Elissa, just pick up the phone and call your damn in-laws," Sean said.

Elissa gave him a tremulous look and started twisting her napkin.

"Well, so, tell me," Willa said hastily. She didn't have the slightest idea what she was going to ask; she just felt a pinch of anxiety when she saw Elissa's expression. "Are you two, um, do you two live in a house now, or an apartment?"

"Apartment," Sean said. "Out Loch Raven a ways." Which meant nothing to Willa, of course. "It's really nice," he said. "Got a balcony, separate dining alcove, study we can use as a guest room—"

"Ian is going to be our first overnight guest, we think," Elissa piped up.

"Ian!"

Sean said, "Yeah, I think I've about persuaded him to come visit in September."

"Come visit . . . here?"

"He's got a week off then, he mentioned."

"I didn't know that," Willa said.

"Yeah, well, he says if he doesn't use some of his vacation time soon, he's going to lose it."

"I see," Willa said.

She had planned to pick up the check, but when it arrived (Sean and Elissa having declined dessert as well as coffee, to Willa's disappointment), Sean said, "I'll get this."

"Oh, no, I want to do it," Willa said.

"Well, it doesn't seem right that Peter should have to pay for a meal he's not even here for."

"Peter?" she asked, bewildered. "It's me who's paying, not Peter."

"What: you're not using his rich-guy hoity-toity uranium or whatever credit card?"

"No, I am not," she snapped. Now she was annoyed. "I do have my own money, you know. I've held a job for a whole lot more years than *you* have, by a long shot."

Sean held up both hands. "Sorry!" he said. "Geez."

So Willa paid, extravagantly overtipping as a kind of declaration of independence even though Sean wouldn't know about it.

When the three of them stepped out onto the sidewalk, it still wasn't dusk. Willa asked Sean, "What are you driving these days?" merely as a delaying tactic. It was a question that men seemed to find important, she'd noticed, but Sean didn't treat it seriously. He shrugged and said, "Oh, same old thing."

Whatever that was.

"Well, I am parked around the corner," she said.

"We're back here," he said, gesturing in the opposite direction. "Okay, Mom, good to see you," and he bent to kiss her cheek. Then Elissa moved forward to shake her hand, but Willa gave her a kiss instead, because that was the formula, after all. How many of Sean's girlfriends had she kissed goodbye? And a few of Ian's, too. "Take care," Elissa told her.

Peter would have said, "Take care of *what*?"

Sean and Elissa walked off to the left, and Willa walked off to the right.

Most people would automatically know how to drive back to the place they'd started out from, but Willa wasn't one of them. She'd written all the turns in reverse on the other side of her instruction sheet, and now she went over them in detail before she started the car.

In the rearview mirror she saw that new wrinkles had developed around her eyes and her foundation had dried in her pores. She had fallen into particles over the course of a single evening.

She headed back through the commercial section, back through the residential section and the jumble of small shops. She turned onto Northern Parkway and traveled east, unhampered now by the traffic she had dealt with earlier. The houses grew smaller and humbler. The landscape grew familiar.

Ian was going to visit Sean?

He could have come to see Willa and Peter!

He and Sean weren't even all that close.

Why, one time long ago, when the boys were still in their teens, Willa was leading them down a street when she realized they were no longer with her. She had turned to see Ian lying flat on the sidewalk in nothing but his underpants and Sean standing over him, triumphantly waving a pair of jeans and a T-shirt. Yet no more than three minutes had passed since she had last looked back!

Willa had been furious at the time, but now the corners of her mouth twitched and then she smiled outright.

Well, never mind. Think about where she was driving to; think about Dorcas Road. Soon she'd be home playing Scrabble. Maybe she'd even try a slice of that pizza if any was left.

9

On Wednesday, Denise managed to make her way upstairs by sitting on the bottom step and scooting backward to the top. "My own bed again!" she crowed. So Willa and Cheryl carried her belongings up to her room, which instantly fell into its former state of chaos. Her hairbrush and cosmetic bottles reappeared on her vanity, pieces of cast-off clothing littered the floor, and a stack of celebrity magazines slithered across her bed—all of this before she had spent a single night there.

That afternoon she said that now that she was more mobile, she thought she might try going in to work for a couple of hours. "You and Cheryl could drive me over to the school," she told Willa, "and drop me off and then pick me up later."

"Just as long as you give me directions," Willa said.

Getting Denise to the car turned out to be the hard part, though. First she teetered out to the porch on her crutches; then she laid the crutches aside and, leaning heavily on Cheryl and Willa for support, lowered herself to a sitting position at the top of the porch steps. After she'd plopped step by step to the bottom, Willa grabbed her

by both hands to haul her upright again and Cheryl gave her back
her crutches and she staggered toward the curb. It wasn't a great
distance (Willa had owned rugs bigger than Denise's front yard), but
it took her forever, and by the time she reached the car they had col-
lected a small crowd of onlookers, all hovering uselessly and offering advice and encouragement—Erland and Mrs. Minton and Dave
Raeburn and a tiny, dainty old lady who'd been heading toward
Ben's office. "Where is Sir Joe when we need him?" Mrs. Minton
wondered aloud, but it was two o'clock on a weekday afternoon
and Sir Joe was off with his truck. "I am here," Dave said, looking
offended. Dave had the build of a half-deflated balloon, though, so no
one stood aside to let him hoist Denise into his arms.

Then, once she was settled in the car—the back seat again, so
that she could stretch her leg out—she remembered she'd left her
purse in the house and Cheryl was sent to fetch it. Willa and Denise
waited in a comfortable silence, the only sound Denise's breathing as she recovered from her efforts. In the rearview mirror, Willa
watched the old lady inching down Ben's side path. She must have
arrived by city bus; there was no sign of a car. Or else she had walked
from someplace nearby. This neighborhood had a whole collection
of halting, faltering old folks.

"Peter claimed I could drive one-footed," Denise spoke up from
the rear, "but I bet that's one of those things that look easy till you
try it. I don't think one foot is enough. You have to kind of brace
yourself with the other when you're pushing the pedals."

"Oh, well, what does Peter know?" Willa said.

She had spoken to him just once since he left, and it was she who
had placed the call. After waiting all Monday to hear from him she
had phoned him late Tuesday afternoon, avoiding the morning hours

completely in case he was sleeping late. "Hello?" he'd answered in a questioning tone, although of course he would have seen who it was, and she had said, "Hi, honey! How was your trip?"

"Abysmal," he said hollowly.

"Oh, I'm sorry."

"You know I had to do the first leg of it in steerage."

"No, I didn't know that."

"Rona couldn't get me an upgrade. On top of that, I had a middle seat. The guy by the window slept the whole way and snored like a Mack truck, that stop-and-go kind of snoring where there's a blessed silence and then a sudden huge snort that gives everybody a heart attack. And the woman on the aisle weighed two hundred pounds at the very least and the minute she got settled she dug into this giant tote that was crowding my feet and brought out a foot-long salami sub with enough onions to kill a horse—"

"That sounds awful," Willa said.

"—and twice before they turned the seat-belt sign off she pressed her call button to ask when drinks were going to be served, and when finally the cart showed up she ordered two Bloody Marys—this was before most people's breakfast time, mind—and an extra pack of snack mix. Snack mix! Ha. Which was no food known to nature, believe me; some kind of crackerish objects coated with sidewalk salt. After the sub she dug out a slice of Boston cream pie wrapped in a sheet of wax paper that kept blowing off her tray into my lap because of *course* she had her overhead fan on, and then around Kansas or someplace she ordered a lunch box with the most mysterious kind of salad in it; I swear there wasn't a single piece of greenery, just gloppy white dressing and croutons and so-called bacon bits. When we were getting near the mountains she unwrapped a—"

"Did you have anything to eat yourself?" Willa asked.

"Oh, God, no."

Then he said he had to go because he had a golf game. He didn't ask about anyone in Baltimore; he didn't ask about her evening with Sean.

Nor had Denise asked about Sean; she'd still had company, after all, when Willa came back from dinner, and for the whole next day her one reference was, "So you got to meet Elissa, I guess."

All Willa had said was "Mm-hmm" before changing the subject.

Now, though, just as Cheryl came bounding out onto the porch with her mother's purse slung over her shoulder, Denise said, "I don't suppose Sean and Elissa said anything about inviting you to *their* place, did they?"

"No," Willa said, "they didn't."

"Would you believe the whole time I knew her, that woman never once had me inside her house?"

"Goodness," Willa said.

Then Cheryl yanked the passenger door open and piled into the car, and no more was said on the subject.

As it turned out, the school was fairly simple to get to. First Denise instructed Willa to drive three blocks south on Dorcas Road, past the stuffed rabbit still asking "Did You Lose Me?" and the sign for "The Bicycle Guy," and then to turn left at the baseball diamond worn into the weeds on a vacant lot. A couple of blocks later they dead-ended at one of those faceless brick school buildings that dated from the 1940s. A new-looking white wooden sign reading "Linch-pin Elementary" very nearly covered the older letters etched in the granite above the front door, and some of the windows featured posters and children's paintings that had faded over the summer.

Willa parked as close as she could get. She had barely maneuvered Denise out of the back seat before two young women rushed out to help—the two whom Willa had met in the hospital, in fact. "Easy, now!" "Don't rush her!" "I've got her," they said, fluttering and wringing their hands and getting in each other's way. Willa stepped back and let them take over; Cheryl followed behind with Denise's crutches. When they reached the front door it magically opened and Mrs. Anderson stepped out, crying, "Careful, ladies! Give her some room!"

She was the one who took the crutches from Cheryl, while the other two made a huge fuss about getting Denise up the front steps and through the door. "Hey there, hon," Mrs. Anderson told Cheryl.

"Hey, Grandma."

"Hi," Willa said.

"Still here, are you."

"Yes . . . for a while."

"School starts in just five weeks, you know. You going to be around that long?"

"Yes!" Cheryl said, wheeling toward Willa, but Willa smiled and said, "I'm afraid not," and once again Mrs. Anderson lost all interest in her. "Now, Ginny," she told one of the women, "you go get Lawrence from the boiler room and let him know Denise is here. Lawrence says he can carry you to my office," she told Denise.

"I don't need carrying," Denise said. "Just find me a typist's chair." Then she turned to Willa and asked, "You want I should phone you when it's time to come pick me up?"

"Yes, whenever you like," Willa said.

"You sure you know how to get back, now."

"I'll be with her!" Cheryl said indignantly.

"Oh, right."

She vanished into the building, surrounded by her attendants.

"School's going to start in five weeks," Cheryl said to Willa as they returned to the car. She spoke in a wheedling, enticing tone, like someone promising a treat.

Willa said, "Yes, summer always seems to fly, doesn't it?"

But evidently she'd missed the point, because Cheryl looked crestfallen and gave a kick to the right front tire before she got back in the car.

Peter called while Erland was sitting in the kitchen. Erland had come over to see if Willa might need help bringing Denise home again—a trumped-up excuse if she'd ever heard one. (Could Erland maybe have a *crush* on Denise?) As she glanced down at her phone screen he asked cheekily, "Who dat?" She didn't bother answering him. She felt a weight lift from her chest when she saw Peter's name, and she punched her phone and said, "Hi, honey!"

Peter said, "How you doing there?" His voice was perfectly friendly.

"Doing fine," she said. "I'm just making a grocery list for supper. And Cheryl's off swimming in the Dumont girls' grandma's pool, and Erland's here in the kitchen."

"Very cozy," Peter said.

"I'm thinking I might fix my chicken-rice dish."

"As for me, I'm going to eat at the club," he said. "The usual something-stuffed-with-something, I suppose. Jim and Sarah Burns invited me."

"That'll be nice."

"Well, as long as Sarah doesn't get going on those genius kids of theirs," he said.

"Is everything all right with the house?"

"Yep. Manuela came to clean this morning. I think she asked me where you were, but you know I can't understand a single thing she says."

"You did see to it she got her money, though, right?"

"Of course I did. How's it going with Denise?"

"It's going fine," she said.

She didn't tell him Denise could manage the stairs now. Or that she'd gone back to work.

After she hung up, Erland asked, "Who *was* that?"

"Peter, of course," she told him. "Who else would I call 'honey'?"

"Well, Sean maybe."

"No," she said, and then she wondered why it was any of Erland's business, and what gave him the right to sprawl here so intrusively with his long stringy legs stretched halfway across the kitchen floor and his elf hat pulled over his ears. She frowned at him, but he was too intent on prying into her life to notice. He asked, "How come Peter left before you did? Did you-all have a fight?"

"No, we did not have a fight," she said. "He just needed to get back to work."

"His lawyer work, right?"

"Right," she said. She was dragging a step stool over to the cupboard above the stove now, hoping to locate some rice.

"Is he the kind of lawyer for criminals, or what?"

"No, for mergers and acquisitions."

"What're those?"

She didn't answer, because she couldn't imagine that he really wanted to know. She stepped up onto the stool and peered into the depths of the cupboard.

"It would be handier if he was a criminal lawyer," Erland said in a thoughtful tone.

"Handier in what way?" she asked. Oh, good: rice. A cup or so in a cellophane bag. She grabbed hold of it and got down off the stool.

"Like if you were ever arrested, for instance," Erland said. "When the cops allowed you one phone call, you would have someone to call."

"That does set my mind at rest," Willa told him. She put the stool back in the broom closet.

" 'Because otherwise, what would a person do? Me, for instance: I would have no idea who to call."

"Why not Sir Joe?" Willa asked.

"Sir Joe is not a lawyer!"

"No, but he could ask around for one."

"Who would he know to ask?"

"Well, Erland?" she said. "It looks like you'll just have to not get arrested."

He slumped in his seat.

"My recipe uses breast meat," Willa said, mostly to herself, "but I'm thinking I'll change that to thighs and just up the baking time. Thighs have a lot more flavor."

"When I was a kid," Erland said, "I used to collect all these useful tips for criminals from the back pages of comic books. Well, they didn't *say* they were for criminals, but who else was going to need them, right? They told how to cover your footprints and all; how to not leave fingerprints. Like, did you know you can make an impression of a key by mashing it into a warm Hershey bar? If you wanted to steal someone's keys without them finding out, let's say. Only thing I couldn't figure was, when you asked the locksmith to cut you a key from the pattern on a Hershey bar, wouldn't he want to know why?"

"Well, or even if he didn't," Willa said, "how would he physically fit the Hershey bar into his cutting machine?"

"Now that I think about it, I bet they just made up that tip to fool little kids with," Erland said.

He started chewing on a fingernail. Willa hated when people did that. She looked away; she wrote "chicken thighs" on her grocery list.

"Could Peter be a criminal lawyer right now if he wanted to, or would he have to go back to school first?" Erland asked, speaking indistinctly.

"I'm not sure," she said. She glanced over at him again. "Stop *doing* that," she said.

He took his finger out of his mouth and sent her a cowed look.

"Sorry," she told him. "It makes my teeth twang when I see people biting their nails."

"Okay," he said meekly.

"Sorry," she said again. She really was sorry; she knew she'd been rude. To make amends, she said, "Wouldn't you like to take your hat off? You must be roasting."

"Naw, I'm okay."

"How come you wear a knit hat in the summertime, anyhow?"

"I've got this real frizzy hair," he said.

"Well, I know what *that's* like."

He obviously didn't believe her. "No, like even my frizzes have frizzes," he told her. "If I was to take my hat off, right away every hair on my head would be zinging up a storm. I'd look like those circus clowns with the big poufs of curls sticking out on both sides."

He had those anyway, but Willa didn't point that out. She said, "When I was a teenager, I used to squeeze my head into a tied-off length of nylon stocking every night at bedtime. It didn't work, though. Now I just get treatments."

"Treatments?"

"At my beauty parlor."

He squinted at her skeptically.

"You'll see what I'm talking about if I stay around much longer," she told him. "Already it's beginning to feel a little bit crinkly."

She lifted one hand to her hair and made tiny pinching motions to demonstrate, but Erland didn't seem impressed. He started biting his nail again, and then stopped himself. He said, "I wish I was a grownup."

"Well, kids can get treatments too, you know. Not that I'm saying you should."

"I just hate this not being in charge of my own life," he said.

"Oh. Well. Right," Willa said. She had never been one of those grownups who told young people they were lucky to be young.

"Did you-all get a phone call from that cop guy?" he asked suddenly.

"What cop guy?"

"The one that was going around before asking who saw the shooting."

"No," Willa said, "I don't think so."

"He phoned Sir Joe last night. He said he was checking did any of us have any new thoughts on the subject."

"Denise didn't mention it," Willa said.

He gave a furious swipe to his nose with the back of his hand. Willa looked at him more closely. "Erland?" she asked.

No answer.

"Erland? Is something wrong?"

He made a giant sniffing sound. Willa passed him a paper napkin from the basket on the table, and he took it without looking at her and blew his nose.

"It was me," he told her in a muffled voice.

"Excuse me?"

He folded the napkin to a dry spot and blew again. "I'm the one that shot her," he said.

Willa pulled a chair out from the table and sat down.

"I didn't do it on purpose, honest," he said. "I was just trying to stop this guy from waving a gun around. I didn't *mean* to shoot her."

"Better start at the beginning," she told him.

He drew in a breath and said, "Well. I've got this friend, right? Or kind of a friend. Magnus, his name is. I know him from my chemistry class; he was the Locker Bomber."

"The what?"

"But don't tell anybody, okay? I mean, he doesn't do that anymore. So anyhow, on the day I'm talking about I ran into him at the deli. And when we left he started walking alongside me and so I was like, Whoa! Magnus the Locker Bomber is walking alongside of me! Because he'd never acted all that friendly up till then, see. And I was hoping he wouldn't split at the next corner or whatever, so, I don't know, I just happened to mention that my brother had a gun."

"Sir Joe has a gun?"

"Right, and so—"

"What does he have a gun for?"

"What do you mean, what for? He just does. And I was, I don't know, making small talk and I happened to tell Magnus about it. And he said he'd like to see it. And at first I was glad, because that meant he'd have to come home with me, and I said 'Sure.' So we went to my house and I unlocked the front door and Cheryl was all—"

"Cheryl was there?"

"Yeah, she was out front because *lots* of people were, they're watching this noisy truck across the street, and she and Airplane are watching too but she stops watching and comes after us saying, 'Hey, Erland, what you up to? Who's that you got with you? Where you-all going?' and like that. But I told her, 'None of your business,' and me and Magnus went on inside. Sir Joe keeps his gun in his mukluks, so—"

"In his what?"

"In these boot-looking Eskimo slippers that some girl gave him for Christmas one time. He says only fools keep their guns in their nightstands, because that's where a burglar looks first. So me and Magnus go up to Sir Joe's room and I get the gun from his mukluks and Magnus right away grabs it. He's acting all expert, checking it out, looking down the barrel . . . He tucks it in the waist of his jeans and I say, 'Okay, give it back now, hear?' But he pays me no mind; walks out of the room with the gun still jammed in his jeans. 'Magnus?' I say. I'm following him. I'm starting to get mad. I say, 'Come on now, Magnus, I'm serious,' but he says, 'What you in such a sweat about?' and heads on down the stairs to where the front door is standing open and Cheryl is shading her eyes and looking in through the screen with Airplane next to her."

"Cheryl!" Willa said.

"Yeah. I already told you. So Magnus says, 'Out of my way, fatso'—talking to Cheryl, you know—and she steps back real quick and he walks onto the porch. And I'm following; I'm saying, 'I mean it, Magnus,' but he says, 'Oh, Erikson, you are such a fag. Relax.' And he takes hold of the gun and sticks it out straight-armed like he's aiming across the street. I know he wouldn't really have pulled the trigger, he's not a total moron, but I was so damn *mad*, you know? I felt like the whole situation was just getting past my control. You know how when you're mad you hear this kind of rushing sound in your ears? So I hear this rushing sound and I reach out and yank the gun away from him. I didn't even think I'd get it! I thought he'd be hanging on too tight! But I guess he wasn't expecting I'd grab it and so all at once it was there in my hand and then it kind of, you know. Went off."

Willa groaned.

"I didn't mean for it to," he said.

She said, "What were you *thinking*? You could have shot Cheryl!"

"I know," he said. "Or Airplane."

"You're an idiot!"

"But it went off all on its own, I swear! I thought it would be locked or something! And I'm so surprised I just drop it, and I'm standing there looking down at it and when I look up again, Magnus is clear to the street and walking fast. And first I think, Whew! Nobody noticed, because they're still watching the truck; only one looking at me is Cheryl. Cheryl is, like, shocked. And then I see that Denise is sitting flat in her front yard and I think, Uh-oh."

"You had no business letting that boy come anywhere near this neighborhood," Willa said.

"I know! I know that! I just got carried away. I was trying to make an impression. I mean, Magnus *Alden*, Willa. And you don't get what things have been like for me. I don't have any friends. I've only been here two years and everyone else at school has known each other since kindergarten. And girls don't like me, and teachers hate me, and the only sport I don't suck at is baseball but the one time the coach let me play I made the final out and had to wear the Backpack of Shame."

Willa looked at him blankly.

"Pink," he said. "Pink satin. With rhinestones spelling out 'Desiree' across the back."

"That is absolutely no excuse," Willa told him.

"No, I realize that," he said humbly.

"So Cheryl knows how her mother got shot?"

"Right."

"Why didn't she tell anyone?"

"She doesn't want people finding out it was Sir Joe's gun, is why. You know how she is about Sir Joe."

"Still, though," Willa said. "Under the circumstances . . ."

"But what's bugging *me* is Sir Joe finding out himself," Erland said. "I did put the gun back again exactly where I found it, but sooner or later he's going to notice it's been fired."

"Good," Willa said.

"He can't, Willa. That can't happen. Sir Joe's my only relative."

"So?"

"He'll tell the police. He'll let them send me to reform school; he'll say I can't live with him anymore. He didn't want me in the first place, you know. I had to beg and plead with him. He said he wasn't around enough to take good care of me and blah-blah-blah but I pleaded on bended knee, and even so he would have said no except I'd have had to go to a foster home and everyone's heard what *those* are like."

He dabbed at his nose with his napkin. Willa looked away.

"Maybe you could just clean the gun and reload it," she said after a minute. "Or no, not that"—because she remembered all those newspaper stories about people who got killed cleaning guns. "Forget that," she said firmly.

He looked relieved.

"Maybe he'll just never take the gun out again," Willa said. "Why would he, anyhow?"

"To shoot a burglar, maybe? And he'll pull the trigger and the gun won't fire and the burglar will shoot *him* instead?"

"But it must have other bullets in it, don't you think?"

"I don't know," Erland said.

"Isn't there one of those . . . chambers that you spin around and put bullets in?"

"I think those are only in westerns."

Willa was silent a moment, considering.

"I thought of maybe just disposing of it," Erland told her.

This didn't seem like such a bad idea, at first glance. "In the garbage," Willa agreed. "Buried beneath eggshells and coffee grounds and such."

"But then how about when a burglar shows up?"

"Though why would a burglar show up in this . . . not-rich neighborhood?" Willa asked.

Erland shrugged. "He might not *know* we're not rich?" he suggested.

The front screen door slammed, and Cheryl called "Willa?"

Willa said, in a hurry, "You have to tell Sir Joe."

"No!" Erland said.

"There's no other way," she said. "Trust me. You have to tell him the honest truth, and throw yourself on his mercy."

"I can't," Erland said.

"I'll go with you, if you like."

"What good would that do?"

But then Airplane came bounding into the kitchen, followed by Cheryl and the Dumont girls, all three of them with damp hair and sunburned noses. Cheryl said, "Guess what . . ." and then she said, "Erland? How come *you're* here?"

"Hey, Cheryl," he said morosely.

"What are you two talking about?"

Willa said, "Oh, nothing," at the same time that Erland said, "I told her about you-know-what."

Cheryl drew in a sharp breath. So did Patty and Laurie, which made Willa glance toward them in surprise. Patty clapped a hand to her mouth, and Laurie said, "Uh-oh."

"You told *them*?" Erland asked Cheryl.

"Well, you told Willa," Cheryl said.

"That's different! Willa just . . . wormed it out of me. Jeepers, Cheryl! Why not put an ad in the newspaper?"

"We swear-hope-to-die we won't say Word One," Laurie announced solemnly. "We would *never*. We will carry it to our graves."

Willa said, briskly, "Well, anyhow. We're all going to forget this ever happened, isn't that right?"

"Right," the three girls murmured, and then they edged out of the kitchen, sliding their eyes toward one another.

"I'm done for," Erland moaned once they were gone.

"All the more reason you have to talk to Sir Joe," Willa said.

Erland still looked unconvinced, but at least this time he didn't refuse outright.

In the evening they watched *Space Junk*—Denise and Cheryl and Willa and Airplane, along with Hal, who had taken to hanging around a lot lately. Denise sat pointedly at the opposite end of the couch from him with her eyes fixed firmly on the screen, and Hal kept leaning forward to say things like "Denise? Are you having trouble sleeping now that you're alone? Because I am, I don't mind telling you." And Denise would say "Huh." And Cheryl said "Ssh!"

Willa had grown very fond of *Space Junk*. Just the sound of the *woo-hoo* music made her feel happy and anticipatory. And Cheryl and Airplane felt the same way, of course. But Denise was clearly watching only because Cheryl had coaxed her into it, and Hal didn't even bother pretending. From time to time he would yawn aloud, "Ho-hum," and then "Denise?"

"Ssh!" Cheryl told him.

Even while Willa focused on the show, though, a part of her was running through Erland's confession. She wasn't the least bit worried that he would be sent to reform school, because after all, the shooting had been purely accidental. But she was sure this could get Sir Joe into a lot of trouble. There must be some sort of law about adequately securing your firearm, wasn't there? And although she doubted that he would go so far as to throw Erland out of the house, she really couldn't be certain.

Until now she hadn't stopped to consider Erland's lonely position in life. No parents, no blood relatives . . .

She thought of a time right after Sean was born when she had become obsessed with her own mortality. For a short while Sean had had something the pediatrician called a milk rash—tiny red pimples on one cheek where he'd lain against a damp blanket. It had turned him homely and pitiable, and it had made her love him even more than when he had been perfect. Who else but a mother would feel that way? she had wondered. No one. Not even his father. And she had been terrified by the thought of how easily she could die and leave him unprotected.

Not only did the aliens in *Space Junk* fail to notice differences in skin color, age, and class; they also appeared oblivious to the fact that their captives spoke different languages. Spanish, English, Mandarin, whatever: the aliens would reply in kind, without visible effort. There weren't even any subtitles; the producers just seemed to assume that the viewers would understand too. Willa enjoyed this. She asked the others, "Wouldn't it be wonderful if this were the way the real world worked?"

"Huh?" Cheryl said.

"If everyone could understand all those different languages?"

"Well, *you* understood what Jose just said to the spaceship captain."

"That was only Spanish, though," Willa said.

As if neither of them had spoken, Hal leaned toward Denise again and said, "Maybe you and me could go to a movie sometime, do you think? To make Sean and Elissa jealous."

Without taking her eyes from the screen, Denise said, "Sean and Elissa could care less if we went to a movie."

Couldn't care less, Peter would have corrected her.

The doorbell rang, and since the inner door was open Denise just called, "Who is it?"

"Me," Ben Gold said, and he let himself in and came to stand in the living-room archway. "Oh, good, *Space Junk.*"

"Hi, Ben," Denise said. "Have a seat."

"I'm looking for Robert," he told her, but he headed for the armchair anyway. "Maybe just for a minute or two," he said as he sat down.

"Who's Robert?" Willa asked him.

"My cat."

"I didn't know you had a cat! Is that the gray tabby I see out on the street sometimes?"

"Afraid so," Ben said. "He's supposed to stay indoors, but you'd never guess it. Which episode are we watching?"

"The one where Li Tang tries to escape," Cheryl said.

"Ah, one of my favorites."

"I was just telling Denise that me and her should go to a movie," Hal said to Ben. "Good for what ails her, right, Doc?"

"Hmm? Sure," Ben said, but he didn't seem to be listening. "You know, the guy playing Li Tang is actually a famous actor from Hong Kong. It was quite a coup when he signed on for *Space Junk.* And he was the one who approached *them*; it wasn't their idea."

"What else has he been in?" Willa asked.

"If you hadn't asked, I would remember," he said reproachfully.

She laughed and said, "Sorry."

Cheryl said, "I bet you understand Chinese, Willa, don't you?"

"Oh, lord, no!"

"Willa speaks about ninety-eight languages," Cheryl told Ben.

"Is that a fact," Ben said.

"Or five, to be precise," Willa said.

Ben peered at her over the top of his glasses. "Which ones?" he asked her.

"Spanish, Italian . . . I was planning to be a linguist, once upon a time, but I ended up in ESL."

Cheryl said, "What's ESL?"

"English as a second language. Teaching English to foreigners," Willa said.

Cheryl's attention returned to Li Tang, who was fumbling now with the latch on the spacecraft door, but Ben said, "You know how to teach English to foreigners?"

"That's what I was trained in."

"You should come with me sometime to the Blessed Book Church," he told her. "We've got all these immigrants there who can't communicate with us."

"You belong to a church?" Willa asked

She hadn't meant to sound so surprised. Ben chuckled and said, "Well, if I did, it would be a synagogue; but no, I just volunteer there. Blessed Book runs this clinic; you wouldn't believe all the different languages."

"I bet Willa speaks every one of them," Cheryl told him.

"Not quite," Willa said drily.

There was a tap on the screen door, and then Callie's loud, flat voice: "Denise? Is Ben in there?"

"I'm here," he called.

"You still looking for Robert? Because he's out by Sir Joe's truck."

"Thanks," Ben said, and he heaved himself to his feet and shambled toward the foyer. A moment later they heard him out front, calling, "Robert? Robert! Come here, you rascal."

"If you don't like movies," Hal told Denise, "we could try that new fried-chicken place up on Ballycroft."

"Fried chicken gives me the gas," Denise said.

Li Tang burst out of the spacecraft door and floated off into the ether.

10

Willa had expected she would have to nag Erland repeatedly before he agreed to tell Sir Joe about the gun. But no: bright and early Thursday morning, as she was waiting on the back stoop in her kimono while Airplane took his first pee of the day, Erland popped out on his own stoop, wide awake and fully dressed. First he yawned aloud and stretched, gazing at the sky. Then he turned toward her and gave a theatrical start and called, "Oh! Hey there!"

"Morning," Willa said. She'd never seen him at this hour before.

"So," he said. "By the way! I've been thinking. I think maybe I *should* talk to Sir Joe."

"Oh, good."

"Because he'd probably see my side of it, right?"

"I'm just about sure he will," Willa said. "And you'll feel better afterward, I guarantee."

"Yeah. Okay. So . . . I'm wondering, were you serious when you said you could be there too?"

"Of course."

"Well, then," he said. He heaved a loud sigh.

"Shall I come over after breakfast?" she asked him.

"Breakfast! You mean, like, today?"

"Sooner is better than later."

"Yeah, but today is Thursday," Erland said.

She waited.

"He's always real busy on Thursday," Erland said.

"How about Friday, then?"

"Friday. Well. You know what? Let's just wait till the weekend."

"The longer you put it off, the likelier he'll find out on his own," Willa said. "And *that* wouldn't be good."

"Look, at least I'm doing it, okay?"

"Okay," she said, strategically retreating. "You're the boss."

"Maybe Saturday?"

"Saturday's fine with me."

"Say ten o'clock Saturday morning," he said. "I'll come over and get you."

"Oh, you don't have to do that."

"Because if you showed up on your own, it might look like telling him was your idea," he said. Clearly he had been giving this some thought.

Willa said, "Oh. Okay."

Actually it *was* her idea, but she saw his point.

Erland gave a sharp nod, looking uncharacteristically decisive, and turned and went back into his house.

On Saturday morning precisely at ten, somewhat to Willa's surprise, he knocked on the front door. You could tell he was under some stress. His face was white and stiff, and when Willa said "Good morning," he said a frozen "Morning" without returning her smile

She nudged Airplane aside with her foot—he seemed to be imagining that he'd been invited too—and stepped out onto the porch and followed Erland across the yard to Sir Joe's yard. Erland was walking in that spiky, teenage-boy way with his hands jammed in his rear pockets and his elbows jutting out. Willa had to take a couple of extra skips to keep up with him.

She was feeling almost as nervous as if it were she who was about to confess.

They climbed the steps to Sir Joe's porch. Erland pulled the screen door open and walked in first (nothing chivalrous about Erland), and she followed. "Yo," he called out. "Look who I found!"

Sir Joe's house smelled like bacon and coffee. The foyer was empty except for a wooden bench bearing a motorcycle helmet, and the living room was painfully neat. It held just a giant flat-screen TV and a couch and a coffee table. No rugs, no lamps, no knickknacks, no pictures on the walls. No Sir Joe, either, but just then he walked in from the dining room, wearing his weekend outfit of black leather pants and white T-shirt and carrying a mug. He stopped short when he saw Willa and said, "Well, hey there, pretty lady."

"Hi," she said.

"What brings *you* here?"

"Oh . . ."

She looked at Erland. He was jittering on the balls of his feet, hands still in his rear pockets. He caught her look and visibly swallowed. Then he turned to Sir Joe. "I was just telling her I had, like, something to talk to you about," he said, "and she said she might like to be in on it."

Sir Joe cocked an eyebrow at Erland and waited.

"It's about, *you* know, that gun of yours," Erland said.

Sir Joe glanced swiftly at Willa, no doubt because he didn't want her knowing the gun existed. Willa stayed impassive.

"See, the other day it, like, accidentally went off," Erland said.

"What!" Sir Joe said with a start. "Went off? Went off where?"

"Um . . ."

"Where was this?"

"Well . . . on the porch?"

Sir Joe drew back a bit and blinked.

"I was just, like, showing it to this guy I know? From school? And he took it out onto the porch. I didn't *let* him take it; he just did, and I tried to get it back from him and by accident it, um . . ."

Sir Joe said, "Goddammit to hell, Erland. You could have shot someone!"

Both Erland and Willa held their breath.

"Oh," Sir Joe said. "You *did* shoot someone. You're the one who shot Denise."

"It was an accident! I swear it was. I was only, like, trying to stop this guy from waving it around."

Sir Joe said, "You brought a friend here when I wasn't home. Flat-out going against the rules."

"I was just—"

"You went into my mukluks."

Willa felt an absurd urge to giggle.

"And you," he said, wheeling on her. "What's *your* interest in this?"

"I came because I know Erland is really, really sorry," she told him. "I just wanted to make sure you realized that."

"And now I guess you-all are going to sue or something."

"Sue?" she asked. It was so unexpected that for a moment she thought he was referring to a *person* named Sue.

"That's what folks like you do, isn't it?"

"I don't know what you're talking about."

"What, then?" he said. "What is it you want?"

"I already told you: I want to make sure you understand that Erland is sorry." She paused. Then she added, "And he's worried you'll tell the police."

"Police," Sir Joe said. "Oh. Well."

There was a silence.

"I'm not real sure about the police," he said finally.

More silence.

"I mean, as I recall, I got that gun some time ago. In maybe not the most licensed way."

"I see," Willa said. She put on a nonjudgmental expression.

"I don't mean I stole it or anything."

"Of course not."

"But considering I don't have a permit to show, I'm thinking I might just not bother them with it."

"That makes sense," Willa said.

She glanced at Erland. He was chewing his lower lip, keeping his eyes fixed on Sir Joe.

"Then also," Willa told Sir Joe, "he's afraid that you won't let him go on living here."

"Huh," Sir Joe said. He seemed surprised. He took a sip from his mug. "Yeah, I'll need to think about that," he said. And then, after about fifteen seconds of ostentatious pondering, "Nah, what the hell."

Willa wasn't sure of his meaning.

"It kind of sucks, being fifteen," he said finally.

"Oh! Yes! It does!" Willa said enthusiastically.

"Geez, the kid can't even get a driver's license yet."

Willa made a tsking sound.

Erland said, "So I can stay?"

Sir Joe shrugged. "I guess," he said.

Erland pulled his cap off—whole *pinwheels* of hair! Slinky toys of hair!—and said "Phew!"

"But no telling Denise," Sir Joe told him.

"Oh, why not?" Willa asked, and Erland said, "I was thinking I could apologize."

"Nah," Sir Joe said dismissively.

"I been wanting to do that for ages."

Willa said, "And I bet she'd feel a whole lot better if she didn't think someone had shot her on purpose."

"Why would she think *that*?" Sir Joe asked. "Face it," he told Erland, "she is the one who'd likely go to the cops."

"You think? Gosh. Okay, Sir Joe," Erland said in a meek voice.

Willa wanted to argue with that, but she supposed they should just be grateful Sir Joe had taken the news as well as he had.

On Tuesday afternoon, Willa and Cheryl drove Denise to her ortho-pedist's office. Denise was hoping to exchange her plaster cast for a walking cast. When she announced this, Willa felt a twinge. Once Denise was in a walking cast she wouldn't need Willa anymore. It seemed a little too sudden.

Somehow, Willa's stay in Baltimore had stretched on without her noticing. The guest room had acquired the settled, slightly shabby feeling of home; the people she met on her morning walk greeted her with a smile; the man who passed the house twice daily towed by his three Westies had started commenting on the weather; and the stuffed rabbit on the corner had been claimed at last, or else discreetly discarded. She and Denise were like longtime roommates: she knew not to expect Denise to act sociable before breakfast, and they both liked a glass of chardonnay in the evening, and Denise had begun counting on Willa to finish her sentences for her. "That other side of the street is so full of themselves," she would say. "So conceited and stuck-up and over . . . over . . ." and Willa would say, "Overbearing? Overweening?" If she stayed around much longer, she thought, they'd start correcting each other's anecdotes.

"Is this just your sneaky way of leaving me?" Peter had demanded during a recent phone conversation. "Are we turning into one of those couples where the wife stays on permanently in the country house while the husband lives in the city?"

"Goodness! Don't exaggerate," she'd told him. "You should be glad to have some time to yourself."

It was he who phoned *her*, most often. This was only reasonable, since she had no way of knowing when he'd be out playing golf or eating at the club or whatnot. But then when she answered he would be surly and laconic, as if the call were her idea, and so even though she was happy to see his name on the screen she found the conversation hard going. She pretended nothing was wrong, though; she made a point of sounding breezy and animated. She brought him up-to-date on Cheryl's baking projects, and she joked about how Airplane was desolate without him.

She was less forthcoming about Denise. She still hadn't told him that Denise had started going in to work now, and she had made no mention of the walking cast.

When Denise came out of the examining room, she was wearing a chunky blue canvas boot that stopped halfway up her shin. A young girl in pink scrubs carried her purse and her crutches, but Denise was making her way unsupported. "Look at me!" she called to Willa and Cheryl, and when she was closer she said, "It fastens with Velcro; I can take it off for showers. I cannot *wait* to shave my legs."

"Here you go," the girl said, handing Denise's belongings to Willa. "You be careful now," she told Denise. "Don't overdo; remember what the doctor said."

"Yah, yah," Denise said on an outward breath. She raised both fists above her head. "Free at last!" she crowed.

Though she did need Willa's arm as they left the building, and she leaned on her heavily when she settled into the car.

"Denise is in a boot cast now," Willa told Peter that evening.

"So does this mean she can start driving?"

"Not yet. But she's managing without her crutches."

"Can she make it up the stairs?"

"Well, just by sitting down and scooting up backward," Willa said. "She's too wobbly yet to risk walking up."

She failed to tell him that Denise had been sitting down and scooting up backward for some time now.

There was no reason, though, to feel guilty about staying on a little longer, because it turned out that Denise was still not ready to drive. And simply getting around the house was such a laborious process that she continued to rely on Willa for any serious fetching and carrying.

"At least we can say the end is in sight," Willa told Peter. "It won't be long before she can manage on her own."

"So why not call Rona right now and make your plane reservation?"

"Oh, well," Willa said, "I'll just wait a bit for that."

The next evening while Willa was fixing supper, Richard and Barry rang the doorbell. Cheryl was the one who answered—calling "I'll get it! I'll get it!" and racing off to the front of the house with Airplane close behind. She brought the two men back to the kitchen, where Willa was slicing bread and Denise was setting the table.

"Look at *you!*" Richard told Denise. "Walking around big as life!"

"Staggering around is more like it," she said.

Richard was dressed casually, for once, in jeans and a polo shirt, but a clipboard hung from one hand and he had a businesslike air. Barry, wearing his baggy drawstring pants, came ambling in behind him with a giant tape measure.

"We're on a mission," Richard said. "Like to check out your powder room."

"Why's that?" Denise asked.

"Mrs. Minton is selling her house and I'm going to handle it for her. I told her she'll get a lot better price if she puts in a powder room first."

"Mrs. Mitten is moving?" Cheryl asked.

"Right. Can you believe her place has no downstairs bathroom?"

Willa said, "My goodness, how has she been managing?"

"I have no idea," Richard said. "So Barry would like to see what you've got here; yours is the same house plan."

"Go ahead," Denise said, and Barry trudged back out to the foyer. They heard him open a door, close it again, and open another. "Interesting," he called. "It's in that alcove across from the stairs instead of underneath them."

"Underneath the stairs is my coat closet," Denise said.

"So I just found out," he said. His voice was muffled; they heard the zipping sound of his tape measure.

"Where's Mrs. Minton moving to?" Denise asked Richard.

"New Jersey, I believe."

"You'd've had a good two more feet if you had put it under the stairs," Barry called.

Denise said, "I didn't put it *anywhere*. My landlady must have done that; it was here when we moved in."

She was limping out to the foyer now, so the others followed. She peered over Barry's shoulder into the powder room. "What's this space used for in Mrs. Minton's house?" she asked.

"Just a big old bureau, I think," Barry said. "Right, Richard?"

"Right, with about six doilies on top."

Barry snapped the tape measure shut and told Denise, "I'd love to know where your landlady got that itty-bitty sink from."

"Come over with us and take a look," Richard told everyone. "The space beneath her stairs is what I would vote for, but I guess it depends on the plumbing connections."

"Cheryl's going to miss her," Denise said. They were all moving toward the front of the house now; evidently the whole group was headed next door. "Aren't you, honey? You know how she is," she told Willa. "Always looking for a grandma."

Willa felt a pang, but she smiled noncommittally.

They walked out to the porch and down the front steps, Denise hanging on to Barry's arm as they descended. Airplane led them toward Mrs. Minton's house as unhesitatingly as if he understood their mission. "I'm thinking new shrubbery, too," Richard told Willa. "Give it some curb appeal."

The existing shrubs were nondescript little scratchy things choked by weeds. The front walk was so cracked and broken that it yielded beneath their feet.

"Some young married couple might be interested," Barry said. "Maybe for their starter house."

It was sad, Willa thought, that an elderly woman's longtime home should be merely the starter house for a young couple.

Mrs. Minton was standing just inside her screen door, as it happened, talking with Ben. "You're back," she said to Richard and Barry. "You didn't notice Ben's cat out there, did you? Oh, Denise! You've ditched your crutches!"

"Denise's powder room is in that alcove to the left of the kitchen," Richard told her. "Not under the stairs after all; under the stairs is a coat closet."

"Well, I have just made do without a coat closet," Mrs. Minton said. "When my husband and I had guests, they draped their coats over the newel post."

She turned to lead them into the dimness of the house, clomping ahead with her walker. It was strange to see the empty space beneath the stairs. The foyer itself had a felted feeling because of the thick maroon carpet, and there was a stuffy woolen smell that made Willa want to sneeze.

Richard said, "If we could find a miniature sink like Denise's, we could do the same thing here—put your powder room in the alcove and make this space below the stairs a closet. Buyers like a ground-floor closet."

"What's in New Jersey, Mrs. Minton?" Willa asked.

She was half dreading the answer, fearing a nursing home or some such, but Mrs. Minton brightened and said, "My daughter, Marie. She's got this darling little guest cottage in her backyard, entirely separate from her house but just a few steps away."

"Oh, how nice!" Willa said. "I wish I had a daughter." The words popped forth without her planning them, almost without her thinking them.

Denise said, "Why, Willa, I'll be your daughter any old time!"

Willa felt touched, and all the more so when Cheryl snuggled against her and wrapped both arms around her waist.

"Mine just thinks the world of me," Mrs. Minton said with some pride. "She's been after me forever to come up there."

"Well, aren't you lucky," Willa said.

"But your children feel the same way, I imagine."

"Oh, well . . ."

Cheryl said, "Willa, are you rich?"

"What? No, not really."

Denise said, "Cheryl Carlyle, what on earth would make you ask that?"

"I was thinking she might could afford to build a guest cottage in our backyard."

Willa gave her a grateful squeeze, but Ben muttered, "Little matter of what Paul would have to say about that."

Denise and Willa, together, said, "Who?"

"Paul, Peter . . . *you* know. Her husband," Ben said, and the dismissive tone of his voice made Willa flick a curious glance at him.

"For a long time I resisted," Mrs. Minton told Willa. "I valued my independence, you see. And I worried the move would distress my poor dog; he's old now and set in his ways. But then one day I thought, Why not? Why not go live near Marie? Things have been getting somewhat more difficult lately."

"I can imagine," Willa said. "It's hard to believe you've been climbing those stairs to the bathroom on your own."

"Oh, that's no trouble. I just hang on to the railing with both hands and kind of haul myself along. And then I've got a second walker waiting at the top—my little luxury. Insurance only pays for the one, they told me. No, it's more a question of . . . you know. Figuring out what to live for. That's the great problem at my age."

There was an odd little silence. Then Willa said—she couldn't help herself—"What *do* you live for?"

"Well, one thing is that when you're old, everything takes more time. Bathing, counting out my pills, putting in my eye drops . . . You'd be amazed at how much of the day a person can fill that way."

"Ah," Willa said.

Although this was not much use to Willa. She was still very quick on her feet.

"But sometimes it feels so repetitive. You know? Like when I'm getting dressed, I'll think, These same old, same old colors; I wish I had some new ones. But there aren't any new ones, anywhere on earth. Or vegetables: same old vegetables. Come suppertime and there's spinach, or there's tomatoes, or there's corn . . . Why can't they invent some new vegetables? It seems I've used everything up."

"There's broccolini," Cheryl said suddenly, dropping her arms from Willa's waist.

"What, honey?"

"*That's* a new vegetable."

"Oh. Well."

Ben turned to Willa and said, "What do you live for, Willa?"

"Me!" Willa said.

"It's worse now that Henry is gone," Mrs. Minton said in a thoughtful tone. "Men give a purpose to things, have you noticed?" she asked Willa.

"Yes," Willa said, "I have noticed."

"Now, here's what I'm going to do," Barry told Mrs. Minton. "I've got this professional plumber friend, and me and him are going to come back tomorrow and figure out your pipes."

"Well, if you think you can," Mrs. Minton said dubiously.

They were heading to the front of the house now. Airplane, who had not been allowed inside, stood silhouetted on the porch with his nose pressed to the screen. When he saw them coming, he wheeled and raced down the front steps and then pivoted to watch them approach, wagging his tail encouragingly.

The outdoors felt refreshingly airy after the stuffiness of the foyer. Denise hooked her arms through Richard's and Barry's and hobbled between them; Cheryl threw a stick for Airplane, who dashed off after it, ears flapping joyously. Ben told Willa, "You haven't answered my question."

"What question is that?" she asked, putting on a look of puzzlement.

Instead of repeating it, he said, "I've been thinking about your father's advice. About breaking your days into moments. Do you suppose that might be going at it the wrong way?"

She wrinkled her forehead.

"I mean, sometimes when I'm feeling sorry for myself, I try the opposite approach: I widen out my angle of vision till I'm only a speck on the globe."

"Well," Willa said, "but doesn't that make you feel kind of . . . puny?"

"I *am* puny," he said. "We all are. We're all just infinitesimal organisms floating through a vast universe, and whether we remembered to turn the oven off doesn't make a bit of difference."

That he considered this to be comforting made Willa laugh, and he smiled at her without appearing to take offense. Then he said "There he is!" and off he shambled toward the street. "Come here, you devil," he called. He returned carrying Robert looped over his forearm like a shawl, and that was the end of their conversation.

Willa was playing I Doubt It with Cheryl and Denise after supper when Peter phoned on the landline. Cheryl was the one who went to answer. She said, "Hello?" and "Oh, hey, Peter!" and "Let me see," and then she pressed the receiver to her chest and told Willa, "He wants to know can you talk."

"Thank you," Willa said. She dislodged Airplane, who was lying on top of her feet, and went out to the foyer.

"She's coming," Cheryl told Peter. "We're in the middle of a game, though." And then, holding the phone out to Willa, "It's your turn next, don't forget."

Willa said, "Hello?"

"Where *are* you?" Peter said. "I've been calling and calling your cell phone."

"Oh, I must have left it up in my room. I'm sorry. How is everything there? Have you been having a nice day?"

"Not really," he said.

"What's wrong?"

"What do you think is wrong? I'm rattling around this house all on my own; I supposedly have a wife but I'm forgetting what she looks like; I can't find anyone to go to supper with tonight and there's nothing in the house I feel like eating."

"Don't we still have some of that seafood stew in the freezer?"

"Nothing I *feel* like eating, I said."

"Well, I'm sorry to hear that," she said. She laced her fingers through the coils of the telephone cord and looked toward the living room. Cheryl and Denise were watching her with identical crinkled expressions, waiting for her to come back.

"Is that all you have to say?" he asked.

"What?"

"Willa, are you paying attention, here?"

"Of course I am," she said, although in fact she was only half listening. But then, when she went back to the others, only half attending the card game.

11

They'd had very pleasant weather lately, everyone agreed: hot but not unbearably so, and a bit less humid than usual. They did need rain, though. The grass—what there was of it, in the little yards lining Dorcas Road—hadn't had a good soaking since Willa's arrival. In fact, when a gentle shower began before dawn on Thursday, the sound was such a novelty that she woke imagining it was the automatic sprinkler system watering the golf greens back in Tucson. For one anxious moment she tried to recall just when and under what circumstances she had made the flight home.

At breakfast, Denise announced that she was skipping work on account of the rain. And Cheryl just assumed that she and Willa would not be taking their usual walk with Airplane. When Willa set out anyway, having borrowed an umbrella from the coat closet, it emerged that Airplane had been assuming the same thing. He lifted a leg beside the hedge in a desultory fashion and then turned and looked at her expectantly, plainly hoping they could go back indoors now. "What a sissy," she told him. She had begun counting on their morning walk. It made a kind of entranceway to her day. But she gave in and let him scamper back up the porch steps.

Even when the weather cleared, in the early afternoon, Denise didn't propose going in to work. Instead she said, "Maybe this would be the time to have me try my hand at driving. Don't you think?"

"Oh, good idea," Willa said.

Although she felt a little jog of resistance, to be honest.

So they tied a plastic grocery bag around Denise's boot to protect it from the damp ground, and the two of them went out to the car. First Denise had to reposition her seat and all the mirrors, which were adjusted for Willa. Then she made a production of where to place her injured leg. There was plenty of space for it, but she said, "It just feels so clumsy! Like it might be going to get in my way if I suddenly stomped on the brakes."

Eventually, though, she inched the car out into the street and they proceeded at a stately pace to the end of the block. They took a painfully slow right turn and then three more right turns and finished up back at the house, at which point Denise said "Phew!" and yanked the keys from the ignition and held them out to Willa. "That's enough for now," she said. "You're just going to have to keep on being my chauffeur a while longer, Willa."

Willa was amused to think she could be anybody's notion of a chauffeur, but it was true that she was a good deal more comfortable behind the wheel these days. She knew her way to the accustomed destinations—the supermarket and the school and the ATM and such—and she had mastered the quirks of Denise's elderly car. In fact she almost enjoyed her trips.

The next day, same as always, she drove Denise to work, but it was dawning on her now that she wouldn't be doing it for much longer.

She began to look at everyone here with an eye to losing them, the way she used to look at her sons when they were about to go off to college. Denise's dark-blond hair, shining like bands of satin even when she shoved it unbecomingly behind her ears; Cheryl's dear, soft, pudgy cheeks; the elegant whorls of fuzz on Airplane's nose—she *dwelt* on them, committing them to memory. She felt some prophetic nostalgia even for Erland's elf hat, and for Hal's hound-dog gazes at Denise, and for Ben Gold's bushy white eyebrows poking out like two antennae in the direction of whomever he was speaking to.

But still she made no move to reserve her flight home, and when Peter offered to call Rona for her, she countered with transparent excuses. Denise was not really driving yet, she said for openers; and Peter said, "So? She can get a neighbor to drive her. I'm sure your doctor pal would be willing."

"My doctor pal," Willa repeated.

"What's-his-name."

Willa sighed.

"It's not only the driving," she told him. "She can't do heavy housework. She can't get down the basement steps."

"Why would she need to?" Peter asked, and Willa said, "That's where the washer and dryer are, remember?"

"Which Cheryl is fully capable of operating herself, remember?" Peter asked.

"Well, yes, but—"

"Little one. Today's Friday. If you come in over the weekend, I can pick you up at the airport."

"Oh, you don't have to do that."

"I want to," he said. "Besides, that way I can be sure you won't take it into your head to turn around and fly back again once you land."

"Ha ha," Willa said. "How are things at the house?"

"Lonesome," he said. "Even your saguaro is lonesome. It hasn't been looking so good."

"Oh, no! What's wrong with it?"

"It's kind of, I don't know; kind of pale."

"Pale? What do you mean, pale? It's always pale."

"There's this wrinkly look to its skin."

He was making it up. Willa was just about positive that slow-growing creatures like cacti didn't go downhill as rapidly as all that. "Oh, well, too bad," she said heartlessly, calling his bluff.

"Huh," he said. "So what do I tell Rona: Saturday, or Sunday?"

"You talk like someone who still goes to work," she said. "What does it matter to *you* if it's a weekend or not?"

It was late afternoon by now and her thoughts were turning toward what to serve for supper, so she hadn't chosen her words as carefully as she might have. Peter let a significant silence develop—an iciness in the air that she could feel almost physically. Then he said, "Right. Well, don't let me keep you," and he hung up.

On Saturday, Willa had a call from her sister. She would have missed it if she hadn't been upstairs near her cell phone at the time. "Elaine?" she said when she answered. "Is everything okay?"

"Where *are* you?" Elaine asked. She sounded cross. "I've been calling you and calling you."

"You have? You've been calling my cell phone?"

"No, your home phone."

"But I told you, I'm in Baltimore," Willa said.

"You told me that ages ago. You're still there?"

"Right."

"Well, darn. I'm in Phoenix for a conference."

"You're in Phoenix, *Arizona?*"

Elaine didn't dignify this with an answer.

"I had no idea!" Willa said. "Did you leave me a message?"

"No," Elaine said, "I just hung up. I was afraid I might have to talk to Derek."

"To . . . ?" Willa said.

"I mean Peter. Sorry. Peter, Derek: same difference really, right?"

No matter how accustomed Willa was to her sister's blunt manner, she could still be shocked by her. She sat down on her bed abruptly, pressing her phone to her ear.

"Hello? Are you there?" Elaine asked.

"I'm here."

"So it sounds like you won't be home in time. I'm leaving tomorrow evening."

"Well, I wish I'd had some warning," Willa said.

"Why? Would you have flown back early?"

"I might have," Willa said. "It seems like forever since I've seen you."

In fact, when she imagined Elaine nowadays she had to remind herself to add in the grown-up details of her—the threads of gray in her hair and the settled shape of her body.

Elaine said, "Well, you can't say I didn't try."

"No," Willa said. "I'm sorry I'll miss you."

But the sister she missed was a six-year-old sitting at a long-ago breakfast table, not the heavy-voiced woman at the other end of the line.

As Willa was putting her phone back in her purse, she noticed she had a text message. She clicked on it, and up came a photo of Ian. He was standing in front of a log cabin with an older man in a park ranger's uniform and a hefty young woman in hiking clothes. Ian himself wore jeans and a faded windbreaker. He'd grown a beard several years ago that still took Willa aback every time she saw it, a close-cut, pointed beard that accentuated the sharpness of his face; and he had new glasses, the rimless kind that people used to call granny glasses. "Hi mom just down here getting supplies hope you're ok," he wrote. Where "here" was he didn't say. She studied the photo for clues. The log cabin must be a grocery store; a sign above the door read "Bennett's," with a Coca-Cola disk at either end like a thumbtack. The woman seemed the right age to be Ian's girlfriend, but it was hard to know for sure; they were standing next to each other but not touching. Though on second thought she was so unselfconscious, so carelessly slouched and indifferent-looking, that she was probably just an acquaintance.

Willa did manage to figure out how to send back an answer. "Good to hear from you, still in Baltimore," she wrote. Then she went downstairs and showed the photo to Denise. "This is Ian," she said. "Sean's brother."

"Gosh, they don't look much alike, do they?" Denise said.

"They never did, really. I can't tell if that's his girlfriend. What do you think?"

Denise peered at the photo more closely. "Nah," she said finally. "I doubt it."

"He's had a few over the years but they don't seem to last," Willa said. "I'm really beginning to wonder if I'll ever be a grandma."

"Well, look at it this way," Denise said, returning the phone. "If you don't have grandchildren, you won't have to worry about them going through the death of the planet."

This made Willa laugh. "There is that," she said.

Then, on Sunday afternoon, Denise got a phone call from Patty and Laurie's mother.

Willa had never met her, so when Denise said, "Oh, hi, Fran," it meant nothing to her. "You do?" Denise asked next. And then, "Say *what*?"

Willa and Cheryl, who were baking gingersnaps together, looked over when they heard the edge to her voice. She said, "You're kidding."

They couldn't make out what was said on the other end of the line.

"Who else knows about this?" she asked. And then again, "You're kidding." She pressed a palm to the crown of her head like a skull-cap. "Well, thank you, Fran. Thanks for telling me. I'll take it from here. Bye."

She hung up and turned to Willa and Cheryl. "So," she said. "Fran Dumont says Erland was the one who shot me."

Willa and Cheryl froze.

"And you knew this, Cheryl. And you too, Willa. You knew all along."

Willa said, "Well, not *all* along . . ."

"You knew and didn't tell me."

Willa felt herself flushing. And Cheryl, she saw, had a fine white line tightening around her mouth.

"I had to hear it from a third party," Denise said. "Were you two *ever* going to tell me?"

Neither of them answered.

"Who else knows?" Denise asked Willa.

"I don't think anyone," Willa said. "Well, Sir Joe, of course, but—"

"Sir Joe knows?" Cheryl said.

Willa nodded.

"What'd he say?"

"What *difference* what he said?" Denise demanded. "I'm the one that matters here. Jesus! Seems like everybody was in on this but me. I feel like an idiot."

"Oh, please don't think that way," Willa said. "We weren't . . . conspiring or anything, I promise! We just didn't want to get anyone in trouble."

"'We,'" Denise said bitterly. "You and Cheryl: isn't that cozy. I should have known you'd come between us; you always put on this lady act, so cheery and polite and genteel and super . . . super . . ."

". . . ficial?" Willa suggested sadly.

Denise glared at her. "But underneath, meddling," she said. "Meddling and interfering with your busy little dainty fingers."

Then she wheeled and plunged out the back door, clunk-step-clunk in her boot cast, letting the screen slam behind her.

Willa and Cheryl looked at each other. Cheryl said, "She was *mad*."

"You should go talk to her," Willa said.

"You come with me."

"I shouldn't be there. It has to be just the two of you."

Cheryl didn't look happy about it, but she turned finally and trudged out the back door.

Up in her room, Willa crossed to the open window and listened for voices. Not that she would have eavesdropped; she just wanted to know if Denise and Cheryl were speaking to each other. But it was a side window and she couldn't hear a thing out in the backyard.

She felt so miserable that she took her phone from her purse and sat down on her bed to call Peter, but then she thought better of it. She could guess what he would say. "Didn't I tell you?" he would ask. "What did you expect, getting caught up in other people's lives? People you don't even know, for God's sake!"

So instead, she started checking for a flight home. Home! Even the word was a comfort. She didn't want to wait till Rona's office opened on Monday; she wanted to leave immediately. This very evening, if it could be arranged.

But it couldn't. Or maybe she was just inept; she had never made a reservation online before. At any rate, the first flight she found left early the next morning—6:45. That was bearable, she supposed. All she had to do was get through the night. If she went to bed early, she wouldn't have to interact with Denise for more than a few hours.

After she had entered her credit card information (taking way too long at it, forced to start over twice), she did call Peter, but she dialed their landline in the hope she could just leave a message. To her relief, the call went to voice mail. "Hi, honey," she said. "It's me. Just to let you know I'm coming home tomorrow morning, arriving at eleven twenty in case you still want to pick me up." Then she gave him the flight number and caroled, "Bye now!" She was almost sure she sounded perfectly normal.

Although the instant she ended the call, she allowed her face to go slack and she slumped on the edge of her bed.

From beginning to end, she thought, she'd done everything wrong. She should have told Erland right away that he had to confess to Denise, but instead she had focused on Sir Joe—on what his reaction might be and on how to protect Erland from it. And also, face it: she had been so pathetically pleased to find herself in the role of confidante. Denise had been the last person in her mind. No wonder she was angry!

Nothing terrified Willa more than an angry woman.

Well. Anyhow. She rose and went to the closet to haul her suitcase out.

When she had packed everything that she wouldn't need that night and draped her travel dress neatly across the other bed, she smoothed her hair and refreshed her lipstick and gathered herself together to go back downstairs. Denise was on the couch in the living room. She was reading the newspaper; all that Willa could see of her was the opened-out *Baltimore Sun*. Willa continued through the foyer to the kitchen, where she found Cheryl at the table doing nothing at all. She had her hands clasped in front of her; at the center of the table sat a plate of freshly baked gingersnaps.

"Oh, didn't they turn out nicely!" Willa said.

Cheryl said, "They're okay."

"They look delicious."

Cheryl was silent.

"What do you think we should fix for supper?" Willa asked her.

"I don't know."

"Deviled eggs? Tuna salad?" They'd had their big meal at noon, since it was a Sunday.

Cheryl shrugged.

"BLTs?"

"I hate BLTs."

"Goodness! You're the only person I ever heard say that."

"They scratch the roof of my mouth," Cheryl said. Then she said, "Grilled cheese sandwiches might be good."

"Well, I hate grilled cheese sandwiches," Willa told her.

"We could heat up a pizza, maybe."

"Good idea," Willa said. "Do we have one?"

She was almost hoping they didn't. A trip to the supermarket would fill some of that gaping stretch of time. But no, she found a pepperoni pizza in the freezer. "And we could fix a salad to go with it," Cheryl said. She was beginning to look happier; she slid off her chair and went to the fridge to see what was in the crisper. "Can I make up my own dressing?"

Willa said, "Absolutely."

She might as well have been in a play—some amateurish, wooden high-school play whose only virtue was that the actors did remember their lines, more or less.

Not until they were eating supper did Willa announce she was leaving. They were sitting in their usual places around the kitchen table but keeping very quiet—Denise perched on her chair with perfect posture, her manners impeccable for once; Cheryl looking alertly from one of them to the other but saying nothing. "So," Willa said finally. She set aside a crescent of pizza crust and wiped her fingertips on her napkin. "Tomorrow, I've got an early flight back to Tucson. I thought I should mention it now because I'm leaving before you two will be awake."

Denise stopped chewing.

Cheryl said, "You're *leaving*?"

"I've got a 6:45 reservation," Willa said. "I'm going to tiptoe out of the house like a mouse."

Denise said, "You don't have to go."

"Oh, I know that!" Willa said brightly. "But Peter's going to think I've deserted him if I stay away any longer."

"Well, there's no need to overreact," Denise said.

"No, of course not, but . . . is it all right with you if I print out my boarding pass on your printer?"

After a pause so long that it almost seemed she wasn't going to answer, Denise said, "Sure."

"Thank you," Willa said.

They finished supper in silence, and then Denise picked up her own dishes and set them in the sink. For a moment she stood watching as Willa and Cheryl cleared the rest of the table, but eventually she left. A kind of bleakness hung over the kitchen once she was gone.

Willa filled the sink with hot water and squirted detergent in. Cheryl fetched a fresh dish towel from the drawer. She said, "Willa, can't you stay a little bit longer?"

"I wish I could," Willa told her, sponging off a handful of forks.

"I was even thinking you would maybe build a guest cottage in our backyard," Cheryl said.

This made Willa smile. She said, "But what about Peter?"

"Peter could live there too, and you could be a resource at my school. Mrs. Anderson is *dying* for resources!"

Willa turned to hand her the rinsed forks and found Cheryl staring up at her expectantly. She reminded Willa of those little girls on Victorian valentines—her cheeks touched delicately with pink, her upper lip a curly Cupid's bow, her eyes a lustrous gray and fringed with long, thick lashes. She really was the most beautiful child, Willa thought.

She had read somewhere that human infants were born with the belief that they were entitled to two parents—that this explained why children reacted so catastrophically to divorce. Since coming to Baltimore, Willa had begun to wonder if they also felt entitled to grandparents. And certainly the reverse was true, because it seemed unthinkable that she didn't have any grandchildren.

Even if they *would* have to deal with the death of the planet.

After she'd printed her boarding pass Cheryl suggested a game of I Doubt It, but Willa said, "How about Crazy Eights?" because I Doubt It worked best with more than two people and Denise had pointedly reclaimed her computer by now. The whole time Willa and Cheryl played (speaking in loud, obvious voices, slapping their cards down dramatically), they were haunted by the silhouette of Denise in the dining room, her profile set like stone toward the screen in front of her.

At eight thirty—not even Cheryl's bedtime, let alone Willa's— Willa announced that she'd better say good night because she was getting up early in the morning. "Should I take Airplane out first?"

she asked. She was thinking that Denise would volunteer to do it later, since she was perfectly capable of standing on the porch while Airplane peed, but Denise said, "If you like," and went on gazing at her screen.

"Does he even need to go yet?" Cheryl asked.

Willa sent a glance toward Airplane, who stood up and wagged his tail. "Well, I guess you do," she told him. "Let's be off, then."

Outside a night breeze was stirring, and tattered clouds were whisking across the face of the moon. Willa trailed Airplane down the front walk to the street, where he peed against a lamppost and sauntered on, tracking some scent that had caught his attention.

The sound of her heels on the concrete reminded Willa of how she used to wish for sidewalks when she was a child. She had dreamed of living in a real city where she could fall asleep every night listening to the gritting of strangers' shoes beneath her window. And now look: here she was, heading down a city sidewalk perfectly at home.

Cheery and polite and genteel and superficial.

If Willa were to invent a clock dance, it wouldn't look like the one the three little girls had shown her. No, hers would feature a woman racing across the stage from left to right, all the while madly whirling so that the audience saw only a spinning blur of color before she vanished into the wings, *pouf!* Just like that. Gone.

Airplane raised his head and made a snuffling noise; he was eyeing a cat picking its way along the hedge in front of Mrs. Minton's house. "Robert?" Willa said. The cat paused and glanced her way. Willa started walking toward him, meanwhile giving the impression that her attention was elsewhere. She avoided Mrs. Minton's crumbling front walk so as not to make a crunching sound; she approached the cat stealthily and then darted forward to snatch him up. He allowed it, to her surprise. He neither resisted nor snuggled against her but perched like a figurehead within the crook of her arm, waiting to see where she took him. "Let's get you home," Willa told him.

She walked on past Mrs. Minton's house and turned in at Ben's, with Airplane ambling after her. Now Robert made a move to escape, but she tightened her grasp and climbed the porch steps and rang the doorbell. The light clicked on overhead and Ben appeared behind the screen. "Robert," he said in a disgusted tone. "Thanks," he told Willa. "I didn't even know he was out."

He opened the door to take the cat, and Willa brushed gray hairs off her blouse. "He was under Mrs. Minton's front hedge," she said.

"Won't you come in?"

"No, thanks, I've got to get back. You know, when I was a little girl cats went outside all the time. Some of them even lived outside; the barn cats."

"Same when I was a kid," Ben said. "But now we know that every year, cats in this country kill something like three billion songbirds."

"Really! Well, I see your point, then," Willa said.

"I shouldn't even own one, but I can't have a dog because he'd set up a ruckus every time a patient arrived. Not to mention that I happen to be a sucker for cats."

"Oh," Willa said, "I always think it's a good sign when a man likes cats. It shows he doesn't feel the need to be in constant control of things."

"Well, I certainly have no illusion that I'm in control of Robert," Ben said amiably. He turned to let the cat pour from his hands like a liquid and stalk off into the interior of the house.

"Anyhow, this gives me a chance to say goodbye," Willa told him. "I'm going home tomorrow."

He raised his eyebrows. "So soon!" he said.

"I think Denise has had enough of me."

"Oh, I can't believe *that's* the case."

"No," she said, "take my word for it: we need to get on with our separate lives."

"Well, it was awfully nice of you to come all this way to take care of her," he said.

The kindness in his voice made her feel almost teary. "I don't think it counts as 'nice,'" she told him, "when it was mostly for my own benefit. I was sort of looking around at the time wondering what to do with myself, to tell the truth."

"Oh, it still counts," he said. Then he said, "Darn. I had this devious scheme in mind: you were going to buy Lucinda Minton's house and come help out with our immigrants."

"That would have been fun," she said.

"Why, we've even got some Syrians!" he told her.

He sounded as artlessly boastful as a schoolboy; it made her smile. "You do?" she asked.

"They seem to have trouble with the P sound."

"The P sound," she repeated, intrigued. "Is that a fact." But then she caught herself. "Well, maybe in my next life," she said. "So, goodbye, I guess," and she held out her hand.

He took it and asked, "How are you getting to the airport?"

Airplane, sniffing around Ben's sneakers, pricked up his ears and looked at him, perhaps fancying he'd heard his own name. "I'm going to arrange for a cab," Willa said.

"Let me drive you, why don't you."

"Oh, thanks, but you wouldn't believe how early I have to leave," she said.

"How early?"

"Um, four forty-five or so? I'm kind of a nervous Nellie about catching planes."

"All the better," he said. "I can get back in time for my patients."

"Well . . ."

"It's a deal," he told her. "See you then," and he clicked his tongue at Airplane and turned to go into his house.

When Willa got back to Denise's, Cheryl was nowhere in sight and Denise had moved to the couch and was leafing through a magazine. A half-empty glass of wine sat on the coffee table in front of her. "Here's Airplane, safe and sound!" Willa told her, and Denise said, "Hmm? Oh, thanks," and turned a page.

Willa climbed the stairs to her room, feeling bruised around the heart.

There was a light shining under Cheryl's door, and so she crossed the hall and knocked softly. "Cheryl?" she whispered.

She heard Cheryl's feet thudding to the floor, and a moment later Cheryl opened her door. She was in her pajamas but she hadn't gotten into bed yet; her pillow was still propped upright against her headboard.

"I just wanted to say goodbye," Willa told her. "You won't be awake yet when I leave for the airport."

Instead of answering, Cheryl flung her arms around Willa's waist and pressed her face against her. "She didn't . . ." she said, and then something unintelligible, her breath warming Willa's midriff.

"What, honey?"

Cheryl drew back to look up at her. "She didn't *mean* it, that you were super-whatever."

"Oh, well," Willa said, "even if she did, it's all right."

"Really she didn't. She's going to get over this in, like, just a day or two; you'll see. Did you notice she's not telling the police?"

Willa hadn't stopped to think about that, but it seemed in keeping with Denise's lackadaisical attitude—her tendency to shrug off events like Amstel Light pregnancies and truncated college careers. She told Cheryl, "Well, good. I guess Erland can stop worrying."

Then she kissed the top of Cheryl's head and said, "Bye, honey. I'll miss you. Take good care of my cactus for me, will you?"

"What do I have to do for it?" Cheryl asked.

"Just water it from time to time, but not too much. It can stand a lot, remember; it doesn't need to be pampered."

"Then will you come back in a while to see how it's doing?"

"Of course," Willa said. Because she didn't want to admit she had no intention of coming back.

She had planned to phone Sean before she went to bed, just to say she was leaving and tell him she'd enjoyed meeting Elissa. But why, really? Considering that he hadn't been in touch since their dinner, she doubted that he would much care if she was leaving. And in fact she had *not* enjoyed meeting Elissa, not really.

These were ungracious thoughts, she knew, and she tamped them down almost immediately. But even so, she didn't call him. Nor did she try calling Peter again. He had her message by now; let him come to the airport or not, as he wished. She was perfectly capable of finding her own way home.

She set the clock on her bureau to wake her at 4:15. It wouldn't take her more than half an hour to dress, and she would grab coffee once she got to the airport. She changed into her nightgown and packed what she'd been wearing; she washed her face and brushed her teeth; she turned off the light and slid into bed and gratefully closed her eyes.

It had been a very, very long day.

12

Willa had no idea whether Ben was the punctual type. He might arrive late, or he might not show up at all. But at 4:45 exactly, just as she was tiptoeing downstairs with her suitcase, she heard a muffled knock. She set her suitcase at the bottom of the stairs and opened the door. "Good morning," she murmured, and Ben growled "Morning" on a whiff of peppermint toothpaste.

It was lighter outside than inside—a flat, opaque gray-white that made him a featureless outline, his expression unreadable. "Is this all you've got?" he asked, stepping in for her suitcase.

Before she could answer, a stirring sound came from the living room. The two of them turned to see a column of white approaching: Denise, wrapped in a sheet. Nothing showed of her except the oval of her face, but she must have been wearing her day clothes because her footsteps made that boot-shoe-boot sound on the floorboards. Behind her came the click of Airplane's toenails. "Hey," she said to Ben. Her voice was a little bit hoarse.

"Well, hey there," he said.

She rotated toward Willa—all of a piece, imposingly. "Listen," she said, "you don't have to leave on *my* account."

Willa said, "Well, it's time, really. I should let you have the house to yourselves again."

"Oh, why do you have to take everything so *personally*?" Denise asked her. "Here I thought we were doing great! I even had this plan in mind where you'd go on living in the guest room forever. I mean, I know I flew off the handle, kind of, but look at my side of it! You and Cheryl all lovey-dovey, with your private secrets; I *hate* when someone keeps secrets from me! Sneaking around behind my back, whispering on the sly, let's-keep-this-from-Denise-shall-we . . . I just hate it! For me of all people, after what Sean did! That was hurtful, Willa."

How did it happen, Willa wondered, that people apologizing for their anger so often got angry all over again? She said, "Well, I'm sorry, Denise. I didn't mean to be hurtful. I hope you can forgive me."

She stepped closer and gave Denise a hug, but Denise made no move to hug her back. Although maybe that was only because she was swathed in her sheet. Then Willa bent to lay her cheek on the top of Airplane's head, which smelled like a well-worn sweater. He made a small whining sound that she chose to read as regretful. Reluctantly, she straightened. "Ready to go?" she asked Ben.

He hesitated, but finally he nodded and stood back to let her pass through the door. "So long, Denise," he said. "I'll check on you later, if I may."

She was silent. She must have stayed there looking after them, though, because Willa didn't hear the door close behind them as she and Ben walked toward the street.

His little Corolla stood at the curb, its headlights glowing and the engine running. Above the hum of the motor Willa heard a few sleepy-sounding birds chirping in the trees, but otherwise the neighborhood was silent. No windows were lit, no cars passed. She felt she would be disturbing the peace if she so much as whispered.

Ben put her suitcase in the trunk while she slid into the passenger seat. His car had the musty smell of old newspapers, and a Post-it reading "wiper fluid" was plastered to the dashboard. When he settled behind the wheel she saw by the light from the ceiling bulb that he hadn't shaved yet; his whiskers made tiny white sparks across his weathered cheeks. He wore one of his plaid shirts with the sleeves rolled, so that he looked more like a farmer than a doctor.

"You and Cheryl been keeping secrets from Denise?" he asked as he pulled away from the curb.

Till now Willa had been impressed with his forbearance, but naturally he would be wondering. "Just about the shooting," she said. "It turns out it was an accident, but Cheryl didn't want to tattle."

Ben snorted. "Of course it was an accident," he said. "No one's going to shoot a gal like Denise on purpose."

He didn't ask *whose* accident, to Willa's relief.

They crept past Callie's house, and then Hal's. So many people on this street sleeping alone and then waking alone, rising to go about their solitary routines. Willa already missed them. She pictured Callie tripping off to work on her tiny, brightly shod feet, a go-cup of coffee clutched in one plump hand, and Hal slouching toward Denise's house on the off chance that today was the day she would finally agree to go out with him. And Denise herself making one of her emphatic declarations that ended with a "So . . . yeah!" like a stamp of self-approval.

"Now, you're sure you want to do this," Ben said, as if he could read Willa's mind.

But she said, "Yes, I'm sure."

They took a right onto Reuben Road. Here too the houses were dark and the porches were empty. Ben's radio had been playing at a very low volume—a news program—but now he reached over and switched it off.

Willa took her boarding pass from her purse. For some reason, Denise's printer had made a horizontal white scratch through every tenth line or so. One of the scratches ran smack across the bar code, and this worried her. (She could always find something to worry about when she was taking a trip.) She made herself look out the window again because she didn't want to get carsick; they had left the residential streets behind and were speeding down the Jones Falls Expressway. Then they took an exit into the downtown area, where people were already stirring. Delivery men unloaded vegetable crates from their double-parked trucks; a woman cranked open a grate in front of a café; a man in a red apron hawked newspapers on a median strip.

"You can always change your mind," Ben said, as if no time had passed since they had last spoken. "I could turn around right now and take you back."

Willa smiled. She said, "Oh, well, Denise might have other ideas about that."

"Denise would love it," he said.

"Are you kidding? She just told me I was stealing her daughter."

"She most certainly did *not* tell you that," he said.

"In a way she did."

"I was there," he said. "Remember? She objected to your keeping the truth from her, that was all."

"I was sneaking around, she said. I was whispering behind her back."

"Well, choose to believe what you like," he said.

"I'm not *choosing*."

"You can creep away, all meek and wronged, or you can say, 'You're right, Denise. I should have been more forthcoming, and I promise this won't happen again.'"

"I am not *meek*," Willa said stiffly. "I am not *wronged*."

"Okay. Have it your way."

They left the city behind. The sky was growing lighter now above a wasteland of widely spaced warehouses and storage tanks and electrical pylons. Willa kept turning her head to watch different scenes slide past, as if that would explain her failure to keep up the conversation.

"My wife used to say that her idea of hell would be marrying Gandhi," Ben said.

"Doing what?"

"Think about it: Gandhi was always the good one. Everyone else looked so rude and loud and self-centered by comparison."

Willa sat considering that. They overtook a stretch limousine with windows so darkly tinted that it might have been unoccupied.

"I believe my mother may have married Gandhi," she said finally.

Ben flicked a glance at her.

"My father was so mild-mannered that he thought it was impolite to pick up a telephone in mid-ring," she said. "He always allowed a ring to finish before he answered."

"Ha," Ben said.

"It was marry such a person or *be* such a person, I used to figure," she said.

"You might want to rethink that," Ben told her.

"Excuse me?"

"Those aren't your only two choices, you know."

"Well, it can seem that way when you're eleven," she said.

"Sure, when you're eleven."

"Anyhow," Willa said. She put her boarding pass back in her purse.

They were far out in the country now, and the horizon was turning pink. The silence in the car began to feel wrong, like the silence after a quarrel, but Willa couldn't think how to break it. Whatever subject she considered—the scenery or the weather or the traffic—seemed contrived. Ben may have felt the same way, because when they reached the airport turnoff he said, "So! Getting close," as if he were relieved he'd soon be done with her, and he clicked his blinker to veer left. They began to see signs for long-term parking lots and motels and car-rental firms. "Which airline?" he asked.

He sounded like any random shuttle driver, and she answered him as crisply as any random passenger.

They passed the first terminal, where glaring overhead lights made them both wince. They passed a line of stopped cars. People were unloading baggage from their trunks, buses were wheezing to a stop behind other buses, taxicabs were honking, and everybody seemed rushed and frantic and startlingly wide awake.

They drew up behind a station wagon where a woman was making kissy lips toward the grid of a pet crate that her husband had just hoisted from the rear. "Don't bother getting out," Willa told Ben. "Just pop your trunk." But he opened his door as if she hadn't spoken, and so she opened hers and stepped into the tumult.

He took her suitcase from the trunk and set it on end and pulled the handle up. She said, "Thank you, Ben. I appreciate the ride."

His shoes were high-top black sneakers such as a schoolboy would wear, she noticed now. They made her remember how much she liked him. She stepped forward to give him a hug, but he was already holding out his hand. "So long, Willa," he said.

She said, "Goodbye, Ben," and they shook hands, but then he went on gripping hers. "You know," he said, "I've always meant to tell you that I like the way you look at people."

"The way I . . . ?"

"Like when you're watching Cheryl's face while she's talking. You know? The corners of your mouth twitch as if you're trying not to smile. Or Denise says something outrageous and you just stare at her all wide-eyed and innocent. Or you send Sir Joe this mocking little tease of a glance when he thinks he's being suave."

Willa felt a twinge of disappointment. It took her a moment to understand why: she had fancied, for an instant, that he'd been going to say he liked the way she looked, period.

"So. Anyhow," Ben said. "Okay." And then he dropped her hand as abruptly as if he were throwing it away. He wheeled around and plunged toward his car, leaving Willa there on the pavement.

She should have told him that she liked the way *he* looked at people, too.

The security line was long and zigzagging, but it moved quickly. As she was nearing the scanner, though, everything came to a halt behind a man who seemed never to have flown before. He had to be told to take his shoes off, take his belt off, take his laptop from his bag, and every new instruction caught him completely by surprise. Then, wouldn't you know, he set off the alarm when he walked through the X-ray booth, and he had to return and empty his pockets of coins and keys and Rolaids.

Peter would have muttered something underneath his breath, and Willa would have had to mollify him with a secret, sympathetic smile.

Her gate lay at the end of a high-gloss corridor that opened out finally into banks of waiting areas. Occasionally she passed lone passengers gazing at their phones among a sea of empty seats, or janitors listlessly pushing wheeled bins, but it didn't seem to be a busy time of day for this particular terminal. And her own waiting area, when she reached it, was sparsely populated, although that may just have been because she was so early. She sat down in a chair that had several empty chairs around it, and then she took her phone from her purse. She was thinking she would send an e-mail to Cheryl—just a note for her to wake up to later, something casual and affectionate.

But when her screen came on, she saw she had missed a call. Peter's, she saw. He had phoned at 8:40 last night, when she must have been walking Airplane. She was annoyed with herself for not thinking to check. He'd left a message, though. She pressed Play and raised the phone to her ear.

"Willa," he said, "it's Peter." He spoke so sharply that she had to move the phone an inch or two farther away. "Tomorrow I'm tied up. I do have a life, after all, whether or not you're aware of it. So you know what, Willa? You'll just have to find your own way home. Bye."

There was a click.

Willa lowered her phone and looked at the screen.

It was not quite five thirty, she saw. In Tucson it would be night still. But she called him back even so, because she knew he turned his phone off before he went to bed. She listened through several rings until his voice came on, smooth and cordial now, suggesting that she leave a message. "Please speak slowly and distinctly," he instructed, speaking slowly and distinctly himself as if to demonstrate.

"Hi, honey," she said, "it's me. I'm sorry I didn't think to ask if you'd be busy. I'll just grab myself a taxi, no trouble at all, and see you at the house later. Love you!"

Then she tucked her phone back in her purse and reached for her suitcase and set off to find a cup of coffee.

Something about the way her suitcase trundled behind her brought to mind the oxygen tanks that heart patients dragged around.

On the plane she had a middle seat, but neither of her fellow passengers seemed likely to be any trouble. The man by the window wore one of those puffy neck pillows that made her think of a cushion with a severed head on top, and he went promptly to sleep as soon as they were in the air. The woman on the aisle—gray-haired and plump, although not so plump as to require more than her fair share of space—merely gave Willa a smile and opened a handicrafts magazine. Willa wouldn't have to worry about getting a crick in her neck from talking with anyone next to her.

For a while she gazed out the window at the countryside shrinking below, the miniature rooftops forming segmented lines that resembled centipedes. But then the view changed to nothing but white—not individual clouds but unremitting blankness—and so she took out the paperback mystery that she had started on the way to Baltimore. She had to start it all over again because she'd forgotten the beginning. It was full of meaningful-sounding details that she should probably pay close attention to, but this struck her as a lot of work. After a few chapters her lids began to droop, and finally she closed her eyes and let her head tip back.

She had assumed she wouldn't sleep. She seldom did when she traveled. But all at once she found herself in a city that she knew to be foreign, with cobblestone streets and ancient, moss-covered buildings. Ahead of her a child was walking alone, a little girl in a gingham dress. Willa felt that this child would be very happy to learn Willa was behind her, and so she opened her mouth to call her but all that emerged was a broken high note, an *ee-ee-ee* sound that woke her up. Her own squeaky voice was still ringing in her ears. Mercifully, the woman next to her hadn't noticed; or maybe she was just being tactful.

Willa briefly closed her eyes again, but she had lost the dream for good.

She must have slept longer than she'd realized, because the woman next to her was sipping from a glass of ice water. Evidently the flight attendants had passed through at some point with their cart. Willa sat forward to see where the cart was now—she supposed she ought to stay hydrated—but it was nowhere to be seen and anyhow, she wasn't thirsty. She sat back and listened to a couple behind her arguing about whether someone named Dink should get his allowance even when he didn't make his bed. "All the books say a child's allowance shouldn't depend on his doing his chores," the wife announced, and the husband gave some response that Willa couldn't hear. The wife must not have heard either, because she said "What was that?" and the husband said, loudly, "Hogwash."

Willa's seatmate stuffed her paper napkin into her empty glass and stood up with it and headed toward the rear of the plane. Willa waited a minute or so before she stood up herself; she didn't want to look like a copycat, but she liked to schedule her restroom trips for when she wouldn't have to dislodge anyone.

When she got back, of course, the woman did have to be dislodged, because she had gotten back first, but at least she was expecting it and hadn't refastened her seat belt.

The man by the window was still asleep. Willa was always amazed when people made it through a long flight without a bathroom break.

By now she had reached the point where she felt the trip would never end. She didn't think she could bear another minute of droning engines, canned dead air, young men in suits discussing "asks" and "reaching out" and "taking a meeting." She imagined ringing for a flight attendant and announcing, in a pleasant voice, "I'd like to get off now, please. If you would be so kind as to fetch me a parachute, I'll just be on my way."

But this mood passed, eventually, and she closed her eyes and fell into the kind of half-sleep where she never lost her awareness of her own tensed, furrowed forehead.

At long, long last she felt a barely perceptible change in altitude, a shift in the sound of the engines, and she sat up and looked out the window and saw the sand-colored landscape of Arizona below. It wasn't *her* landscape, not her natural landscape; but it would do.

The instant the plane touched down, all the passengers switched their phones on. Everywhere around her Willa heard dings and tweets and chimes. She checked her own phone, just in case Peter had changed his mind and left another message. But she had no new calls, and no e-mails or texts, either, although she waited several minutes with her eyes fixed on the screen to make sure. Nothing.

This wasn't a disappointment, she found. Instead she felt a distinct sense of . . . gratification, she would have to call it.

She lowered the phone and stared at the seat back in front of her.

When she stepped into the terminal, she had the illusion that everyone here had been frozen in position all the weeks she'd been gone. Those rumpled, tired-looking mothers with their fractious babies, those elderly couples in mammoth jogging shoes, those businessmen with their laptop cases slung across their chests . . . they could have been *painted* here. They looked as settled in as dollhouse dolls.

She walked past the rows of burnt-orange chairs with their indolently slanting backs. She walked past the white-lit shops displaying chocolates and electronics. She reached the moving staircase that led down to the airport exit, and the people in front of her stepped onto it one after another, but at the very last minute Willa veered to one side, nearly tripping a young boy bent beneath an oversize backpack. "Sorry," she murmured, and she looked around for the ticket counters.

In her new life, she will rent a room somewhere. Or she will live in Mrs. Minton's house, or find herself an apartment with a swimming pool Cheryl can visit. She will teach English to Ben's refugees, or Spanish to Cheryl's classmates. Or she might try something new that she hasn't even imagined yet. There is no limit to the possibilities.

She sees herself as a tiny skirted figure like the silhouette on a ladies' room door, skimming the curve of the earth as it sails through space.